VIRAL

Helen FitzGerald is the bestselling author of *Dead Lovely* (2007) and nine other adult and young adult thrillers, including *My Last Confession* (2009), *The Donor* (2011), *The Cry* (2013), which was longlisted for the Theakston's Old Peculier Crime Novel of the Year and the *Guardian*'s Not the Booker Prize, and most recently *The Exit* (2015). Helen has worked as a criminal-justice social worker for over ten years. She is one of thirteen children and grew up in Victoria, Australia. She now lives in Glasgow with her husband and two children.

Further praise for *Viral*:

'It's got all the juicy components to keep you hooked: a Magaluf sex tape, a suspicious supporting cast, an angry mother who is also a judge. Read it.' *Stylist*

'My favourite contender for the inevitable title of "the next *Gone Girl*".' *Independent*

'[A] high-velocity thriller . . . As the plot veers back and forth between Scotland and Spain, FitzGerald adds an emotional current in the form of the complex nexus of relationships between mother, daughters and sisters.' *Metro*

'FitzGerald's offbeat psychological thriller features first-rate dialogue and fascinatingly complicated characters.' *Sunday Times*

'A fast and well-written thriller with a topical theme, this is a more thoughtful novel than just a mother/daughter/viral sex tape romp.' *Daily Mail*

'This is a real psychological roller-coaster, dealing with themes of victimisation and vengeance with great subtlety and tenacity. It is enhanced, too, by some pleasingly gritty, choppy dialogue and smatterings of FitzGerald's signature dark humour, making it highly readable, as well as being an important morality tale for the internet age.' *Scotsman*

'A compelling tale about the darkest aspects of contemporary humanity told with intelligence and surprising wit.' Lisa Ballantyne

'This is a fast-paced tale that never goes quite where you expect. Laced with FitzGerald's trademark black humour, it is by turns funny and sad, scary and bittersweet.' *Independent on Sunday*

'I loved Helen's book . . . In one page-turning thriller, she covers heredity, the internet, shaming, sexism, sibling rivalry and cultural identity . . . A rare treat!' Julia Crouch

'Fresh and uncompromising, reliably topical and filled with unexpected reversals and twists, *Viral* is the latest gripping and darkly funny novel from one of crime fiction's most daring and original voices.' Chris Ewan

'A nuanced and perceptive look at social media and misogyny.' *Guardian*

'A dispatch from the front line of contemporary life to enlighten the pre-social-media generation.' *Literary Review*

'Powerful with fully realised, strong characters.' *Sunday Mirror*

'Combining elements of a coming-of-age novel with a chase that leaps from Magaluf to Barcelona and Korea, *Viral* skilfully navigates the dilemmas of life online. Fast-paced, witty and touching, it also has an unexpected underlying message of empowerment.' *Financial Times*

'A compelling and *au courant* thriller about the internet, shame and retributive justice.' *Tatler*

'Funny, smart, moving and beautifully written.' Steve Mosby

'This is a timely thriller about a leaked sex tape and a mum's attempt to hunt down the men who shamed her teenage daughter online.' *Good Housekeeping*

'The Australian author's depiction of the notorious party town feels very realistic and her no-nonsense writing style frames this story about lies, vengeance and family loyalties well.' *Irish News*

'If you are up for a provocative read, which will fuel book club debates for months to come, this is just the thing.' Crime Fiction Lover

'Viral is all too chillingly believable. I couldn't put it down.' Crime Warp

'Helen FitzGerald does an amazing job tapping into very up-to-date moral issues . . . *Viral* gives the reader much to think about. It reflects badly on our society; how quickly we all judge and how the private becomes public at the touch of a button.' Northern Crime

Viral

HELEN FITZGERALD

FABER & FABER

First published in 2016
by Faber & Faber Ltd
Bloomsbury House
74–77 Great Russell Street
London WC1B 3DA
This paperback edition published in 2016

Typeset by Reality Premedia Services Pvt Ltd
Printed and bound by CPI Group (UK) Ltd, Croydon CR0 4YY

A CIP record for this book
is available from the British Library

ISBN 978-0-571-32350-0

FSC
www.fsc.org
MIX
Paper from
responsible sources
FSC® C101712

For Anna Casci

Chapter One

I sucked twelve cocks in Magaluf.

So far, twenty-three thousand and ninety-six people have seen me do this. They might include my mother, my father, my little sister, my grandmother, my other grandmother, my grandfather, my boss, my sixth-year biology teacher and my boyfriend of six weeks, James.

Where r u? A text from James, the latest of umpteen.

I'm not going to tell him, or anyone.

Twenty-four thousand, one hundred and forty-three. My netball coach maybe, the guy at the Spar on Lang Road. Barry Craig, the boy next door. *That's not . . .* he'd be saying to himself in his bedroom. *No! Zoom in, pause. Is that? Oh my God, Su.*

The incident at the Coconut Lounge brings the total number of times I have performed an act of oral sex to twelve. That's right, never before. Not even when Greg Jamieson pointed it at me in the bushes on the Duke of Edinburgh trek, not even with James, who only got to second base a few weeks ago. I am prudish, virginal Su. I'm the one who usually stays at home to study or, if I do go out, the one who distributes water and buys the chips and calls the taxi. I don't ever feel the need to swear, and I don't like it when others do, unless it is the only accurate way to convey the information (as with the first line above).

Is my chin really as pointy as that? Can't be me. I'm not dirty or dangerous or a rebel. Leah is the rebel in the family. Leah gets drunk every weekend. Leah inserts expletives in sentences that would be more powerful without them. Leah's slept with loads of boys, and some full-grown men, too. It should be Leah on that screen.

I have to keep my phone plugged in so I can play it over and over. That's my floral green top certainly, my hair, my mouth, eyes. Chin? It is me, it is, and my mother and my father have watched it and might be watching it now.

This room is so cold. It's on the third floor of a four-storey, two-star hotel on the outskirts of Puerto Pollensa. It has a small double bed, a window that doesn't open, and a tiny but aptly named wet room that is always very wet, even if it hasn't been used for some time. The wallpaper is peeling on the ceiling and water-stained in three spots which are not pleasingly spaced. The bed is against the wall, by the window. One wobbly bedside table is jammed at the other side. The only light is a dull, energy-saving bulb dangling unevenly inside the Chinese lantern on the ceiling.

The film was uploaded by 'Xano' at 3.20 this morning. Xano describes himself as a 'UK film director'. He's not very steady with the camera, or phone, or whatever he's using to film me with, so he needs to work on that if he wants to call himself a director. Xano is the only faceless person in the film. I count forty-seven people in the crowd. Twelve males surround me in a circle, ready to be next. Everyone else stands behind them, drinks in hand, shouting me on. A few phones are pointing at me, but if the people holding them were filming me, they didn't post it, or haven't yet.

I've paused and screen-grabbed and zoomed in and so far I recognise five people in the crowd. There's the PR guy. He's shirtless in order to show off his glistening six-pack and the two-bird tattoo on his hairless chest. He was the one who lured us inside ('Good evening, ladies? Free drinks, ladies? Jäger bomb, ladies?') and he is one of the folk who is pointing a phone at me. At one stage, he laughs and some drink spurts out of his mouth. Millie and Natasha are at the back, each holding one side of a bucket of blue alcohol, straight-faced like they're scared, but mouths still on their windy straws, not worried enough to stop drinking or to stop me. I recognise the shoes and shorts of one of the guys in the circle. I can only see the bottom half of him. He's getting his thing ready. He'll be the fifth receiver and he's yanking away, panicking that it'll still be wee and soft when I get to it and that – let me check – *twenty-four thousand, one hundred and seventy-one* people will know his thing is tiny and that he can't get it up. His shoes are white, trainer-style, but go up to the ankle, with white laces threaded through black eyelets. His shorts are also white and folded at the bottom. His boxers are grey. His name's Euan. Millie had tried to have sex with him on the third night but he said she was doing it all wrong. She was planning to try harder with him after the Coconut Lounge if she couldn't find anyone better. He's still soft when I get to him, and – yes – my mouth doesn't alter that, so Millie's probably thinking at the back there that she'd better find someone else quick smart as it's our last night in Maga, her last chance for no-strings holiday sex, and she'll require a functioning penis. I pause the shot after Euan zips his shorts and skulks off. Millie's scanning the room for other options. And there's Leah, my sister. She's at the back, peering over shoulders, smiling, clapping, shouting 'Go, go, go!'

Please please, where are you? Darling, don't be scared. It's going to be okay. Let me know you're all right. A text from Mum, the latest of seventeen from her and twenty-three from Dad and thirteen from Woojin and seven from James and three from Ashleigh and two from Jen and none, not one, from Leah since I failed to appear at Palma airport.

I wonder if Mum is texting from court. She's a Sheriff: not one with a gun and an American accent, but with a wig and a West-of-Scotland one. People have to call her 'My Lady' and when she's annoying that's what Leah calls her too. Or she could be at home, having taken time off for the first time since her dad died five years ago. Or she could be at the police station. She could be reporting me missing! She could be tracking my signal!

I take the SIM card and battery out of my top-of-the-range Ri7 and stomp on them, which makes no impact bar hurting my bare soles. I bend the tiny SIM card till it snaps, flush it down the loo, my feet in half an inch of freezing water as I watch it sink to the bottom but not disappear.

Millie must have pulled that night. Leah and Natasha too. I was alone when I woke up on the bathroom floor of the two-bedroom apartment we'd rented. My phone was going crazy in the distance, zzz, zzz, zzz. After being sick several times, I crawled towards the noise, and eventually located the phone in the kitchen sink.

It was Millie. 'Su, are you sitting down?'

I left my suitcase and most of my belongings in the holiday

apartment. I ran to the nearest cash machine, withdrew everything but twenty euros from my Thomas Cook cash card, used fifty-five to get a taxi from the other side of the island to here, and the rest for a week in this room. Mum knows people. She'll have traced my signal. I grab my bag and leave.

I have no money and no idea where to go. At a bank a few blocks from the hotel, I withdraw what I had left yesterday – twenty euros – but when the receipt comes out it says the balance is 620 euros. Mum, bless her.

I withdraw another 300, buy a baseball cap and sunglasses, get a cab to the ferry port and purchase a ticket on the next boat to Barcelona, which is leaving in twenty minutes. I know I should ring Mum and let her know I'm okay, but I can't handle a direct conversation with her or with anyone else. She'll know I withdrew the money, so it's not like I'm making her suffer. She'll know I'm alive. My plan is to hide away until another video goes viral. It'll need to be good, like the 2013 triumph involving the branch. In that particular video, a teenage boy was recording his friend with his phone. In the background, the friend's dad was using his new birthday present, a chainsaw, to chop off a tree branch that was getting too close to their house. The boy's mother was holding the ladder steady, but not very well, because the man lost balance, holding his precious chainsaw as he fell, and decapitating his wife en route. That's the kind of Oscar-winning stuff that's out there. It'll be difficult to top mine – a trampolining kitten wouldn't do, for example, nor an obese guy dancing poorly but with gusto in unflattering Y-fronts. It'll need to be horrendous, outrageous. But I'm confident someone will eventually do something worse and, when they do, I'll drop down the screen in Google Search results and a fresh sorry soul will replace me on this never-ending circle of disgrace. Once I'm off the first page, I'll ring Mum, go home, explain to James, and go to Uni. It's all going to be okay. I'm a sensible girl, and I know there is a very good chance that this will pass and that I will survive.

I'm a survivor, you see. Even when my birth mother dumped me on a doorstep in Seoul, things came good for me. And she didn't dump me in the relative safety of a baby box. It'd be years after my birth that Pastor Lee Jong-rak would build a baby-sized post box at the front door of the Jusaran Orphanage in Seoul for disgraced young women to deposit their errors. Years till the public outrage at his solution, matched equally with public respect. No baby box for me. I was left in a frayed wicker basket with no lining, outside a police station with a note from my mother in Korean that said: 'She is Su-Jin. I am 17. Please look after her.'

Mum and Dad gave me the note when I was six, right after they sat me down to explain that I was precious because they had chosen me. As if I didn't already know there was something different about me and Leah. She's white. Her name's normal. Mum and Dad had always called me Su-Jin before that meeting, age six. Not long afterwards I asked them to cut the Jin because I wanted to be Su. I have been Su ever since, except with Leah, who has called me Su-Jin since puberty turned her nasty, with an emphasis on the Jin to make her point. She also started calling me Chinky when we were thirteen, and I never once called her pizza face even though she was one. Boy oh boy, did the Chinky thing annoy Mum the first and last time she heard her say it. 'That is not a word we use, young lady. It's a derogatory slur used by people who feel threatened and weak and inferior. The term for people like that is racist. Do you understand, Leah? Here, I've printed out some information about the territory of Korea and the sovereign states of North and South Korea. Look at the map – China is a different country from Korea. Look up the words "derogatory" and "racist" and never say that word again.' Leah has said it since, but never in front of Mum.

The adoption agency had given my birth mother's note to Mum and Dad when they collected me. It was written on the back of a napkin in red pen. Dad framed it and a translated version and hung them side by side on my wall. For months my bedtime routine after Mum and Dad kissed me goodnight and turned off the light and shut the door behind them was to turn the light back on, sit up, and stare at the framed note and its translation on the wall.

My name is Su-Jin.

My mother was seventeen when she had me.

She was polite. *Please* look after her, she wrote.

She either borrowed or owned a red pen and she could write straight. The napkin was square and white (yellowing now), like the ones you get at Starbucks.

Mum and Dad told me the police station was in Myeong-dong. I've checked it out a lot on Street View. The building is red brick, with an arched doorway. It's welcoming: looks more like an art gallery. The streets around it are full of shops (including Starbucks) and there are people in jeans. There are neon lights, and food stalls with sea snails, pancakes and spicy rice cakes that I wish they sold in Scotland. The roads

7

have bicycle lanes. The doorstep to the police station is a flat concrete slab, hence not a doorstep at all. And there is no wicker basket with a baby in it on it. For years I have crept around that place, clicking the cursor right then left, zooming, about-facing, noting everything around the spot where my birth mother last laid eyes on me. To an alien looking down, as I am, Myeong-dong is a happy place. Rather than dumping babies, the women sip mango mojitos there.

My mother may have lived pretty close to that non-doorstep. She may have walked there, in the rain I can assume, as I was born midway through *jagma*, the wet season. There is no date on the note, but a young volunteer in the orphanage told Mum and Dad I was dumped on 2 July within hours of my birth. So my biological mother may have walked to Myeong-dong station in the rain if she lived nearby, or she may have cycled in a bicycle lane all the way from wherever it was she lived, with me in a sling against her stomach, or in a backpack, or swinging in the frayed wicker basket in her hand. All I know is that not long after my mother wrote the note, I was allocated to Ruth Oliphant and Bernard Brotheridge (Solicitor and Musician respectively, from Glasgow and Oregon respectively) and allocated the most Anglo-Saxon, pretentious, and excruciating-to-spell-out-loud hyphenated surname in living history.

A baby box would have been cooler than a basket, and a way better story. I've lied twice about it. Ashleigh and Jen, I told, in the backyard of Peter McAllister's house. It was his sixteenth birthday party. They were both: *Oh my God!* and they liked me much more than before because I'd been totally *posted*.

8

As well as hanging the note on my wall, Mum and Dad hooked up with another couple who had a Korean kid. Once a month they'd drop Leah at Gran's or Aunty Louise's and we'd drive to a rainy play park or a beach and Korean Kid 2 and I would stare at each other over beach-sand or sandpit-sand while our parents swapped dumpling and Gamjatang recipes. After the discussion age six, Dad and I also spent an hour a night learning Korean using CDs by Rosetta Stone. Together we repeated:

My name is Su Oliphant-Brotheridge.

Do you have water?

I'm sorry, but I do not understand.

and

Where is the toilet?

Basically all this effort by my folks ensured that I would never have identity issues because I knew everything there was to know about my mother and my culture, and if I ever went to South Korea, I could ask for water then ask for a toilet to dispose of it in.

They adopted me after years of trying to conceive: multiple miscarriages, IVF, the lot. The process was gruelling apparently. There's a whole album in the living-room cabinet devoted to the process of collecting me and bringing me home. There's the photo of the first time they saw me in the orphanage. Me in the hotel room. Me on the plane to Glasgow. Me in the room they'd spent weeks (and loads of money) decorating to 'make me feel at home'. On one wall was a huge painting of the South Korean flag. As a kid it did nothing but worry me – the blue and red swirl seemed to wink at me. The four black markings surrounding the swirl meant something that

9

I did not understand, something sinister. On another wall was a map of South Korea. On another, the note my birth mother wrote and beside that, the translated version which Dad had typed and printed, both in thin black frames. Above my bed was a painting of a woman's hands which had nails about three inches long that were decorated in bright thick candy-stripes. The woman had a peacock feather on her wrist.

(Note to prospective parents of an adoptee from South Korea or a child of any description: If you want your precious darling to have night terrors, decorate their bedroom as above.)

Mum discovered she was pregnant one month after they brought me back to Scotland. It happens all the time, apparently. Suddenly, if a couple hasn't thought about it for years, hasn't wanted it, needed it, taken temperatures, counted days, injected hormones, suddenly, boom.

Leah.

She has mum's blue eyes and Dad's dark brown hair but no one ever says either of those things even though they are all thinking it. Leah has Gran's mouth and Grandpa's lips and white skin like every Oliphant and every Brotheridge except me. My skin's dark but not very, as if my Asian-ness has been left out in the rain all these years, wishy-washy, nothingy-wothingy, not a colour, but not not one either.

But Leah's! When we had baths together as little ones, my skin against hers looked as dark as a proper Korean's. Oh how I would scrub at it.

The ferry gate's open. Time to cross the seas and disappear for a time.

Chapter Two

Ruth Oliphant was used to wearing a wig. Usually it was short, grey, had three curls above each ear, cost £2,000 (according to the *Daily Record*), and complemented her classic black skirt and red robe. The wig she had on now was bright pink, bob-shaped, straight bangs, and it complemented her low-cut slinky black dress and the pink 'Hen Party' sash which crossed her torso and back. For fifty-two, she was pretty damn hot. Good skin from years of water-drinking healthy-living. Slim, toned body from years of organic-only vegetarianism as well as a twenty-mile round-trip cycle from home in Doon to the court in Kilbarchie. People laughed that she cycled to work in Lycra, showering and reappearing in 'My Lady' clobber.

She wasn't the only Hen in the jam-packed club, but she was the only one over the age of twenty-five, the only one without a gaggle of at least ten others with an identical sash, and probably the only one who was about to spike a man's drink.

'Think you've got the wrong place, lady. The bingo's two doors down.'

'Does an attractive cougar threaten you?' She sipped her 'Multiple Orgasm' as sensually as she could, leaning forwards to show some cleavage.

'What makes you think you're attractive?' He wasn't looking at her face when he said this, so it was working.

'The fact that I am.' It had taken a long time to find this man and Ruth's quest to find him had been as mercurial as her plan once she did.

'Can I wear your wig?' He stroked her pink hair and looked into her eyes but didn't recognise her. She smiled at his glorious stupidity and slipped a pill into his beer.

No, she would not let him wear her wig.

*

She'd been in the afternoon's custody court when her husband phoned. Wig on, she'd sat through three breaches of the peace, one of them a domestic, an assault to injury, a dangerous driving, a housebreaking, and a few more that she can't recall now. She was in a good mood by the end of the afternoon session, she remembered that much. Michael MacDonald was defending a few of the cases, and he'd always entertained her, since the first time she'd seen him in court. It was two years ago, and he was defending an unusually dapper man in his early twenties. Ruth had studied the defendant – his designer suit jarred with his tacky billiard ball ring – and had thereafter thought of him as 'The guy behind the 8-ball'.

'The defendant experienced a spontaneous and unprecedented moment of rage,' Michael had said, 'when he came home and found his partner had cut his designer shirts into tiny little pieces. One of the shirts was a Louis Vuitton worth £450.'

The guy behind the 8-ball had expressed his rage by setting fire to his partner's dog. Silver Fox didn't argue hard on this occasion. Like most people, animal cruelty upset him more than violence against women and he did not consider appealing against the eighteen-month custodial. It was a memorable case for Ruth, watching Silver Fox in action for the first time, but also because of the threats the guy behind the 8-ball hurled at Ruth from the cells below her afterwards: 'I'll get you for this, bitch'; 'I know where you live'; 'You'd better watch out'. Ruth decided to ignore the muffled noise, confident that the guards would quieten him, and continued the session.

Shortly after this first encounter with Silver Fox, Ruth was surprised to see him singing in the East Kilbride Gilbert and Sullivan Society's performance of the *Pirates of Penzance*. She had to admit he was the very model of a modern major general. He was exceptionally charismatic, and never more so than today, it seemed. Ruth would never smile in court, but she found this difficult as he spoke about the last defendant of the session, a short and painfully thin twenty-one-year-old man called Barry Andrew Malone, who had somehow managed to find a suit three sizes too small.

'Mr Malone suffers from Oppositional Defiant Disorder, My Lady.' MacDonald gestured towards the glaikit defendant, whose grey suit sleeves ended three inches before his yellowing shirt and who looked like he wanted to punch everyone in the room. 'This is a recognised condition which means he finds it difficult to comply with requests and is often argumentative. In layman's terms, My Lady, Mr Malone has been diagnosed as clinically naughty. On the afternoon in question he was suffering quite badly from naughtiness and did not wish to wait in the queue at Greggs the Bakers on Queen Street. My Lady, the defendant was in dire need of a cheese and onion pasty at the time of the alleged incident. It was 3 p.m., M'Lady, and he'd had no breakfast and no lunch. The alleged victim confronted him, saying . . .' MacDonald pushed a flop of silver hair away from his face as he leant down to read the transcript: *'Wait ya turn, ya knob.'* Head and hair upright again, MacDonald continued. 'My Lady, at this point, I'm afraid the psychological disorder reared its ugly head, which as I've explained is outwith my client's control and My Lady, this is why Mr Malone used his elbow to shove the alleged victim, a Ms Ellen Dalkeith, who was first in the queue at Greggs on the afternoon in question and hoping to purchase two strawberry tarts.'

Ruth bit her lip to suppress a smile and spoke flatly and without looking up. 'He's pleading not guilty?'

'Yes, My Lady.'

As requested by Sheriff Ruth Oliphant, the defendant stood, revealing suit trousers that bulged painfully at the groin and ground his teeth as trial dates were announced by the clerk of court. Ruth gathered her papers as everyone stood and lowered their heads. She exited via the back door, and giggled all the way to her chambers.

There were two messages from her husband on her mobile. 1: *Ruth, call me as soon as you can.* 2: *Ruth, my darling, I'm in the car park across the road and I'll still be here when you're done. Come as soon as you get this. I need to talk to you. It's urgent. I love you.*

Bernard was an affectionate and kind man. Since they'd fallen in love – in Yosemite, it was – he'd often called her 'my darling' and most days he told her he loved her, but when Ruth heard the messages she knew something was wrong. Her first concern was for Bernie. He'd never been into fitness like she was, and while he wasn't overweight, he was definitely cuddly. Last November, he'd complained of a fluttering in his chest. The only hippy notion he'd inherited from his parents was that he disliked hospitals and medicines. He refused to go to the doctor about it and instead cut out almost all fats from his diet, and all alcohol, drank green tea rather than coffee, meditated each morning on a mat in his music room, and prioritised a good night's sleep. Had Bernie had a mild heart attack? Was he waiting for her in the car park, too stubborn to call an ambulance or too scared to take himself to the hospital? She tossed her wig and gown to the floor and raced out of the court to the car park, barely breathing. As she ran, she began worrying that it wasn't Bernie at all – he wouldn't have been able to drive here if he'd had a heart attack. *Not one of my girls,* she thought. *Please, not one of my girls.*

When Bernard told her the real situation – that a lewd video of her beloved eldest daughter was all over the internet and that she hadn't caught the plane home with Leah – Ruth let out a huge breath and said, 'Thank God.'

Bernard did not understand her relief and yelled for the first time since the palpitations of last November. *'Thank God?'*

She kept her voice low and soft. 'I thought you were going to tell me one of them was dead.'

'Sorry, but this . . .' He looked at the phone in his hand, his eyes red and puffy from crying.

Ruth took the phone from him. 'How hard is it to find?'

Bernard lowered his head till it rested on the steering wheel. 'Just type "Magaluf".'

Ruth always read her case papers three times before a trial. The first she called 'an emotional scan'. How did the incident make her feel? It was easy to become hardened in this job, she often reminded herself, and important to remember what the victim felt: the pain, the fear, the alarm. The second time she read to establish the facts so far. What is known to have happened? What law is alleged to have been broken? The third she asked herself what was missing. What questions haven't been asked? What questions remain unanswered?

In the car beside her husband, she pressed play for the first time to commence the emotional scan.

The screen is filled with mostly topless men and almost naked women, all with drinks in hand. The camera rattles from one drunken face to another, bumping from side to side and from floor to ceiling. There's a lot of noise: talking, laughing, ugly music like the rubbish Leah plays in her room. There is Leah at the back, in tiny orange shorts and a blue bikini top, guffawing at something, her beer spilling from the bottle with the force of the joke. Millie and Natasha are there too, drinking from a supersized shared cocktail.

'State your name.' The man with the camera demands, moving the shot to the floor where everyone seems to be looking.

That's not Su. Is that Su?

There's a girl sitting on the dance floor, which appears to have been cleared for her. She looks up at the camera and smiles. We see the cameraman's hand gesturing for her to stand. The girl manages to get to her feet, and moves her face towards the lens, holding one eye up against it for a second, then she jumps back, star-shaped: 'Da-da!' Her usually straight torso bends to one side. She begins to move her arms loosely to the music. She follows the lights with her lolling eyes. She turns to the left and then to the right, curtseying to the men who have circled her. The crowd shuffle in closer, two deep behind the men.

'Name!' the cameraman demands a second time.

'I'm Su Oliphant-Brotheridge!' Oliphant is said with extra vowels and Brotheridge as one syllable. She yells it a second time. 'My name is Su Oileeeephiant-Bridgggge and I'm from Doooooon!'

'You want a free Jäger bomb?'

'Aye!'

'Yes?'

'Yes!'

Cheering from the men in the circle, then chanting from them and the crowd. 'Su Elephant! Su Elephant!'

Black for a moment, an edit, and Su is now on her knees before one of the men in the circle whose shorts are at his knees. She lifts his flaccid penis and puts her mouth over it. 'Su Elephant from Doooon! Su Elephant from Doooon!' The chant gets louder.

'Go go go,' shouts Leah, as if watching the football.

Su moves her mouth to the base of the man's penis, which isn't difficult – a soft two inches – then upwards again. Down up, down up, her black hair knotted and messy. The shot moves to the back of her head: down and up four more times before another pair of shorts shoves its way into the frame. The limp two-incher plops from Su's lips. She slides her knees two feet along with some difficulty, and pulls the next pair of shorts down.

'Go go go!' Leah's chant has taken hold of the crowd.

'Fucking slag,' is the cameraman's whispered commentary. He sounds as if he's hard with hate. 'You fucking cow. Suck it, whore. Take it all the way, dirty bitch.'

Just over halfway through the first viewing and Ruth was already confident about what happened and how she felt about it. Her beautiful daughter had been drugged and gang raped. About fifty people made this happen, let this happen, watched this happen. And thousands are complicit by watching it online.

Ruth felt the heat of a stress rash take over her cheeks, then her neck, closing her eyes as the horrific commentary continued – *Dirty cow, slut. . .*

'That's enough.' Bernard took the phone from her, turned off the video, and dialled a number. 'Su, hon, it's Dad. We both know what happened and we're not mad with you. Not at all. It's going to be okay. Please call us. We love you.' He hung up. 'I've called and called. She won't answer. Or her phone's out of juice or money.'

Ruth's father, also a successful lawyer, was hit by a truck one morning. An embarrassing way for a seventy-seven-year-old man to die, Ruth had thought at the time: popping out to fetch the milk, never getting it. She hated herself for having this thought but could not deny having it, even still.

He must have been swinging his arms as he walked along the too-narrow pedestrian strip just around from the Clover roundabout. He was probably whistling, because he was always whistling, when a huge petrol lorry turned sharply from the roundabout and screeched alongside the strip he was walking on. His right arm got caught in the cavity above the wheel, apparently. The driver didn't even notice till a lady with a pram waved him down fifty metres on. They had to close the street for hours so no one would see the various pieces of him being scraped up.

She felt a familiar mix of grief and mortification now, and felt similarly guilty about the latter. 'Of course. We have to find her. You don't think she'd. . . You don't think she's. . .'

'I'm sure she'll be fine.' Always so calm, Bernard. Always so comforting. 'She'll be hiding out somewhere. Leah said she left the club alone before they did. And she answered the phone to Millie this morning. She's safe. Just, you know, scared.'

'She'll need money. Let's go to the bank.'

Ruth had agreed to fund the holiday if the girls went together. Su, being the sensible one, would look after her sister, she'd thought. Su was reluctant to go – she'd heard about these trips – but didn't argue about it, probably because she, like Ruth, hoped the trip would bring the sisters close again. Leah argued aggressively ('I won't go then! I hate you! You ruin everything!'). She even got a part-time job at the dry-cleaners where Su worked to try and raise the money herself, but was let go after sleeping in twice, and eventually gave up. Once resigned to going, Su said she had enough money in her Santander account to pay her own way (Su never slept in, and had saved over £5,000 in the last three years). Ruth refused to take Su's hard-earned university money, made her promise to leave her Santander card at home, and gave the girls a Thomas Cook cash card each. She had a second card for both in her wallet, so she could put more money in their accounts if they ran out. At the Clydesdale around the corner from the court, Ruth deposited the equivalent of 600 euros into Su's cash card, and continued texting and phoning her as Bernard drove home.

Front door closed, Ruth realised this was nothing like her father's death. Her daughter was missing, not dead. The incident was ongoing, not over. Over twenty thousand views now? Yes, well over that. There were no flowers on the doorstep, no calls on the answerphone and no one would come by with casseroles.

As Ruth dialled work, she yelled for Leah, furious that she'd caught the plane home without her sister. She should have stayed and searched. 'Leah! Leah?' No answer from Leah, but her secretary had picked up the phone.

'Hi Anne, I'm sorry I had to run off—'

'It's all right.' Anne Rinaldi was usually business-like and deferential, but she sounded embarrassed as she interrupted. 'Bill told me to say you should stay off as long as you need to. He's organised Dunmore for tomorrow.'

'Right.' God, they all knew. Of course, thousands of people knew. By tomorrow, the whole world would know. 'Thanks. I'll be in touch in the morning.'

She poured herself a whisky, screamed for Leah again ('Get down here!'), and phoned the police. Bernard took the whisky from her hand and replaced it with a mug of camomile tea.

He'd made a cheese and pickle sandwich too, which he put on the telephone table. She'd always been the one to make arrangements and fight battles. She was good at it, and Bernard wasn't threatened by her competence. He had his own roles – to provide emotional support, and food. For anything else, Ruth felt he needed her clear instructions. He put a fresh pad and a pen in front of her so she could make a note of everything, and paced the hall as she talked to the police.

It was PC Anstruther who answered. He'd given a dodgy statement in court a month or so ago. Twenty-five and bald already, she could tell he'd have a lengthy, successful and spectacularly corrupt career. 'Can I speak to DC Campbell please? It's Sheriff Oliphant from Kilbarchie Sheriff Court.'

There was a snigger in his voice as he said, 'I'll put you through.'

Davy Campbell was one of the good ones. She never doubted his statements; never felt he valued results for results' sake. He was known in the area for being fair with offenders, or at least there were no rumours that he beat them up in the back of vans. 'Sheriff Oliphant. Are you okay?'

Ruth asked him to trace Su's mobile phone, her withdrawals from the Thomas Cook cash card, and agreed for him and a colleague to come by at 7.30. In her own shorthand, she made a note of everything that was agreed. 'So how do I get it off the internet?'

He hesitated. 'Report it to YouTube. Hopefully it'll be taken off shortly. But to be honest, it's not going to be possible to keep up.'

'But surely—'

'It's everywhere.' People were usually too scared, or in awe, to interrupt Ruth. In the last five minutes, it had happened twice. 'Folk are sharing like wildfire.' Davy Campbell had no fear or awe in his voice. He could have been talking to anyone. 'You can report all day every day and you won't stop it. I'm sorry, but you'll never get rid of this. You should focus on finding your daughter.'

'And you'll focus on the men?'

'The men?'

'The one who filmed it, and uploaded it. The ones who practically *gang raped*—'

'I'll go through everything with you in person when I see you at 7.30.'

'7.30. Thanks. Bye Dav—' He'd hung up. Ruth put the phone and the mug down. She grabbed the whisky, drank it in one, and turned to a still-pacing Bernard. 'Get on your computer and report every site that's hosting the video.'

'How do you—'

Sheriff Ruth Oliphant was the only one around here who was allowed to interrupt. 'I don't know! Jesus, Bernard, find out, and do it, and don't stop doing it till it's gone.'

'Okay, I will. And we need to warn your family.'

Shit, he was right. 'Can you talk to Louise and Marie, make sure they don't speak to the press. Get them to break it to Mum, in person?'

'I'm on it.'

Ruth took a deep breath, and headed upstairs to Leah's room.

As Ruth climbed the stairs, fury rising with each one, she couldn't have imagined that Leah would make this worse. But she had, by being curled in a ball under the duvet, head and all. She always did this when she was upset, ever since she was big enough to have a bed. Standing at the door, Ruth fought the urge to take Leah's precious MacBook from her bedside table and smash her over the head with it. 'Leah, sit up. Come out. Leah. LEAH!'

Leah's head appeared from under the duvet. 'Please don't be too mad at her.'

MacBook. Head. Head. MacBook. MacBookhead. 'Mad at Su?' The anger in Ruth's stare seemed to prise Leah's eyes fully open. 'Is Su the one who said Go . . .' Ruth walked over to the bed, paused, and with a tone less flat than before, a little intimidating even, repeated the second word of Leah's Coconut Lounge mantra: 'Go . . .' She bent down till she was breath to breath with Leah: 'Go?'

Chapter Three

Barcelona! I wish Leah could see this, and my wish staggers me. She's been vile to me for years, and I've watched and waited, a desperate victim of unrequited love. But if Leah was with me now, approaching a new, different-coloured city, she would be crazy with happiness and with plans, and her excitement would infect me. I'm pathetic.

She wasn't cruel to me before puberty. I moved into her room when we were six to help her sleep and it was fun. Granted, if I told her to turn the light off and stop reading she sometimes scratched at her sheet for hours to keep me awake, a sound I'd never thought to imagine, and could never have imagined to be so terrible. And I recall several arguments over teddy bears (she got the pink, I got the blue, I wanted the pink, no way was she swapping) and neatness (she was messy, I was neat). But mostly I remember dressing up and dancing and singing and laughing and me having to tell her everything because she wanted to hear it. Dad called us his twins. He said we were two halves of a whole.

The hormones poisoned her slowly at first: she stopped walking to school with me, kicked me out of her bedroom, spent more and more time with Millie and Natasha, wouldn't take me out shopping and help me look pretty. As Leah's happy-girl body was gradually colonised, her hatred of me seemed to intensify. At first I felt confident that she'd come

24

back to me, but hope dwindled over the years. Thank God I had my own friends – particularly Ashleigh from netball and Jen from debating (or the lesbian and the dweeb, according to Leah). At school last term, Leah wouldn't even acknowledge me in the corridor. I think the last conversation we had before the whole us-going-to-Magaluf thing went something like this:

Me: Morning!

Leah: Are those my socks? They're MINE! I am so fucking sick of you stealing my shit. Get them off. (Tries to pull my left shoe off.) Take them off!

Dad (Enters kitchen, has no clue): Guten Morgen and buongiorno! Now what I really want, what I really really want, is a huge mug of (inhaling scent from open Lavazza tin) green tea.

Me (Taking off shoes, handing over socks and talking loudly enough to give Dad a clue): Here, Leah, take them. I didn't know they were yours. I'm sorry I made you so angry.

Leah (Grabbing socks and whispering in my ear): Butter wouldn't melt in your fucking Chinky bitch mouth.

So why am I still yearning for Leah, especially after what happened last night? Because life is never dull with her around? Because she's my twin, my other half?

No, if there are *twins* in our family, it's Leah and Mum. They smile and talk and walk and look the same. They think exactly the same thing at exactly the same time (*No, it's left! Snap! Too much salt. Snap! It was the step-father. Snap!*). They argue so furiously that it makes me shake and then they forget about it but I'm still shaking. They have 50 per cent of the same DNA: a proper mother and daughter. I've never thought about the DNA thing with Dad. By being calm, male, and always around, he's managed to make me feel I have just as much of his as Leah does.

Leah didn't want me in Magaluf and I didn't particularly want to go. I had bags to pack and journals to read. My going-to-university list was five pages long and I'd only made it halfway through the first. After many screaming matches with Mum, and tearful late-night pleadings with Dad, Leah finally accepted that my presence was non-negotiable. For a few weeks, her cruelness towards me strengthened: 'I'm booking a separate apartment for you. Don't think you're hangin' 'round with us.'

I ignored her at first, a strategy I'd been in the habit of for six years. But a week before the trip, when I realised my seat on the Jet2 flight was in row 38 and that Leah, Millie and Natasha were together in row 3, I threatened to pull out. This was a cunning move on my part, as Leah realised she had to at least pretend to be nice to me. Like the loser that I am, I was thankful – no, elated – that she was giving me eye contact, that she changed my seat to row 4 and cancelled my separate studio apartment. She even made polite conversation in front of our parents. Okay, so circumstances had forced it, but Leah was returning to me. We might never be twins again, but I began to hope that her hatred of me was not necessarily a for ever thing.

Following my threat, Leah dedicated herself to honing my look and teaching me how to behave. Glasses were a no-no, and after a few days the contacts stopped freaking me out. My hair, allegedly 'parted like a spaz and dripping like some fucked-up treacle', was handed over to Wesley at Vidal Sassoon who shaped jagged bangs, snipped six inches to chin-length, added curl, weight, caramel bits, and then declared it to be 'Selfie-time! Check yourself out, lady! My work is done.' Marks & Spencer jeans were hidden – I never found out where – and replaced with several pairs of shorts that didn't fit me. Speedos and goggles, no. Bikinis (strapless black, orange floral, fifties polka dot), yes.

Shorts and green halter-neck top on, glasses off, music on, drinks poured, I sat on Leah's floor as she applied the cover-up, foundation, powder, blusher, eyeliner, mascara, lip liner and gloss she'd sourced and bought especially for my dark skin. Each night she'd do it once, wipe it off, cleanse my face, then make me do it again. 'Less, Jeez, not there, not that one, more, now you've gone all drag-Queen, that's it, you lucky bitch, your skin is amazing.'

As instructed, I listened to Leah's Maga playlists each night, watched as she danced in the bedroom, then danced as she watched me. 'Jesus. Close your eyes. No pointing! Feel, can't you feel it? Enough with the seizures already. Drink this, drink it. Now again.'

It was decided I responded best to vodka, which I could tolerate if mixed with cranberry juice or lemonade.

She also gave me swearing lessons: 'Repeat after me: fuck, fucked, fucking.' She'd pinch my arm hard and instruct me to swear in context.

'Ouch, fucking!' Apparently I got it wrong 100 per cent of the time.

The day before we left, she organised a global waxing and eyebrow-and-tache-thread. Back in her bedroom, Mum and

Dad away at the theatre, she sat on the bed to invigilate my final exam. Ever the diligent student, and more-than-ever a competitive one, I set the scene with Maga Playlist 1, sipped vodka and cranberry (with ice, lots), styled my hair, chose denim shorts and white crop top. She watched as I applied the 'eight essentials' she'd purchased at Mac. Three drinks later and I was Maga-ready and dancing to a song with only three words in it (I think she winced a little at one point, not sure, so I closed my eyes and tried hard to feel it). When I opened them she was off the bed and dancing too.

'By Jove, I think she's got it!' She thumbed something on my Ri7 as she moved – how she moved, so unselfconsciously – then handed me the phone. 'But there's one last thing.'

Hey James, her text read. *Come over. I have a surprise for you.*

James was on the St Aloysius debating team and was impressed with my closing argument on the death penalty (I was arguing for, which was hard at first – because I was personally against it – but I even managed to convince myself). I won the competition for our school. He congratulated me afterwards and we met at the Mitchell Library each day of swot vac. Our first kiss was a dry one the day before sixth-year exams. Our second – after we opened our results – was a little too wet. James had a conditional place to read Law at Oxford and his sixth-year results made it official, and the same with me for Medicine at Edinburgh.

'You can't go to Maga frigid and tied to a doofus. You need to be free to lose the big V to an anonymous hottie,' Leah said. 'Practise on him till the olds get home, then chuck him.'

James, shocked by my transformation, managed to strike second base, but only because I took his hand and put it under my T-shirt but on top of my new pink bra, where it stayed for seven awkward seconds before he removed it. That wasn't the first time I'd wondered if James is gay. I didn't chuck him.

After James left – Leah out with mates, Mum and Dad still absorbing *Hamlet* at a disused swimming pool in Govanhill – I took off my make-up, put on my jammies and glasses, played Maga List 5 ('comedown music, matey') and gathered photos of Leah to put on my pin board in Pollock Halls in Edinburgh.

It's sad that there aren't many photos of Leah as a baby, especially when you understand why.

Chapter Four

Ruth's nose was almost touching Leah's. As ever, Leah was recoiling. As ever, she was crying. Ruth should have persevered with breastfeeding. Maybe that would have prevented years of moodiness and howling. But it was a very stressful time, back then. It started when the social worker, Katie Morrison, visited. Su was two months old, and had been with Ruth and Bernard for one month. She'd settled in beautifully, and the social worker's weekly visits had been great till now. They were doing everything right. Baby Su was healthy and content. Mum, Dad, Gran, Grandpa, Aunty Marie and Aunty Louise were all loving and doting. There were no concerns at all.

Ruth hadn't told anyone she was pregnant, not even Bernard. A week overdue and she put it down to the dramatic change in her lifestyle and routine. Two weeks late, breasts tender, she took a test. In the days that followed she waited for it to bleed out, praying it would happen earlier than the last two times, when she'd had to give birth to unformed dead things. She was distracted from the routine she had set herself to bond with Su, which annoyed her. And she felt depressed, which worried her. She wondered how social services would react, as they'd told her she should use contraception to avoid this situation. She'd forgotten a pill or two – life was very hectic, after all, and she wasn't in the habit of pill-taking. Ruth deliberated for days, finally deciding that she would pre-empt the inevitable and terminate the pregnancy.

At 11.30 a.m., Ruth had put Su in her pram and begun the thirty-minute walk to the hospital. The baby always fell asleep on a morning walk and slept soundly for two to three hours. As she entered Kelvingrove Park, Ruth realised that her legs were trembling. By the time she reached Argyle Street, she was crying. She'd thought this through and she knew it was the right thing to do. Why wait for a painful and upsetting miscarriage? But as she passed the art gallery, she couldn't help thinking *What if?*

What if nothing, she told herself as she passed Saskia's bar, doors opening for the day's business. *What if it worked this time? What if I* can *have one of my own?*

She scolded herself for letting those words form in her head, checked that baby Su was asleep, pushed the brake down on the pram, and walked into the bar. To get this done, she needed a stiff drink.

It was bright and sunny outside, so the bartender had left the doors open, which meant Ruth could sit at the table by the door and keep an eye on the baby. Halfway through her whisky, she became so consumed with her thoughts that she stopped staring at the pram and concentrated instead on her glass. *What if?*

By the time she'd finished her drink she'd decided she would let nature take its course. Guilty and panicky now that the drink she'd had might harm her unborn child, she walked four or five steps (no more) from her table to the pram by the door.

31

'Is this your baby?' A blonde woman, around thirty, was standing on the other side of the pram and had her phone to her ear.

Ruth hadn't seen this woman from inside, and didn't feel accused yet. She responded calmly. 'Yes.'

'Hang on, I'll check . . .' The woman had a Glasgow City Council ID badge round her neck. SOCIAL WORKER. Shit. In this city, there were more social workers on the street than cigarette butts. 'You're Mrs Oliphant of 13 Park Street?'

Like almost everything portable that Ruth owned, the pram was labelled with her surname and address. It cost a fortune, this top-of-the-range baby-carrier. Ruth had sewn a label onto the fabric of the inner-hood the day she brought it back from Mothercare. 'I am. Ruth, Ms Ruth Oliphant. This is my baby.'

The girl looked at Su's tiny dark face. 'Really?'

'We adopted her from South Korea. A month ago. You can ask . . .' Ruth stopped herself from suggesting that the girl confirm details with her office. Shit, shit shit shit, she probably already was. She kissed her sleeping baby on the forehead in order to prove her bond. The girl looked at the baby, looked at Ruth, and spoke into her handset. 'It's "mum", thanks, yep, okay, bye.' She hung up. 'Someone could have taken her, y'know.'

Ruth spoke as calmly as she could. 'No they couldn't. I could see her the whole time. Why didn't you look inside? I was just at that table!'

'I can smell alcohol on you.'

'I'm so sorry I worried you. Thanks for being a good citizen.' Ruth unhooked the brake and power-walked home, legs shaking more wildly than they had been before.

Katie Morrison arrived two hours later with a side-kick in tow, a man of around fifty called Samuel Lee. The two of them settled at the kitchen table, each laying out a notepad and pen as Ruth prepared a bottle for Su.

Katie Morrison asked her to go over what had happened at Saskia's bar.

'I'm pregnant, unexpectedly. I was on my way to have an abortion and needed a drink.'

Their expressions filled with horror – the situation was far more complex and serious than they'd anticipated.

Ruth explained that she'd only had one drink. She'd made a bad decision as a result of having to make a very difficult decision.

Katie Morrison asked about leaving the baby unattended on a public road. Ruth explained that she was at a table just inside and that the doors were open. When she realised they might not believe this, or that her behaviour still concerned them even if they did, she began crying. She wasn't thinking, she told them. It was so unlike her, not thinking. She was so sorry.

Katie waited for Ruth to stop crying. 'And you're back already? From the clinic?'

Ruth took a deep breath. 'I didn't go.'

It seemed a long moment before Katie finally spoke. 'What are your plans, Ruth?'

'Plans?'

Samuel Lee took over at this point. He appeared to be Katie Morrison's senior in some way, or just typically male and assuming seniority. 'You know what we mean.'

'You mean have I decided to keep this baby?' Ruth patted her belly with one hand, and noticed the other was holding Su's formula bottle a little too firmly. She relaxed her grip. 'The question should surely be: "Will this baby keep me?"'

'Your answer is yes?' Samuel Lee was writing down everything that was being said.

Ruth took two deep breaths. She had to be careful, work with them, work with them. 'I've never carried to full term. Six times, you'll know that, it's in your file. But if we need to risk manage an unlikely scenario, then okay, let's talk it through. I had a drink in order to gather the courage to abort but ended up deciding against it. I would not have had alcohol if I didn't intend to terminate. I'm not against abortion, but I realise I don't want to do that. If I go to term, all that means is Bernie and I will have two children. A lot of people have two children. If the IVF had worked we'd probably have had at least two. As you know, my marriage is happy, our income good, our house lovely, my extended family close and close by. Su is settled and healthy and we're all very content. If I need help, or if you feel I need help, of course I'll take it.'

Samuel Lee raised his eyebrows. 'There's a lot to talk about. I'm going to arrange a case conference.' He shut his notepad and nodded to Katie Morrison, who Ruth would never refer to as Katie again. A pretty name, Katie. From now on she'd be Ms Morrison to her face, and 'That Dimwit' behind her back.

Ruth was investigated for suspected child neglect and police and social work began their interminable inquiries. Social workers took Su away one month later, after two case conferences in the local social work office, and one children's hearing at the reporter's office. The fact that she was never charged with child neglect did not deter social workers, who argued that there had always been concerns in the department about the mixed race adoption, that their application had been hotly debated, their success a very close call. It was argued that Ruth's behaviour on the day of the planned abortion placed baby Su at risk. This, as well as the pregnancy, now tipped things the other way. It was argued that the couple wouldn't cope with two babies so close in age, that all adopted children need special care and undivided attention. It was argued that the race issue would always have been difficult, but much more so with the added complication of a white sibling so close in age. Issues of cultural identity would apparently now play havoc with attachments. Right-on jargon dominated the arguments and won. It was decided that it was not in baby Su's best interests to be the daughter of Ruth and Bernard now she was going to have a third family member with different coloured skin.

That Dimwit brought Samuel Lee and a police officer with her when they took baby Su away. Ruth and Bernie had decided to get it over with quickly because they didn't want to distress the baby. She was taken from them in the driveway, and they walked inside without looking back. After closing the door, Ruth fell to the floor and cried.

She picked herself up an hour later, and spent her second trimester fighting. She attended alcohol counselling even though she'd never 'misused' alcohol, and had stopped drinking altogether since deciding to go ahead with the pregnancy. She researched social work papers regarding race and adoption so she understood the arguments that she needed to undermine.

She studied the relevant law, read everything there was about similar cases in the UK and the rest of the world. She tracked down a woman who'd gone through the same thing in Australia and had eventually won her case. She hired experts on adoption, race, sibling relationships and attachment theory to produce reports and to help her make a plan that might alleviate some of the concerns social workers had outlined. She contacted the press, and was interviewed on *Reporting Scotland*, where she pleaded for her child to be returned home from her third foster carer, real tears flowing at just the right moment. 'How can it be in my baby's best interests to be taken away from the only mother, and the only family, that she has? She won't even be sent back to South Korea, but dumped into the UK care system. It does not make sense.' Ruth came over well and other television stations picked up on the story. Most newspapers carried it. All were sympathetic.

Ruth barely noticed the baby growing inside her during this battle, which troubled Bernie. 'Perhaps you should rest,' he said when she arrived home at 11 after a television interview in London. A man of playful games and gentle hobbies, his latest was growing vegetables in glasses of water. That night, he was tending the lettuce stump he'd resurrected from the compost bin.

'Perhaps you should *stop* resting.' Ruth mostly appreciated Bernie's ability to remain calm, but calmness would not get Su back and the sight of the lettuce stump made her livid. 'Why are you faffing about with that? They cost 30p, Bernard!'

'Because I don't want to die of stress. And I don't want you or our unborn baby to either.'

Ruth grabbed the jar from Bernie and tossed it in the bin,

lettuce stump, water and all.

Ruth didn't check her pants for blood every couple of hours like she did with the last six pregnancies. She didn't go to the doctor with every twinge. Didn't pray, 'Please God let it be okay this time.' She felt no fear and no anticipation. She wasn't unhappy about it, just distracted, obsessed perhaps, but who wouldn't be?

She was on the phone to one of the lawyers she'd hired when her waters broke. The lawyer had just come out of a hearing with Bernie and they had some amazing news. A contraction made her drop the phone, and she felt intensely annoyed that she had to wait till it subsided to call him back.

She'd won the case. Su would be returned home.

Now, if anyone asks Ruth what labour is like, she tells them it's bloody brilliant.

Baby Su was nine months old when she was returned to her home by a new social worker (also a dimwit). Su looked grotesquely large against her tiny new-born sister, and much darker than Ruth remembered. Ruth handed Leah to her husband after answering the door. She took possession of Su and refused to let her go for weeks, even sleeping with her in the spare bed. She would never lose her again.

The battle for Su's return caused so much distress that Ruth would never know if she also had postnatal depression after giving birth to Leah. The only thing she felt certain of at the time was that her white baby did not seem to need her, and that she was scared of it.

Ruth wasn't scared of Leah now. She sat upright on the end of the bed and took two deep breaths. She needed information.

She could not afford to anger the witness. 'Tell me exactly what happened yesterday, in order, and in great detail, starting from noon.'

Chapter Five

Pension Paula is in the busy Ramblas area of Barcelona. I'd give it a star for location if I was inclined to mooch or feel happy, and maybe another half for price (thirty-seven euros a night), but otherwise it's a dump. It's hard to recall the pretty façade once inside: walls and pieces of furniture that have been patched up over the years, by the elderly owner, I imagine (his name's Carlos); an unstable staircase that smells of dog (his name's Rico); and my narrow single room, which would be okay if it was in an aeroplane, but not on earth. I've been trying to nap for an hour now, but the mattress is lumpy and the pillowcase has a light brown stain on one side and a brownish/red one on the other. I hate to think what the actual pillow underneath looks like. Outside, I can hear English tourists talking about blisters and directions and where to have dinner even though the window's closed (it won't open). Inside, a variety of insects are making a variety of noises. The shared bathroom is on the landing opposite my room and I can almost see particles of faeces and urine creeping in through the crooked gap between my door and the stained green carpet. What I'd do to be in my own king-size bed at home, or even in my bottom bunk in Magaluf.

I slept well in Magaluf. Usually till noon, but yesterday I woke at 1.50 p.m. Leah wouldn't let me set an alarm – it was one of the rules she laid out for me the morning we left.

No non-alcoholic drinks – 'You must match drink for drink'; no talking to boring and/or ugly people; no heading back to the apartment early and alone; no reading; no karaoke singing; no alarm; no unauthorised photo posts; no contacting James; absolutely no haggling – 'if I catch you haggling you're on your own for the rest of the trip'; and no morning runs. My mother's surname had guaranteed body-fascism for the females in our family. Mum, Leah and I all knew that we could not be overweight and an Oliphant. To prevent this deadly combination, Leah didn't eat much, and sometimes vomited if she did, and Mum and I exercised.

At first I missed my fitness regime – I either ran or swam every day, played netball, and regularly raced mini triathlons and half marathons – but I soon surrendered to slovenliness. By the third or fourth day I was waking as late as eleven. By the eleventh, twelve. Yesterday, 1.50 p.m. I remember feeling guilty at first, then chuffed with myself for finally being normal – i.e. lazy and badly hung-over – like the others, who always slept till two, sometimes later, waking with unexplained bruises, bad breath, a need to vomit and – on more than one occasion – a naked male. We'd been at a boat party the day before, moving on later to trawl the six top bars on the strip (Leah let me break the rules because she was almost out of money, and I haggled the price of a Maga Club Pass – or an MCP to us in the know – down to fifteen euros). An Aussie bloke had offered me an ecstasy tablet outside the loos at one of the bars. It was white with a wee thumb imprinted on it and this meant it was safe, apparently, unlike the yellow ones with the butterfly. I was happily drunk, and took it without thinking twice, and without telling the others.

The pill caused me to feel a great deal of love and enlighten-
ment. I told Natasha she was the best kind of clever – a happy
and good and kind clever. I told Millie she should be a hand
model because – man, those hands, can I keep stroking them?
I understood what Leah meant about 'feeling' the music and
went about feeling it for hours. I liked ecstasy. A lot. Next
morning, not so much. Leah must have heard me heaving.

'You okay in there?'

'Aye, think that's it.' My stomach had nothing more to
eject, but it kept trying, noisily.

'Can I come in then? Dying for a pee.'

I retched a couple more times in the sink as Leah chatted
on the loo beside me. 'Can't believe Natasha – what a slag.'

'You mean because of the boat?' Natasha had volunteered
for one of the dodgy games on the deck the day before, baring
her bottom alongside several other drunk girls, to be slapped
by drunk boys who'd answered the Rep guy's question correctly. I'd had several vodka concoctions by that time, and
thought it was funny. Her bum was firm and tiny considering
the size of her boobs, probably why she volunteered.

Natasha's straightened blonde hair, large breasts and nose
ring offset a lack of intensity that boys and girls found irre-
sistible. All the girls wished they could be as popular and as
laid-back as she was. She always said the right thing, diffusing
tension by not giving a toss, moving the subject on so that
fun would prevail. All the boys wanted her, and even though
most of them had managed, her reputation as the pretty, nice,
fun one remained untarnished. Since arriving, she'd slept with
three boys, two in our apartment on the fourth night (seven
hours apart) and one in his hotel the day after. They'd all

messaged incessantly since, and Natasha had replied politely, neither upsetting nor encouraging them. In the thirteen years we'd known each other, my relationship with Natasha hadn't extended beyond '*How are you?* Good. *You?* Yeah, good'. But in Maga I finally understood the attraction. She was relaxing to be around. She was up for anything, and not one to ruminate afterwards.

'You nearly finished? Help, quick. I need in!' I opened the door to Natasha, thankful that Leah hadn't answered my question yet and that she hadn't overheard Leah calling her a slag. Leah leaped off the loo for Natasha to throw up in it just in time.

'Su, Su, look, is that blood?'

Natasha had appointed me chief medical officer on the first night, after she drank from a broken glass and cut her lip. Since then I'd tended insect bites (all four of us), sunburn (all but me, and I forced sun cream on them after), chewing gum in hair (Millie), and a mystery ankle gash (Leah). I'd also talked Natasha through one missing condom, holding her hand and looking the other way as she lay on the bathroom floor. ('Breathe in through the nose, and out through the mouth. Imagine the ocean, nice blue ocean, breathe, feet together, slide them up to your bottom, now just let your knees fall, breathe, good girl, pop a finger in, and . . . okay, let's have a rest and try again.') After Natasha finally located and removed the condom, I'd accompanied her to the chemist and made sure she took the morning-after pill. I also took her to the clinic to be tested (positive, chlamydia), administered antibiotics, given her a lesson about condom sizes and secure application, and planted fresh ones in the girls' handbags (nine handbags altogether) and in every drawer in our apartment.

Natasha's expulsion included several undigested chips and at least one intact slice of onion. 'No, it's not blood, it's the chilli sauce. You're all right.' I held her hair as kebab and pink liquid filled the bowl.

'I fucking love you, Su.' I'd just detached the thick stick of bile dangling from Natasha's lip and wiped her face with a clean, warm flannel.

'Aw, I love you too. Now drink this water, all of it, that's it, hon.'

Throughout Natasha's ordeal, Leah had been removing last night's make-up at the mirror. 'You've put on weight, sis,' she said. 'Your legs are pure trunks.'

'Have I?' It had become obvious that Leah didn't particularly like me fitting in.

As usual, I made brunch for the gang. Fruit salad, cereal, wholemeal toast and jam, and tea. As usual, we then got ready to go to the pool. I was shocked to discover on the first day that it took ninety minutes or more to get ready for the pool. When I went swimming at home – every second morning, forty lengths – it took five minutes. Speedos, yep. Goggles, towel, money, key, yep. Out the door. In Magaluf, pool-readiness required the careful application of day make-up and waterproof mascara. NB: going to the pool did not mean swimming in it.

'Under no circumstances may you put your head and hair underwater,' Leah had instructed that first day.

Then came the choosing of a bikini. The girls had at least

ten each. Being day thirteen, they agonised over having to re-wear one of their earlier choices. Shorts or kimono or crop top selection came next. Finally, accessories.

It was 5 p.m. by the time we got to the pool, late enough for us to find four free loungers together. I could tell Millie was excited to see Euan sunbathing on the next chair with a T-shirt draped over his head, his chest, legs and arms painfully red. She lay on the lounger next to him and played a song on her phone as loudly as she could, hoping to wake him up.

Everyone, including Euan, snoozed in the sun till seven, shade and a slight chill finally telling us to move on. As we walked off, Euan called after us. 'See you on the strip tonight, girls?'

We waited for Millie to answer, which she finally did, without looking back. 'Maybe.'

Millie was the only one in Leah's threesome from an unhappy home. Her parents couldn't stand each other but found common ground in hating their daughter more. In the last year, Millie had been kicked out of home about seven times, either staying at ours or at Natasha's, always retreating to her semi-bungalow in the hope that one parent might greet her with love and an apology. She scared me a bit – I'd heard stories of her punching people in the face on nights out in Glasgow. In Maga, she'd been too busy having sex to punch people. On the first night, she had a threesome with a guy and his ('kind of') girlfriend from Leeds. 'Well I'm not a lesbian,' she announced when she arrived at the pool the next day. Each night after that she'd slept with a different guy. I never engaged in the post-mortems – my virginal input not required, my judgement expected and not allowed – but I listened to the details as she relayed what she could recall. Mostly, she described alcohol consumed, drugs taken (MDMA or ecstasy usually, but cocaine once), penis shape, penis size and penis performance. But she slipped in other details, which painted a sad picture. For example: 'I fell asleep in the middle I think . . .'; 'He told me to leave after, prick . . .'; 'He said I was doing it all wrong . . .'; 'I haven't been crying, it's hay fever.'

Euan was one of her conquests, night three. He'd ended up back at ours and I heard them on the sofa bed in the living room.

'Well maybe it'd work if you didn't stink of puke,' he'd said.

'Shall I brush my teeth again?'

'Nah, it's not your breath. Stop already, it's raw. Jesus, will you give it a rest.'

Millie was pleased with her oh-so-cool 'Maybe' as we left the pool. I wish she could have left it at that, but after a few seconds, she stopped and turned to Euan, who had put the T-shirt over his head again.

'Hey, Euan, what bar you going to?'

This time, he was the aloof one and didn't remove the T-shirt. 'No idea, probably get an MCP.'

'Maybe see you at Roc, say 10?'

'Sure, maybe.' He finally uncovered his face and sat up. 'Are *you* coming?'

Was he talking to me? Boys didn't usually address me. 'Me?'

'Aye, you, I hear you've got something you want rid of.'

Millie grabbed my arm and yanked me away.

'You told him?' I whispered, surprised at how annoyed I felt. Virginity wasn't a big deal to me. I didn't define myself by it.

Millie had gone bright red, so Leah intervened. 'Everyone knows, Su-Jin, just by looking at you.'

'I'm so sorry,' Millie said, loosening her grip on my arm. 'I was pissed, must have let it slip.'

Poor Millie. Ever since I saw her on the first day of school I've wanted to move her into our house permanently and feed her vegetables. At five, she was shorter and chubbier than the rest of us. I remember she sobbed as we formed a line in front of Mrs Benson. I remember that her mum was the only one who didn't shed a tear and who didn't wait till the line disappeared into the building.

We all ordered the usual at McDonald's. Leah and Natasha: cheeseburgers, fries, Diet Coke. Millie: Big Mac, onion rings, Coke. Me: Caesar salad with grilled chicken, water. It was 8.30 p.m. by the time we arrived back at the apartment with the two bottles of vodka that'd get us in the mood for our grand finale.

10.30 p.m., music blaring, outfits and make-up edited and signed off, one litre of vodka and two litres of lemonade finished, Leah opened the second bottle, poured straight vodka into four glasses, ordered us to drink them on the count of three, and began her nightly speech, a kind of coach's pep talk, usually aimed at her threesome (Are we are gonna dance till dawn? Yes! Are we gonna pull? AYE! Are we fucking gorgeous? Roar). But this time, it was all about me.

'Tonight, ladies, we have a mission. Twelve nights in Magaluf and Su here remains tied to an asexual geek. Here, now, before this audience, we shall witness as she unties herself.'

Natasha and Millie chanted 'Untie! Untie!' as Leah dialled James's number on my phone.

My head was already spinning after the three lemonade and vodkas. The straight glass I'd just downed had sent it into orbit. Untying myself seemed a grand idea. I took the handset. I'm still not sure if James had answered or not, but I did believe I was speaking to him, and I did believe that what I was saying was what I wanted. 'James, I want to have fun. You're not very fun, James Frank Morrison-Tweedy. It's over, we're over. It's not you, no it is you. You're . . . what is he, Leah?'

'He's chucked!'

'That's it, you're chucked. Sorry if you're sad, but it's bye-bye now. Bye James, thanks for everything, and good luck at Oxford. You've been great but it's time—'

Leah grabbed the phone from me and ended the call. The gaggle cheered. I climbed on the kitchen bench and bowed to the ongoing applause until I fell off.

Which might be why my shin's got a black and orange bruise the size of a melon.

'Quiet in the coven!' Leah had banged her glass with another glass to get our attention, smashing one, which made us laugh.

'That was only step one. Step two is our main goal, ladies. Su-Jin Oliphant-Brotheridge, your flower must be plucked, picked . . . what is it? Your sheets must be bloodied. Twelve nights and you've not even had a snog. Disgraceful!'

I'm not sure that was entirely correct. On the tenth night we went to Barillo's and I'm almost certain I kissed a boy who had one of those ear things that create a huge gaping flesh hole. His right lobe hung at least two inches lower than his left as a result. But I'm not 100 per cent sure because I was so drunk I fell over, and then crawled from the dance floor to the loo, pretending I was demonstrating a new crawl dance all the way. I can't have spent long with the guy, as associating with someone like him was illegal in Leah's books and no amount of drinking would have made me daft enough to disappoint her. She'd have walloped me.

I was obedient in Magaluf, drinking everything Leah ordered me to. At first I hated the feeling, having never been off my face before, and I'd pretend to go out of whatever bar we were in to 'check out the smoker talent' so I could get some air on my face and sneak a pint of water. But after a few days I started to enjoy letting go, dancing, laughing at things I'd never find funny sober, chanting cheerleader style with my new friends, who had grown fond of me at last. I didn't even hate vomiting, which was a bonding experience, I discovered. I'd never have guessed how lovely it would be to hold a girl's hair back, to take off her heels, carry her to bed, put her head on a pillow, tell her she's going to be okay, reassure her she doesn't look ugly but surprisingly beautiful considering, to hear her tell me: 'No, you, you're the beautiful, much beautiful-er than all the anyone ever.'

It was Leah who said that. I wish I had it on tape so I could listen to it over and over, loser idiot that I am.

Natasha and Millie had been similarly lovely to me, and not only when they were drunk. They'd come to rely on my medical expertise. They giggled at my unconventional dance moves (I do believe I not only created The Crawl Dance but also The Nose. It's good – basically your nose must dictate the moves). They confided in me when Leah was sleeping or away with a boy. Millie's dad hit her and her mum, quite often. Her mum had been hospitalised twice, and had lied to everyone about why. Natasha was in love with head boy Henry, the only male who'd never shown any interest in her. She wondered if it was because she was shallow or stupid. I reassured her that of course that wasn't the reason, but underneath I suspected it may have been. Head boy Henry was intensely clever. The speech he gave about the bedroom tax! The amount of money he raised for Syrian refugees!

In Maga I started to appreciate the benefits of shallowness and stupidity. Thinking about physics and reading about politics not only makes you tired, but also very worried. A sober, well-informed mind is a tense and rightly paranoid one. Basically all I'm saying is that I'd taken to the drink.

'Listen, comrades, and listen hard,' Leah continued. 'Part one of the mission complete, we must now dedicate ourselves to the deflowering – that's the word! – of Su-Jin Oliphant-Brotheridge from Doon. The picker of her cherry is out there waiting.' She took two of the condoms I'd left in her small black handbag, and put them in my brown (and only) purse. 'Are we ready to find this girl some cock?'

Millie and Natasha: 'Yes!'

'Again, are we ready to get Su-Jin cock?'

Millie, Natasha, (A reluctant) Me: 'Yes!'

'I'm not feelin' it, sis. Say the word, say it – *cock*!' Leah was standing on the kitchen bench now. She could be a politician, or a cult leader. We all felt amazing. 'Are you ready to get cock?'

Millie, Natasha, Leah, Me: 'YES YES YES!'

I hadn't said the c word. But I do believe, looking back, that I was ready to get it.

It wasn't a new plan, and it wasn't only Leah's. I thought it was a good idea to have sex with someone in Magaluf, someone I could practise on and never see again. We nose-danced in the small living room of our shared apartment, drank one or two more straight vodkas, and left for the strip.

I remember a bar with a velvet wall, because I stroked it for some time. I remember seeing Euan and his five Manchester mates in a club full of floating bubbles and I remember asking someone if they were real but not the answer. I remember a Looky Looky guy and a bare-chested PR guy with bird tattoos enticing us and Euan's mob into the Coconut Lounge. I remember Leah hauling a boy over to talk to me at the bar: 'Sam here says he'd like to apply for the position.' Natasha introduced me to at least three: 'This is my friend. Isn't she the most beautiful-looking girl you've ever seen?' I remember my chest was drenched. Highly sexy, eh, to have a sweat mark under each breast? I remember feeling hot and angry. The last thing I recall in any detail is Millie putting someone forward: 'John here says he'll shag you.'

After that, nothing is very clear – did I get into a fight? Did someone fall backwards?

I don't want to remember.

I hit myself on the head.

I can't breathe in this room, let alone sleep. It feels like I've been lying here for hours, but I have no idea if that's the case.

I put my denim shorts on. They were always too small for me, but they didn't cut into my groin. Leah was right – I put on weight in Magaluf.

There's an internet café across the road. Baseball cap and sunglasses on, I head over.

Chapter Six

Leah, back against antique headboard, knees to her chest, trembled as her mother looked over the notes she had taken in the fresh Moleskine she'd allocated to this particular case.

'So you went to the Coconut Lounge around one?'

'I'm not sure what time exactly. Probably around one. Like I said, I was really drunk. A Looky Looky guy was harassing us and the PR guy shooed him away.'

'Looky Looky?'

'Street seller: *Looky looky! Designer watch, sunglass for you, looky looky chicken nugget.*'

'Chicken nugget?' The language in Magaluf was obviously not Spanish.

'White trash. Anyway the PR bloke stopped us outside, the one in the video with the tattoo, said we'd get free drinks. We went in. It looked buzzing.'

'What was the PR man's name?'

'I don't remember. I don't know if he ever said.'

'And the Coconut Lounge is on the main strip?'

Leah nodded as Ruth typed the name of the bar into Google on her phone to find the exact address, recoiling when the sex video appeared on screen – 'Jesus' – but persevering till she found what she was looking for. 'Calle de la Punta Ballena,' she added the details to her notes. 'Did you take drugs?'

'No.' Leah cowered behind her knees.

'I'll ask Millie.' Ruth knew Millie's number by heart, but Leah stopped her dialling it. Millie had never lied successfully in her life.

'Millie and Natasha and I took ecstasy. The PR guy sorted it as soon as we got in.'

'And Su?'

'She said no.'

'And you, Millie and Natasha really don't remember who had the idea for Su to do what she did?'

'No, honest. We've questioned each other just like this all day. All we remember is dancing and drinking and taking pills and then suddenly . . .'

'Suddenly you were cheering on a group of men . . .' Ruth stopped herself from heading into the closing argument too soon. 'And the only people the three of you know and can identify in the video are the PR guy with the tattoo and Euan someone from Manchester, who stayed at Hotel Brava with five of his friends?'

'Yes.'

'No one else?' Ruth thumbed at her phone to play the video again. 'Open your eyes, look again properly.'

Leah shook her head.

'Do you recognise any of the faces?' Ruth had been tempted to smack Leah many times, but had only done so twice, both before she'd overtaken her in height. As she played, paused, played and paused, with Leah constantly looking away from the screen, she felt an overwhelming urge to break her nose. 'Concentrate, Leah. You must know someone. You were there for hours!'

'No one else, just us and Euan and the PR guy.'

'Eyes on the screen, Leah, stop blowing your nose. Focus. Look carefully.' Ruth held her daughter's chin to stop her fidgeting.

'Hang on. Pause there. That guy with the red shirt, he's one of Euan's friends, can't remember his name.'

The man Leah was referring to was the seventh receiver in the circle.

'And him with the jeans, same group, don't know his name. I don't know any of the others. No, I don't recognise any of the others.'

After three replays, Ruth was satisfied that Leah had at least examined the video, so she put it away and returned to her note-taking.

'Did anyone buy Su a drink?'

'I don't know.'

'Did she let people buy her drinks?'

'We knew not to, it was a rule. I wouldn't think so, but she was really drunk.'

'The man who took the video, what did he look like?'

'I didn't even know someone was filming it.'

'Whose idea was it?'

'What?'

'They're saying online she did it for a free drink, a Jäger bomb. What is that?'

'Red bull and Jägermeister, energy drink and alcohol.'

'So she was offered one of those as a prize? Because that'd mean someone who worked in the club organised and planned the whole thing.'

'But our ticket gave us free drinks all night I think, so that wouldn't have made sense.'

'Okay, so what happened after? When this film ends?'

'I don't remember how the whole thing ended. I didn't see her after. We were dancing up the other end for ages then we looked for her but couldn't find her.'

'You didn't think to call her? Text her?'

'Um, my phone's been out of juice since this morning. It's been charging.' Leah unplugged the charger and looked through her texts. 'I did! At 04.13, look.' *Whr u? Hows that cherry?* There was no reply from Su.

'What does that mean, "Hows that cherry?"'

'I don't know what I meant. Predictive text maybe, too drunk to type.'

'So you just kept on dancing all night?'

'No, we went to Euan's at some point.'

'You, Millie and Natasha went to Euan's?'

'His hotel. Millie had a thing for him. Natasha was with his mate John.'

'Was John one of the twelve?'

'No, he has a beard. He's not in the film.'

'And who did you have a thing for?'

'I can't remember his name.'

'Was he a pal of Euan's?'

'Yeah.'

'Was he in the video?'

'No.'

'Did the two friends of Euan's who were in the video go back to the hotel?'

'I don't think so.'

'But maybe?'

'No, I only remember us three and them three.'

'*Those* three.' Even at a moment like this, Ruth couldn't stop herself. What a waste of money, private school fees for Leah. 'So you're saying Millie had a thing for one of the men who sexually assaulted your sister, and you and Natasha had things for his two friends, and so without bothering to find out where your sister was, and if she was okay, you all went back to their hotel to make sweet love?'

Bernie halted the interrogation without knocking. 'DC Campbell and another one – Brown, I think she said – are here. Apparently Su withdrew money in Puerto Pollensa earlier this afternoon. She's alive. She's okay.'

Fear crept over Leah's face. 'Of course she's alive!' She obviously hadn't imagined the worst till now, and looked to her dad for comfort. 'You didn't think she'd . . . ? Su would never . . . Dad?'

'How would you feel right now if you were Su?'

Leah looked stunned that her father had not responded kindly, perhaps for the first time ever. 'I'm not Su, am I. I'm not the one in the video, so why are you looking at me like that?'

'I love you, but stop feeling sorry for yourself. This isn't about you. The police are waiting downstairs. I've called Millie and Natasha – they'll be here in a few minutes. I'll get the kettle on.'

With Bernie gone, Ruth closed her notebook and took a breath before taking Leah's shoulders and lifting her back into a sitting position. She prised Leah's hands from her face and placed them in hers, firmly, not lovingly. 'Leah, you let this happen. You allowed your sister to get drunk when she's not used to drinking. You, Millie and Natasha took drugs so you were unable to look after each other or Su. You didn't notice this game or bet or whatever it was kicking off, but when you finally did notice, you did nothing to stop it. You watched as it happened, you goaded and you cheered. It's your fault as much as anyone else's in that film, yours and your best friends'. "The world is a dangerous place, not because of those who do evil, but because of those who look on and do nothing" – Albert Einstein. And now Su's missing. Of course there's a chance she might contemplate suicide. My God, Leah, I could, I just . . .' Ruth wanted to say I hate you, and was impressed that she still had enough control to say 'I am in shock' instead. 'You laughed and cheered when you should have been yelling and screaming for them to stop. No one, not one person in that room tried to stop it. I can't believe it, not one, not even her sister, not even her sister's best friends. You watched them abuse her, rape her, gang rape her, basically, because that's what that is, gang rape. Like in *The Accused*, you were one of the monsters who watched, and those monsters were just as bad as the ones who held her down and raped her.'

'Raped? What are you talking about?'

'Your sister would never do something like this. She would never behave that way.' Ruth removed her sweaty hands from Leah's, which were shaking in sync with her shoulders. 'Now, from this second, you will start to make amends. You and your so-called friends will tell the police everything you remember, and I mean everything, not the scant "I was drunk" crap you just told me. I hear that "I blacked out" line all the time and it's a pitiful defence. Summon the brain cells you have left, and remember every little detail.

'As for your punishment, well as you can imagine, I've given this a lot of thought over the years. Young adults are difficult. Not young enough, not adult enough. So what can I do with you? Withdraw your privileges? MacBook, phone, money, food, so you're forced to get a job or go to college, so you actually do something with your life?'

Leah looked relieved to hear all these ideas, as long as it meant her mother would go away and leave her to cry as loudly as she needed to.

'But I think restorative justice works best at your age.'

'What?'

'Restorative justice. Your punishment, at least part of it, will be to show that you understand the harm you have done, and make it up to the victim. You're going to go and find Su. As soon as the police have gone, I'm going to buy you a ticket to Majorca, leaving tonight if possible. I'm going to stay because I have clout here and I need to hold on to that and use it to keep Su safe and to make things right. I'll guide you. You'll be my woman on the ground. And after you've found her, safe and well, please God, and after you've begged for her forgiveness, which sadly I know she'll offer all too readily, and after you've helped her feel she can face the world . . .' Ruth's voice broke here. Tears almost happened. 'I want you to bring Su home to me. Now wipe the snot and last night's make-up off your face, put a top on that covers your stomach, and get downstairs.'

Chapter Seven

When Ruth and Leah came downstairs, Bernie was sitting on the sofa opposite the police officers. Ruth could tell he was trying to be composed, but his face was pale and his jaw was tight. She perched herself on the edge of the couch beside him while Leah huddled into him on the other side. Even if Bernie wanted to try and soothe her this time, he was not going to manage.

Ruth and Bernard spent their first three years as a couple on the west coast of America. Bernard had a full-time position in the Oregon Symphony Orchestra. It didn't seem fair to move him away when he was doing so well and loving his work so much. Before they met, Ruth had just completed her diploma in professional legal practice and had been informally offered a job with her dream firm in Edinburgh: Hallen, Griffin and Associates, which had a strong reputation for handling civil liberties and human rights cases. The partner who offered her a job over a boozy lunch discouraged her extended holiday, but Ruth had already booked the three-month trip and felt confident she'd start changing the world, or at least Scotland, as soon as she returned. The life she'd planned was to be a serious one. She needed to explore and have fun for a brief period before embarking on it. Alas, she fell in love. Her Scots law qualification was useless in America, so she volunteered for the Crime Victims' programme, comforting victims and witnesses, protecting their right to privacy, and setting up restorative justice groups throughout the state. That first year in Portland was the happiest of her life. She and Bernard would wander the park, go to museums, take the streetcar to the markets, talk endlessly about the world's goings-on, stimulated by shared values, challenged by each other's intelligence. She'd study in the bedroom of their modern apartment, plugs in ears, as Bernard practised in the living room. She'd often cry when she watched him perform in public. He played the same way he loved her – with passion and honesty. Life was pretty close to perfect.

If only Ruth's ovaries hadn't started screaming at her. She'd never expected them to, especially so young, but all of a sudden she wanted and needed a baby. Bernard was the only child of commune-living hippies (Cherry and Bud) who were too busy living off the land and smoking the dope they grew to be helpful grandparents. He was sad to leave the orchestra when they decided to adopt, but understood that Ruth needed to be at home in Scotland; that their application would be stronger if they had a support network around them.

Bernard never made it to head violinist. He was second at the Scottish Opera Orchestra the year they relocated, and won gold at the Glenfiddich Fiddle Championships that same year, but fatherhood took precedence over travel and prestige and he decided to teach. For the last eighteen years, he'd given classes at the Royal Conservatoire of Scotland and at two private schools in Glasgow, dedicating himself to his family with constancy and zeal. Friends and acquaintances probably felt sorry for Bernie. Ruth often worried that people were right to judge him – and her – this way. But when she apologised to him (which she did often) for ruining his career, he'd hold her tight and say: 'That wasn't your decision, Ruth, it was ours. Stop taking all the credit for the best decision we ever made.' And when she apologised after accidentally using her 'My Lady' tone with him (*I will not tolerate this mess in my house!*) which she had done on many occasions, he'd say: 'I bet most wiglets' – he called her cronies wiglets – 'do it all the time and don't even realise, let alone apologise.'

'Really?' In the arms of six-four-four Bernie, Ruth felt wonderfully small and vulnerable. She wished she could tell people what he was like in bed.

'Yes. Anyway, I think it's sexy when you talk to me like I've done something illegal. I think you should send me down.'

Bernie listened attentively as the police asked Leah questions and took notes, unlike Ruth who constantly interrupted: 'Well think harder! Go back, Leah, imagine you're holding that drink. Think!' Occasionally, Bernard would place his hand on Ruth's and stroke it with his thumb, his way of telling her to breathe, keep cool, as he had when That Dimwit had petrol-bombed their world eighteen years earlier.

Leah didn't manage to think at all, her piddling mind still devoid of details. Ruth hoped Millie and Natasha might be more useful, but as soon as they arrived, hope dissipated. Millie didn't remember being at the Coconut Lounge at all, and Natasha was too busy crying and apologising to make any sense. Ruth had always liked Natasha best out of Leah's friends, but this wasn't difficult as they were all idiots. She welcomed Natasha's remorse – at least she realised that she should be sorry. The phone rang as the police were winding up with the girls. It was Woojin.

'Su emailed me an hour ago, but I just noticed it,' he said. *Tell Mum and Dad I'm okay.* Su had written. *Don't try and find me. I'm getting rid of this email account now, and my Facebook's gone, no phone, no use replying. Want to be left alone.* While this was welcome information at first, it didn't make Ruth feel better for long. She already knew Su was alive as she'd withdrawn money from the Thomas Cook card. And the email meant that DC Campbell could conclude his half-hearted interview by saying: 'We won't be filing a missing person's report. She's not missing. She's been in touch and she doesn't want to be found.'

Ruth practically had to beg Campbell to trace the origin of Su's email. 'I'll do my best,' he finally agreed.

'So you'll trace it tonight, and phone me on my mobile?' Ruth wrote her mobile number on a piece of paper and handed it to him.

'Like I said, we'll do our best.' He gave the piece of paper to the young female officer, who didn't seem to know where to put it. 'Stay calm, Ruth. I'm sure she'll be fine.'

Ruth was beginning to realise that she'd have to deal with the situation on her own. No one was going to help her find Su. No one was going to try and stop Su from hurting herself if shame and despair got the better of her. No one would be charged with anything because no crime had been committed. Su had consented to the sex acts, Campbell had stressed, playing the exchange between the 'director' and Su at start of the video as proof: *You want a free Jäger bomb? Yes?*

Yes!

'But she's drunk! Look at her! She's not consenting.'

'Come on, you know that'd be ripped to shreds in your court. Listen to what she says. Look at what she's wearing. Look at what she's doing.'

What Ruth would do to get Campbell in the witness stand right now. She'd find a reason to do him for contempt of court, the misogynistic, arrogant, insolent piece of shit. She'd always thought of him as a good guy, but from this viewpoint – from the other side – he was just as bad as the rest of them. 'Well what about the guy who filmed it, posted it, the people who are sharing it?'

'A month ago, when Su was still seventeen, it would have been illegal to post images or content of a sexual nature. Not now, though, she's an adult. As for the person who uploaded it in Magaluf, or anyone sharing it abroad, I'm afraid we can't do anything about that, probably couldn't even if it was here in the UK. You must know there's no offence here, Ruth, just an unfortunate case of involuntary pornography.'

When Campbell had arrived at the door, he'd stumbled over what to call her. 'Hello Sheriff-Mrs-Oliphant,' he'd said, and she hadn't helped him out. She should always be Sheriff or My Lady to the likes of him. Less than an hour later, 'Ruth' rolled off his tongue. Campbell nodded to his toddler co-worker, and she closed her notepad. Interview over, it seemed.

It had been seventeen years and eleven months since That Dimwit had taken Su, seventeen years and eleven months since Ruth had felt this kind of rage. She stood in the drive-way and watched the police car disappear around the corner of her leafy street. She watched Millie and Natasha skulk off into the darkness in the opposite direction, arm in arm.

Across the road, old Mrs Gray closed the curtains of her front room, where she'd been standing and watching, and Frieda in the modern monstrosity to her right turned out the lights in the hall, the show over. Now, as then, Ruth funnelled her rage into action. She stormed back inside, slammed the front door and grabbed her laptop.

'Bernie, can you book a taxi to Glasgow airport for Leah? 4.30 a.m.' The police had only been gone six minutes, and Ruth was already printing the boarding pass. 'It leaves at 7.10, Glasgow international.'

'I should go with her.'

'No, you need to stay here and keep reporting those sites. Your job is to try as hard as you can to make this thing disappear.'

'I can drive her at least.'

'No, we can't waste time and resources. Leah, go upstairs and pack what you need into a cabin bag. Here's your passport. Don't forget your phone, charger – ring EE and extend that roaming deal for another week. I need you to be contactable and online at all times. Also, send me all your photos from the holiday, and any videos you took, and ask Natasha and Millie to do the same. If you three made any friends over there – if they're on your Facebook or if you have phone numbers or whatever, send me those too. Here's my Nationwide card. Get out 300 euros at the airport, withdraw what you need over there. The PIN number is 3789.'

Bernie put his arm around Leah's shoulders as she sobbed on the sofa, passport in hand.

Ruth pressed the number herself and handed him the phone. 'For 4.30 a.m. Stop crying, Leah, get yourself together.

What's my PIN?'

'Um . . . 3 . . .'

'3789, for God's sake. Say it.'

'3789.'

'Say it again. Thirty-seven, eighty-nine.'

'Thirty-seven, eighty-nine.'

'And take Su's Santander card too – give it to her when you find her. She'll hate spending my money. Right, now upstairs and pack.'

By 7.30 a.m., Leah was on her way to Majorca. Bernie had contacted the Internet Watch Foundation, the police in Magaluf, YouTube, Google, Twitter, Facebook, and about 120 other websites and blogs. Google alerts pinged into his inbox as new sites emerged, the pings coming in faster now it was daylight – ping ping ping, it was raining Su.

Neither of them had slept. Ruth had spent the night in her bedroom, reading up on the relevant law, taking notes on cases of revenge porn and involuntary porn, looking for a way to seek justice. It would be possible to prosecute some-one for distributing explicit images of an ex-partner without their consent, or if Su was under eighteen (just one month younger!), or if there was blackmail involved, or threaten-ing and abusive behaviour, or stalking, or improper use of a public communications network – but DC Campbell was right, none of this legislation would wash in Su's case. A new law on revenge pornography had been agreed in England and Wales, mostly due to celebrity campaigners, but had not been passed there yet. It was also being discussed in the Scottish parliament, but was a long way off. And anyway, this wasn't a case of revenge porn. It was 'involuntary pornography' apparently: a ridiculous term, like some kind of sneeze. She realised the only way to fight this battle was by launching or joining a campaign to change the law – to organise meetings, call for signatures on a petition, write blogs and newspaper articles, be interviewed on television and radio – all of which would keep the story and the film alive, which was exactly what she didn't want.

By 5.30 a.m. she'd reconciled herself to the fact that she was going to do nothing. She would ignore it; wait for it to go away. She would use all her energy – and all her Shrieval power – to find Su and bring her home. She'd help her lie low for a month. She'd dye Su's hair, cut it short, get her a new wardrobe and a new look, maybe change her name, organise counselling for her. If necessary, she'd move house, shire, country. By the time Su was living in halls in a different city and a university filled with fresh-faced strangers, no one would recognise her or even remember that there was a video. She promised herself that she would remain calm and focused so that she would not make things any worse for Su.

Bernie hadn't moved from the kitchen table since the police left the night before. She made them both green tea and porridge, and sat beside him. 'Maybe you should get some sleep.'

He pushed the tea aside and poured what remained of the strong black coffee in the six-cup plunger he'd made. 'I can't stop.' Ping ping ping, three new alerts. 'I'm pasting my complaint and sending it to each new site. Most have ignored me so far but I think it's worth doing. I've also been looking at this company in the States – The Reputation Defender. Their strategy is to flood the internet with positive stories and images of the victim till the offensive one's flushed out. They cost a fortune to hire, but I think we can do what they do. Gregor's coming over to help me set up a blog and Twitter accounts and things. What would Su's Facebook password be?'

'Why?' Ruth looked at the screen. To her horror, Bernie was trying to reactivate Su's Facebook page, adding failed password attempts to a long list on a piece of paper on the table. Methodical as ever, he'd worked his way through Su's friends, hobbies, favourite films, books and places, and was now typing 'Seoul'.

'Stop that, Bernie. The last thing she'd want is to be on Facebook at the moment.'

He typed Myeongdong, which didn't work, and added it to the list on the table.

'Bernard! Are you listening to me?'

He typed Myeong-dong. 'Bingo!' Su's Facebook page reactivated and appeared on screen. She had 743 notifications and 96 messages.

'Deactivate it!'

But he wouldn't listen. He deleted the messages and notifications, and uploaded a photo of Su receiving her Dux award, adding the caption 'Look what I got!' He chose 'public' on the privacy settings and tagged her name. 'It takes time, but it works. Trust me.' Ruth handed him a spoon and pushed the bowl of porridge closer to him. 'Bernie, honey, the way to be invisible is not to advertise.'

'I know what I'm doing.' He posted the Dux photo and started looking through his video files.

'You don't! As usual, you have no idea what you're doing.

What you know how to do is grow leeks in glasses. Go and do that, and get off the computer. I said get off!' She snapped the lid shut before he could post the video of Su's winning death-penalty debate. 'The damage is done and we need to be discreet and ignore for a while. I've been reading all night and we can't undo it, the law won't punish the guy who posted it or the guys who – you know – or anyone who watches it and shares it. The film exists and it always will.' She removed the coffee mug and plunger from the table and put them in the sink.

'I have to try.'

'But you have no idea what you're trying to do. Take her Facebook off, tell Gregor you won't be needing his help, and for heaven's sake do not start up blogs and Twitter accounts about our family. Now eat the porridge, and stay near the phone.' Ruth stood. She'd only managed two mouthfuls herself. 'I'm going to work.'

Ruth locked her bike in the basement area of the court. One of the G4S vans was emptying prisoners for the morning session. It had poured with rain from Doon to Kilbarchie, and Ruth looked more ragged than the men filing out of the van and into the cells. Before showering in the staff bathroom, she checked her phone. Leah and Millie and Natasha had texted their holiday photos and videos, as well as details of the new 'friends' they'd made in Magaluf. She'd look at those later. First, she had to text Leah.

1. Go to police in Magaluf and say your dad has already been in touch. Make sure they've filed a missing person report. Show them the attached photos of her. Tell them what clothes she had and might be wearing etc. Tell them she withdrew

money from MASTERCAJAS, ILLES BALEARS 7470. Tell them she emailed from somewhere over there – give them her mobile number and email address. Give them your mobile and contact details and mine too.

2. Go to Magaluf apartments and ask if anyone saw her leave. Write down everything – names and contact details of people you talk to, and everything they tell you.

3. Go to the Coconut Lounge. Get names of owner, PR guy, staff, anyone who was there that night. Ask if they have CCTV and if so, find a way to get it.

4. FIND OUT WHO FILMED IT.

5. Go to Puerto Pollensa. Ask in shops etc. if anyone has seen her – focus on area near the ATM where she withdrew money (address above).

6. Text as soon as you get this to confirm you have received instructions. Text information as it comes in, immediately.

Dressed and showered, Ruth walked along the corridor towards her chambers. Two middle-aged male fiscals stopped laughing when they saw her coming. Her young secretary, Anne, coughed an embarrassed 'Morning'.

David Dunmore, a jolly travelling sheriff of fifty-nine, was sitting at her desk, reading over the reports for the morning session. 'Ruth, what are you doing here?'

'I'm really sorry, I didn't get time to call. I'm fine to work today. Business as usual. You can go home. I'll make sure you're paid for the trouble.'

He peered over the top of his gold-rimmed glasses, eyebrows raised. 'You're sure?'

'Why wouldn't I be?'

Dunmore slammed shut the file he'd been reading and picked up the newspapers on the desk. (Anne always laid out the morning papers on her desk.) He tossed them in the bin, touched Ruth's arm with a sad nod, and left.

She rescued the papers immediately, cowering by the door so Anne wouldn't see her expression as she read the first headline: *Judge's Girl in Sex Tape Scandal.* She scanned all three papers, certain words and phrases burning into her brain – Shameful, Slut, Shagaluf, Sheriff's disgrace, daughter in hiding.

'This is not the first scandal for Sheriff Ruth Oliphant,' her favoured broadsheet argued. 'One month after adopting Su-Jin, she left the baby unattended while getting drunk in a pub in Glasgow's West End. As a result of her neglect, the baby was taken into care. The Lord President must now ask the question: how can this woman command any respect at the bench? Eighteen-year-old Su-Jin, who has not been seen since performing multiple sex acts in exchange for a free *Jäger bomb* in Magaluf, is due to start studying Medicine in one month. Edinburgh University must similarly ask: how can this prospective medic command the respect of her intended profession?'

The clerk was knocking at the door. Ruth shoved the papers back in the bin, put on her wig, grabbed the reports she should have read, and headed to Court Four.

Ruth dealt with two breaches of curfew, a shoplifting and a dangerous driving as professionally as if she was the same person as yesterday. It was the domestic assault trial that caused her to slip. Almost half the cases in court nowadays were domestic, much more than that after a bad football result, or after a good one. The plague of violence against women in the country angered her at the best of times. There was no political will to address the issue, and hence no resources, so much of Ruth's time was spent listening to bullshit that made her want to scream – (*Lawyer X: She gave as good as she got. Psychology Report X: His wife was going through menopause and was uninterested in sex*) – and all she could do was send hungover men to prison to ruminate about the crazy bitches who'd put them there.

Silver Fox was defending. One of the fiscals who'd been gossiping in the corridor earlier that morning was relaying the case for the Crown. And the defendant, a forty-nine-year-old from Saltcoats with a glass eye, was looking distinctly unremorseful in the seat before her. The man had allegedly 'punched Sarah Marie Johnstone in the face, causing her to fall backwards into the refrigerator, and did repeatedly stamp on her right hand with his foot, and in so doing did break three of her fingers, all to her injury'.

She was finding it difficult to concentrate because of the defendant's expression. He was staring at her with his working eye and there was no fear and no pleading in it. She'd scanned the reports as the fiscal read the complaint, and now knew this one-eyed monster had beaten the bejesus out of his wife on many occasions. Silver Fox was explaining that the man had been drinking since 3 p.m. on the day of the alleged offence and that his wife, sitting three rows behind him in the court, had also been drinking, and had written a letter stating that she had hit him first and that she did not want him to be charged, but wanted him to come home because she loved him and he was a good dad and he was her world and her everything.

'And have you continued to drink since this latest incident in May?' Ruth asked the defendant.

'Hardly at all.' His impertinent stare, the upward turn of his lips, and the raising of the brow above his gone-eye unnerved her, but nothing would prepare her for what he then said: 'Just the occasional Jäger bomb.'

She couldn't be sure, looking back, but at the time it seemed that everyone in the court got the joke. She heard coughs masking giggles. The only person who she felt did not react to the comment was Silver Fox, who tried to move onwards with: 'My Lady, Mr Cowey has since been referred for alcohol counselling and . . .'

The defendant had turned around to face his wife because she was laughing, which pleased him to the extent that he also laughed.

'This is funny, Mr Cowey?' By the time he turned and faced Ruth again, the laugh had ceased but its trace remained.

'And, Mrs Cowey, you think your husband, your "world your everything", is funny?'

The wife turned red and shook her head.

'I will not tolerate insolence in my court! Mr Cowey, you are a disrespectful, arrogant and dangerous man. You have shown your wife no respect, and you are showing me no respect. You've pled not guilty to this offence and I am remanding you in custody until the trial. I am also charging you with contempt of court for your behaviour here today. Miss Williams, dates please?'

The clerk, Lorna Williams, tapped on her computer, arranging trial dates as requested.

The defendant's wife, Mrs Cowey, was now texting

someone, or posting something, not realising she was also in a great deal of trouble.

'Miss Williams, will you take the phone from the defendant's wife and give it to me please? Mrs Cowey, you obviously seek no respect and therefore you will probably never get it. You support the man who broke three of your fingers on this occasion, who gave you a black eye and a cracked rib in August last year, who hospitalised you in January 2012 because you were out with the girls and failed to answer your phone when he called to ask where all the onions rings had gone. I'm reading here that he cracked your rib while your eight-year-old son Robbie was in the bedroom next door and it was Robbie who phoned the ambulance? It's because *you* alerted the police this time, Mrs Cowey, that we're here today, but since then you have taken him back, you have changed your mind, your statement, your story. You have wasted my time, you've wasted the time, resources and a great deal of money of the criminal justice system as a whole, and now you're laughing because it's funny. You're laughing and you've – what . . . ?' Ruth looked at Mrs Cowey's phone, an Ri7, the newest and most expensive on the market. It astounded her that people on benefits still managed to get the latest gadgets. 'You've updated your status on Facebook, *OMG in court sheriff is magasluts ma! LMAO!*'

Ruth wished she hadn't read it out loud. Everyone was now shuffling and whispering.

'Mrs Cowey, I'll see you back here this afternoon because you, too, are charged with contempt of court. I only wish I could place you in the same cell as your beloved.' Ruth was shaking with anger as a very nervous Miss Williams handed her a piece of paper with the trial dates written on it. The room was silent as Ruth read, nodded and handed the paper back, as the clerk read the particulars out loud, and as an officer escorted Mr Cowey towards the stairs leading to the cells. When the defendant got to the top step, he turned to his wife: 'I love you, Vera. I fucking love you.'

Mrs Cowey stood up in order to recite a sonnet of her own: 'I fucking love you, Eddie, I fucking love you! And Robbie fucking loves you. You're a fuckin' amazing dad.'

Mr Cowey smiled at Mrs Cowey. They fucking loved each other. He then tossed a hateful smirk at Ruth, as if to say: 'You think I'm the piece of shit here? You think *I'm* the bad parent?'

Ruth could not contain herself as he disappeared into the bowels of the court. She may have stood up. She may have yelled. She may have directed her words to the offender, or to the fiscals and defence lawyers and clerks sitting at the layers of benches in front of her, or to Mrs Cowey and the dozen or so onlookers still sitting in the court. All she remembers now is the words she said/yelled/who knows. 'I WILL NOT TOLERATE INSOLENCE IN MY FUCKING COURT!'

Ruth stormed out, walked to her office, and slammed the door behind her.

At her desk, she worked quickly, because she suspected the Lord President might call. First, she phoned DC Campbell, and wasn't particularly surprised that he hadn't bothered to trace Su's email. Before he could finish explaining why he hadn't had time to do so – and why he would probably never find or make the time – she hung up on him. She asked Anne to locate Silver Fox and summon him to her office. She packed her work laptop and her work mobile into her pannier bags.

In her work diary, she noted the entry codes to the court and to her office door, and the passwords to the remote information system for her laptop, in case stress deleted these hitherto embedded numbers from her memory, and then added the diary to the other items in her pannier.

And then she took the call she'd hoped would not come, but had half expected. 'Sheriff Oliphant, it's the Right Honourable Lord Kelly for you.' At least Anne wasn't calling her Ruth, she thought to herself.

Thomas Dickson Kelly had been Lord President for three years. As head of the Judiciary in Scotland, he had the power to sack her. She'd met him once at a charity event, and had seen pictures of him many times in the press. He wore a grey toupee and was known in disrespectful circles (usually ones loosened by alcohol: pub, charity event, dinner party) as Tommy-Two-Wigs.

'Lord President, hello.'

'How are you, Ruth?'

She hadn't expected the human touch from this famously dour man. 'I'm fine. She's still missing but I know she's alive, which is the main thing.'

'This must be difficult. I can't imagine. You need to take some time off.'

The human touch hadn't lasted long. 'I said I'm fine.'

'And I'm saying you're taking time off. You can't sit at the bench when people are reading about this in the papers. I expect it'll be on *Reporting Scotland* tonight. We've had calls.'

'So? I've done nothing.'

'Two contempts and one F-word already, Ruth, and you've been at work – what – three hours?'

She wondered who'd been in touch with him about what happened in court. Had he asked the clerk, Miss Williams, to keep an eye perhaps? She hadn't had time to reflect on her behaviour in court, but was doing so now. She was a speedy reflector, didn't take more than a second or two usually. Yes, she'd been unprofessional and had lost control. It was best not to be defensive. 'I believe the contempts were warranted, but if I lost composure, I apologise. I'm calm now.'

'Then there's the neglect charge years ago—'

'There was no charge.'

'Investigation, but it's a catalogue, isn't it? Too many elements. Mainly it's the video. You can't hand out sentences when everyone's judging you. It's not up for discussion.'

'Are you calling a tribunal?'

'I'm just telling you to take some time off.'

Ruth still had her wig on. She rested her hand on it as if to absorb one final moment of power. 'I understand. I'll go home now.' She hung up, slowly removed the wig, and threw it in the bin with the newspapers.

A man called Xano had ruined her daughter's life, and was now ruining hers. A 'film director from the UK' had destroyed everything she loved and had worked so hard to build. She needed to find this man, and was glad the Silver Fox was now knocking at her door because he was the only person she could trust to help her.

Ruth had witnessed Michael MacDonald win the unwinnable, getting his hands on information so deeply buried that no one else could ever have found it. He seemed to have inside contacts in every field – IT, police, criminal gangs, NHS, media. She disliked his methods most of the time, but appreciated his determination, imagination and – particularly – his presentation. Bernie had always been enough for Ruth in the real world, but sometimes in her fantasy world MacDonald would bend her over the desk she was sitting at now.

'Michael, take a seat. I need your help and I'll pay you for it. Whatever your hourly rate is, I'll double it.'

'I'm listening.' They'd made a deal.

'I need you to trace an email my daughter sent her friend Woojin last night. I'll forward it on to you. Can you give me your contact details – email, mobile, everything? I want to be able to get hold of you. This is my mobile etc. Text me your details as soon as we're done.'

Silver Fox handed her his card, then stared at the bin with the wig in it. 'Are you all right, Sheriff Oliphant?'

'Ruth. I'm Ruth, it seems.'

'Are you all right?'

'Yes. Now, the other thing I need . . .' She played the Magaluf video on her phone, and paused it at the beginning, when the man filming it is talking, '. . . is to find this man. He calls himself Xano online. He filmed this and either uploaded it himself or got someone else to. He has a Scottish accent, West of Scotland, Glasgow maybe. He was at the Coconut Lounge the night before last. I'll also send you the photos Leah and her friends took in Magaluf, and details of the friends they made. I haven't had a chance to study them yet, but maybe this guy's in there somewhere. That's all I know.'

MacDonald studied the frame. 'And when I find him?'

'I like that you're saying *when*.'

'I'll find him. But what then? Unfortunately, he's not done anything illegal.'

Ruth paused for a moment. She didn't really know yet. 'Then we'll talk.'

Before leaving her office, Ruth phoned Woojin, who forwarded the email Su had sent the night before, and then sent it and the holiday photos and new Facebook friends on to MacDonald. To her horror, Millie had friended Euan, surname Grier, who was one of the twelve. Ruth was more polite to Anne than usual, knowing she might need her help at some point – access to the office, or to information, for example, she didn't know what yet. It also occurred to her that Anne might be Two-Wigs' informant. She'd never taken the time to notice anything about Anne Rinaldi bar her long dark hair and sharp blue eyes, and now wished she had. If she'd bothered to develop a rapport with her underling colleagues, perhaps she'd be surrounded by sympathetic allies rather than spies with schadenfreude smirks. 'I'll be working from home this afternoon, Anne. Thanks so much for everything, I appreciate it.'

As she unlocked her bike in the basement, Mr Cowey was being shuffled into the G4S van. He wasn't laughing now, but he probably would have had he seen Ruth in her Lycra.

Sun now shining, head down, the fury seemed to do the pedalling for her, and she was three streets from home before she knew it. She stopped by the fish and chip shop on the pier because her phone was ringing.

'Michael here. Su emailed from an internet café in Barcelona. I'll text you the address.'

'Thank you so much. Email me what I owe each day. I'll pay straight away. Sorry, gotta go, another call.'

She was still straddling the bike when she took the second call, but dismounted and dropped it to the ground when she realised she needed to concentrate. It was Merilyn Davies, head of the Medical School at Edinburgh University. 'This is a difficult phone call, Mrs Oliphant. Are you able to talk?'

Ruth sat on the gravel beside her bike. 'I am.' Unlike the one from the Lord President, she hadn't expected this call at all. And she didn't respond to the voice in the same way. 'I don't know if I want to though.' Her voice was fragile, that of a powerless and petrified mother.

'Mrs Oliphant, the University Disciplinary Procedures, set out under section four of the general regulations . . .'

'Are you reading to me from the manual?'

'I'm sorry, I know this is difficult. Yes, I am reading from our procedures, which state that conduct which brings the university into serious disrepute, by causing serious reputational damage, can result in expulsion.'

'But she's not committed an offence! And aren't those regulations only if she's a student, if the behaviour has occurred on campus?'

'The regulations also state that if the behaviour is not in violation of the law or a major offence under the university's general regulations, the college may apply its own regulations and disciplinary processes to the student.'

'So your regulations basically state you can do whatever you want to students. But, you see, she's not a student yet.'

'What I'm saying, Mrs Oliphant, is that she never will be. This is a very unusual situation and we've discussed it thoroughly. We've decided to withdraw the offer because her behaviour impacts our reputation – and we do have the right to do that. I'm sorry, but your daughter will not be studying with us. Are you still there, Mrs Oliphant?'

Ruth held the phone at her shoulder to muffle her sobs. She didn't want Ms Merilyn Davies, head of one of the best medical schools in the world, to hear her cry.

'Mrs Oliphant? Are you still there? I'm so sorry, but we have a reputation and we have rules and we just can't—'

Ruth wished she had something clever to say, but all that came out was how she felt: 'That's not fair. It's her life, her future, it's just so unfair.'

'I've written to your daughter, Mrs Oliphant. She can appeal, but I have to tell you there's not much point and her energies might be better spent applying elsewhere. I'm sorry. Goodbye, Mrs Oliphant.' Merilyn Davies stayed on the line, waiting for Ruth to say goodbye. 'I'm going to hang up now, Mrs Oliphant, okay? Mrs Oliphant? Goodbye.'

Ruth wheeled her bike down onto the beach. She sat and watched the weak waves tickle the sand. This morning she had cycled to work with confidence that this problem could be solved by waiting and ignoring. Ruth felt sure that's what Su had decided too – to hide away and wait till people lost interest in the film. They were so alike: sensible and logical and motivated and single-minded. And, now, because of this video, they were both unemployable, futureless.

Su had wanted to be a doctor since Santa brought her a medical kit at the age of three. She wore the stethoscope around her neck for months. Wherever they were – coffee shop, nursery, grandparents' house, swing park – she'd put the headset in her ears and press the chest piece against the back or chest of whoever would stay still long enough. Already intensely beautiful, with almond eyes, full lips, thick dark lashes that would never require mascara, and deep dark eyes that looked and were kind, it was never hard to find a willing patient. Ruth marvelled as she watched her daughter grow – she had plucked her from a lucky dip, not knowing how her genes would conspire to make her look, think and behave. At three, it was already obvious that she had dipped her hand into a bucket and scored the only bag of gold. 'Cough,' Su would say, and the patient would always obey. 'Again,' she'd demand, trying to sound serious but unable to sound anything other than painfully cute. She'd take notes (scribbles) in her medical notebook, check ears with the plastic otoscope, inject arms with the plastic syringe, and complete her examination with a reassuring pat on the patient's shoulder: 'Take this three times a day and don't spit any out.' Or 'I'm afraid it's very bad news, Mrs Penterland. You have cancer of the hair.' A born businesswoman, she'd then demand an extortionate consultation fee, and haggle for as long as it took to reach their highest limit. Perhaps Ruth pushed her in the direction of Medicine after that. Certainly, she encouraged the watching of medical documentaries and the reading of books with health as a plot or subplot – children's and adults, fiction and non-fiction. Ruth didn't feel the need to limit Su's childhood reading to books considered to be age or subject appropriate. She'd often discuss biology and pharmaceuticals with her, using the correct terminology so she would be comfortable and familiar with the issues and the vocabulary. And, yes, she had steered her towards the sciences when she chose her specialities in third year, but what clever child would select drama over chemistry? In fourth year, she organised for her to do work experience at the Southern General in Glasgow. A tutor or two was hired in fifth year to ensure she got the high As required to get into Edinburgh. As she neared her finals in fifth year, Su had said she was wondering about doing a general science degree, but they talked it over and came to the conclusion that Su was just nervous about getting in. She had no reason to be. She achieved five As (Band 1), won prizes in biology, maths, physics and chemistry, was Dux of the school, and was offered a conditional place at Edinburgh based on her fifth-year results. When she achieved another four high As in all her Advanced Highers, the offer was firmed.

So what now: basic science at one of those ugly modern colleges in Glasgow? No. No no no. Su wanted to be a doctor. She was going to the best medical school in the country. She would be a doctor.

Despite the police and Bernie reporting the video, it was still on YouTube. As Ruth watched it again, she realised that Su had performed the acts with calmness, patience and diligence. Ruth felt she could almost have been watching a home video of three-year-old Su with her toy stethoscope. *Cough. Again.*

One hundred and sixty-seven thousand, nine hundred and eighty-six views. Ruth set the volume on her phone to maximum and played it again. The Lord President had watched this. Anne Rinaldi had watched this. Silver Fox. Merilyn Davies. A conference room full of university professors. Giancarlo from the fish and chip shop at the end of the pier.

They'd all watched this.

'You want a free Jäger bomb?' The cameraman asks. Yes, he had a west of Scotland accent, Ruth confirmed.

'Yes!'

And yes, that was Su's consent. She had agreed to the performance.

'Fucking slag.' Xano snarls to himself, pointing at Su as she performs on her knees. His left hand is in the shot again. 'You fucking cow. Suck it, whore. Take it all the way, dirty bitch.'

As he says the word 'bitch', Xano points at Su and his left hand and some of his arm is clearly visible in frame. Ruth hadn't noticed before, but he was wearing a red fabric bracelet on his wrist and a ring on his middle finger. Just a plain dark band, by the looks of it.

A text from MacDonald diverted her eyes from the scene at the Coconut Lounge. *Su emailed from the café, La Rambla 31, Barcelona, last night at 7.30. Can you call me? Or come over? Working from home today.*

Before responding to the text, she dialled Leah's number. 'Hi, Mum, why haven't you . . . hang on, I can't hear you. Let me go outside.' There was loud music in the background, which gradually faded. 'Did you get my texts? I've . . . Mum? Hello? Reception's bad, I'm gonna text you.'

Ruth had different alerts for texts from different people. For Bernie, a snippet from Mozart's Serenade in G major. Su, an old-fashioned phone bell. Leah's had been set to silent since the first abusive text three years ago (*f you, m'lady*). To her horror, she'd forgotten to change it. She checked her texts now and read the ones from Leah. She was being very efficient:

At 11 this morning: *Spoke to police officer in Maga (name*

Barco). He said Dad has phoned four times already. Told me what he's told Dad – she's been in touch, so she's not missing. Said will talk to bar owner but thinks no law broken. Dad has contact details. Said to tell Dad to stop ringing, they'll ring him. Not helpful.

12.30: *No one remembered seeing her leave apartments.*

14.10 (one minute ago): *At coconut lounge in Maga. Bar tender says there's CCTV. Owner an arsehole, staff hate him. Don't worry I will get it.*

Ruth dialled her number immediately, but it didn't connect – out of battery perhaps.

She changed Leah's alert from *Silent* to *Alarm*.

Next, she texted MacDonald: *What's your address?*

MacDonald's house reflected its owner: old charm, modern flourishes. The plain wife was unexpected, though. Maybe she was pretty twenty years ago, Ruth thought, following Kelly-Anne MacDonald's substantial legs through to the office. 'Let me know if you want coffee or anything.' Kelly-Anne shut the office door before coffee or anything could be requested.

'Millie took this photo in the Coconut Lounge that night.' MacDonald got straight to business, as ever. His dog, a brown and white terrier-cross called Nigel, was curled at his feet. 'Look at this.'

Ruth stood over his shoulder and looked at the photo on screen. He'd zoomed in on a woman's torso. Her white T-shirted chest took up most of the shot.

'Who's she?'

'It's not her. Look.' He pointed at the cursor hovering over a hand and lower arm, which was resting on the girl's shoulder.

He wore a long-sleeved shirt, also white, cuff folded up to just below the elbow. On his wrist was a red fabric bracelet, and on his middle finger, a black ring. 'That's him.'

'So now we know he wore a black ring, a red fabric bracelet and a white shirt folded to the elbow. In the video the ring looks like it's just a band. It's black, see, just a black band? But in the photo . . .' MacDonald clicked on Millie's holiday photo one more time. The ring had twisted around a little to reveal a sideways view of the setting, which was black and bulbous.

'Is it a billiard ball ring?' Ruth shuddered – could the man who filmed Su be the man Ruth had sent to jail last year, the dashing one with Louis Vuitton shirts who set fire to his partner's white Labrador, the 'guy behind the 8-ball'?

I'll get you for this, bitch, he'd threatened from the cells below her court after she sentenced him to eighteen months' custody. *You'd better watch out.*

'I don't remember him having the red bracelet, do you? Then his wrist would probably have been covered in court, or the bracelet could be new. Anyway, he couldn't mastermind a pot noodle, let alone this. Can you get a better shot? Is there a number on the ring?'

'This is as clear as I can get it and you can't see if there's a white circle or a number in the middle, just the black. I agree, I very much doubt it's Jim Docherty or anyone you know. How could anyone plan it? But maybe one of the girls, or someone at the bar, will remember a man with one or more of these details. Worth asking around.'

Just in case, Ruth left instructions with MacDonald to find out if the 8-ball guy was at liberty and, if so, where he was staying. As she cycled home, she pictured dog-murderer Jim

Docherty in jail, filled with hate, planning 'revenge pornography' on the daughter of the woman who incarcerated him. She imagined him following her girls to Magaluf, waiting for the perfect moment. It made little sense, but neither did the ludicrous 'involuntary' option.

Chapter Eight

The guy on the terminal next to me has a beard and is taking notes about TripAdvisor reviews. He jiggles his knee and this makes the whole bench shake, which is annoying. I send an email to Woojin so no one thinks I'm dead and so they leave me alone.

'Can I come hide out with you?' he replies. 'I won't tell anyone. I'm an excellent fugitive.'

Woojin's also an excellent friend. He's always been there for me, especially after Leah started hating me, and I trust him. But I don't want to be near anyone right now. 'Thanks Woo, but I'm fine on my own. ☺'

I go on YouTube to check the extent of my fame. *Seventy-three thousand two hundred and one.* Beardy guy hears me gasp and glances at me. I close YouTube before he glances at that. I'm starving so I walk along La Boqueria. There are many sounds – car engines, voices, birds – but my ears are now fine-tuned to devices. A man walks past with his phone and it pings. A woman sits at a café table with her tablet and it tinkles. The guy at the fruit stall has his phone in his pocket: ping. You have a new message. Tom has shared a video. You have been tagged in a post. Barcelona is showering pings, and each one is a droplet of my shame. Ping – where'd that come from? Ping – whose inbox did I just arrive in? I'm going crazy, hearing pings. They're talking to me: you're disgusting, Su, revolting. I buy oranges and bananas and a paper cone filled with freshly baked sweet potato, and head back to the hovel to get away from the pings, and so I don't have to worry about being recognised. As I'm walking towards the hotel door, I see the beardy man going inside. He sees me, and holds the door open. He's got McDonald's. 'That looks good.' I'm surprised to hear he's American: the beard and Dr Martens boots seem incongruous.

'That doesn't.' I hate McDonald's, can't believe I went every day in Maga with Leah and co. I'm not looking for a friend, so I leave it at that and head upstairs.

The sweet potato is heavenly, the orange just what I need, but the peeled banana in my hand has the power of a hypnotherapist and is drawing out repressed memories. I stare at the fruit, unable to take a bite. Penises are ugly-looking things, especially flaccid. Putting one (or more) in your mouth seems pointless – *See me, I'm a receptacle, a vase! Put a thing in me and take it out, and repeat.* It's accurate to call it a job. Where's the fun for the vase? As I stare at it, a snippet returns to me all of a sudden and I recall one of the penises very clearly. It was long and skinny and semi-hard, and I remember I felt relieved, as it was the first to have shown any sign of response and I'd been feeling unappealing and useless as a result. I remember being aware of a heaviness between my legs when I realised I was having an effect on the guy. He thought I was sexy and I thought I was sexy and I was sexy. I guess pleasing is the vase's reward, then. It's pleasant to please. I'm feeling the heaviness again now and I don't like it.

I hit myself on the forehead three times, smack smack smack, and bite the banana as if to murder it. I rush over the corridor to the loo to spit out the memory and the fruit.

Beardy guy's standing in the corridor knocking on my bedroom door when I head back to my room. 'There you are. I was wondering if you wanna go to the movies. There's a Spanish horror on in thirty minutes, just a few blocks away. Apparently it's the worst horror movie ever made.'

'Why would I want to go and see it, then?'

'To get out of here. To help me write the next chapter of my book.'

Dear me, he's writing a book. He'll probably ask me to read a passage later, and end up making me read the whole thing while he watches for changes in facial expression.

'I'm freaking you out. I just thought she's all alone and I'm all alone and she doesn't look like she's crazy, so I said to myself, why not just ask her.'

I raise my eyebrows. He's sweet.

'*Are* you crazy?' he asks.

I think about the exact thing to say. I always do, Mum says. She likes that about me. 'Not most of the time.'

'You talking 40 per cent crazy? 30? 10? Specify. It's me taking the gamble here.'

My initial thought is to say five because it sounds neat and cooler than the truth, but for the first time in ages, or ever, I don't feel like saying something to fit in and impress.

'I've been alive for 18 years and 30 days, that's 365 multiplied by 18 – 6,570, plus 30, so 6,600 days of Su, and I've been crazy for one of them.' He smiled as I spoke. I think he liked my new personality. 'Which means I am crazy .015 per cent of the time.'

He laughs. 'Holy shit, you need get yourself some crazy, girl called Su. C'mon, it starts at nine. But I'm not letting my name slip. You're never gonna know it.'

He's right about the film: bad, and not cultish bad. There were five other people in the small Indy cinema at the start, but they've all bailed an hour on. Beardy and I, which is what I decided to call him out loud when we bought stale sugared popcorn, stay the duration, talking about every scene like pompous buffs.

At a small bar we drink sangria, which is apparently the worst drink in Barcelona, and this one is the worst he's tasted. He's writing a travel book, he tells me. The deadline for *The Worst Things to Do in the Best Cities in the World* is 9 September.

'So I take it this is the worst bar in Barcelona?'

'Go use the men's toilets and you'll understand.'

'Worst hotel, film, bar, drink. I'm the worst company?'

'So far, but there are seven people I still haven't been out with.'

'What's the worst food here?'

'McDonald's. The editor will demand a re-write, but it is the worst food in every single city in the world, surely? What food could be worse?'

'I dunno, fried tarantula?'

'All natural ingredients. I suspect crunchy; fried so it'd taste like a chip, perhaps with an after-whiff of chicken. Sounds all right.'

'So what cities have you done so far?' He lists five. I've

only been to two of them: Barcelona (to hide) and Paris (Disney World, age eight. Leah and I went on every ride together and shared a double bed in our own room in the Hotel Beausejour in Montmartre. Mum and Dad had an adjoining room, but we felt so grown up. We giggled all night and Leah threw up 'cause she ate a whole Brie). 'Just cities, not towns?'

'The sequel! Thank you, I'll pitch to the Rough Guides tomorrow.'

'If they bite, I know the worst bar in Magaluf.'

'Yeah?'

'And the worst person.'

The sangria is no less awful after three glasses, but I'm definitely less sober.

'That was your *one day*, the 0.15 per cent?'

I must have given something away for him to say that. Or does he have special powers? I nod and gesture for another drink.

'When were you there?'

'Last night. Seems an eternity ago.'

'Aw c'mon, you can't have been that bad.'

'I was.'

'Don't believe you.'

I take his phone off the table and hand it to him. 'Go to YouTube and type Magaluf.'

It feels empowering somehow to watch Beardy watch me on YouTube. His expression doesn't give anything away as I hear my slurred screech *I'm Su Oliphant-Brotheridge from Doon!*

'I don't want to watch this.' He must have reached the

inciting incident. He turns it off, puts the phone in his pocket. 'Shit, Su.'

'Poo . . .dle!'

His 'Ha' doesn't sound anything like laughter. 'You must get that all the time, sorry. But what are you going to do? What are you doing here?'

'Waiting.'

'For what?'

'I feel like I knew the answer to that a few hours ago.' My teeth are probably stained red. I'm drinking too much. I wonder if I'll drink too much for the rest of my life. Maybe I've inherited alcoholism from my mother, who was maybe too drunk to drive to the orphanage and that's why she cycled, or too drunk to cycle and that's why she walked, or too drunk to drive but did anyway because she was an alcoholic. 'Do me a favour, will you please? Put your hand over the screen if you don't want to look at it, but can you just check the number of views? It was around 73 when I was at the internet café before.'

'Well that's okay, not so bad, I mean.'

'Aw, he's thinking 73, no zeros at the end.' I reach over and take the phone from his jeans pocket, which is very forward for me. Beardy swipes the phone on, opens YouTube, puts his hand over the top half of the screen, and then his jaw slowly falls and his eyes lift until they're looking into mine.

Bad, it must be bad. 'Over 100,000?'

'121 and a half.'

I lift my glass and clink his. 'So there you have it. The worst person in Magaluf, hell maybe even the worst person in Europe, this week anyway.'

'You're too scared to go home?'

'Yeah, there's that. But they're better off without me. They would always have been better off without me. They'd be so much happier, just the three of them.' I've never said this to anyone, and if I've thought it I've promptly banished the self-pity, but I am an interloper. If Mum and Dad hadn't adopted me, Leah would have nothing to be embarrassed about: that geeky Asian, always hanging around, on her tail. Dad wouldn't be the unqualified referee of some screwed-up female love triangle. Mum wouldn't be terrified that I feel like I don't belong. And I wouldn't be exhausted from trying to look like I do.

'This must be messing with your head.'

'I've spent the day cringing, recoiling – no, they're not the right words, not gut-wrenching enough. I've taken to hitting myself on the forehead. Boy, I could never have imagined hitting myself a day ago. So yeah, it's messing with me.'

'Must have been a turn-on though, no?'

'You saw it. How could *that* turn me on?' It shouldn't be a lie. How *could* that turn me on? (What is wrong with me? So much, I'm discovering.)

He smiles, which makes me realise that he's being very kind, considering what he's just seen on his phone. 'Because it's naughty, bad, and I get the feeling you're very sexual.'

'I'm not. I'm a virgin.'

He bites his lip. 'You shouldn't go telling people that.'

'I'm oversharing, very un-me. But if everyone else is sharing me I may as well too.'

'You don't have to talk about it.'

He is kind, and pretty. His smile makes me feel pretty too. Perhaps if I'd met him last night he'd have been the one to awaken me. If we'd met at the pool, or in McDonald's, or outside on the strip, or in the bar with the velvet wall, or the one with the bubbles, maybe the whole thing wouldn't have happened. If I'd met him at the Coconut Lounge before my screen debut maybe we would have danced together. Perhaps he would have kissed me and asked me to go for a walk along the beach.

Or: if he'd been at the bar last night – would he have dropped his shorts like the others? Would most men do that? Would all men do that? 'No, I think I need to talk about it. Do you mind?'

He considers his answer. 'I don't mind as long as you're okay.'

'I had a kind-of boyfriend and when we kissed it didn't feel very nice. He had a very small head and a male skull should be larger than a female skull in my opinion.'

Beardy's sizing up our heads. His is larger.

'I'd planned to lose my virginity that night. My mission! I think the plan, plus the drink, made something inside me erupt and I transformed into a porn star. I'm tempted to say it was completely out of character, because that would have been the truth before it happened, but I'm starting to wonder what character I was beforehand, and if she's the one who's not me.' Beardy seems intensely interested in what I'm saying, but I'm suddenly fatigued and bored with myself. 'Let's go back to the hotel, eh? I'm tired. And don't worry, there'll be no awkwardness when we say goodnight in the corridor. I don't want to kiss you or have sex with you. And if you've moved off to Monaco or Marrakech or Madrid in the morning, I won't be annoyed or any more ashamed of myself than I already am. In fact—'

He's leaning over the table and kissing me all of a sudden. When he stops he only moves a few inches away and he doesn't remove his hands from my neck, which I find uncomfortably intimate. 'In fact if I was you, I'd run.'

'Will you stop talking?'

'You should run like the wind!'

'I know something about you that you haven't told me yet.'

'What?'

'Kissing you is the only way to shut you up.'

It feels nice – I wonder if it's because of the size of his head – but his tongue swishing over mine does not induce that now familiar heaviness.

I'm pretty sure I don't want to have sex, but I'm wondering how else to end the night when we get to my room door. I like Beardy. Right now it feels like he's the only person in the world who knows me. But I needn't worry about him wanting to come in. He's a gentleman, and he kisses me on the cheek. 'You were the worst-worst company in Barcelona. Congratulations.' And with a smile he heads along the corridor to his room.

I lie in bed for a while listening for footsteps, worried that he'll knock on my door, worried that he won't. Several scenes play out in my imagination. Beardy whisking me away from the Coconut Lounge before a Jäger bomb is mentioned. Beardy holding my hand as we walk barefoot on the beach. Beardy dropping his trousers in the circle. I hit myself on the forehead. No, not that. Beardy, barefoot on the beach.

The footsteps don't happen, and it's light when I wake. At last, I slept.

I do not spend all day looking for Beardy. I do not go to the shower at 9, and to the loo at 10.15, 11.30, 12.10 and 13.45 hoping to spot him in the corridor. It's not because of him that I wander down to the foyer three times, poke my head out the front door twice, scrutinise passers-by from my window for hours, go to McDonald's and order two coffees and drink them very slowly, my neck stiff from checking and trying not to check as people walk in and out. At 3.30, I don't go to the internet café to see if he's there and I don't leave without sitting down because he isn't and I don't run back to the hotel because his sudden absence is making me feel panicky and angry and much more ashamed of myself than I was yesterday.

I have spent the day looking for Beardy and he's gone. Carlos, the elderly owner, says he checked out at 5 this morning. 'Five! Woke me up to settle the bill. Had a train or a plane to catch.'

'Which one? To where?'

Carlos is looking at me like I'm the kind of crazy stalker who guys run from, like the wind.

This room is hotter than it was yesterday and it has a different smell, perhaps because I've been pacing and sweating in it for some time now. It's stifling. Since I learned of Beardy's departure I've realised no man – not even an ugly, stupid one – will ever want to whisk me away, hold my hand, be my boyfriend. I am no-go Su.

I walk to the market, eat a few mouthfuls of salad on a park bench, and watch holiday-makers having the kind of holiday I wish I'd had instead of the one I did. It's not long before I find myself in the internet café. I type 'Magaluf' into Google and, using Search tools, select the 'last twenty-four hours' option. I'm now on too many porn sites to count. I'm in newspapers and magazines and on blogs and Facebook pages and Twitter and Ello and networking sites I've never even heard of before. One photo and one more video of me in the bar have appeared online, but the video's too wobbly to make anything out and the pic is of the back of my head. I've been online for twenty minutes now, and it's too big a job to add the total number of views. I give up and read articles instead.

They're mostly the same, but the *Mail Online* has discovered something new: 'Edinburgh University has withdrawn Su Oliphant-Brotheridge's offer to study Medicine, an anonymous source revealed today.'

So I'm not going to Edinburgh University. I rejected offers from Aberdeen, Dundee, Glasgow and St Andrews, but I suppose they wouldn't have me now either. I'm not going to study Medicine. I'm not going to be a doctor.

I've wanted to be a doctor since I was three. Mum says I set up a play surgery at that age, and have talked of nothing since. I've dedicated myself to the notion. I've wanted it and expected it.

Haven't I?

I've dreamed of being a doctor. Dr Oliphant-Brotheridge – finally, my excessive surname would seem fitting and marvellous! And then a surgeon. Ms Oliphant-Brotheridge! ('Don't be Miss or Mrs,' Mum had said once, or perhaps twice. 'Men are only ever Mr. Why should women disclose their marital status?')

I've dreamed of curing breast cancer, or dementia.

Haven't I?

Of winning a Nobel Prize.

'You will win a Nobel Prize!' Mum had said once, or perhaps more than once. 'You can and you will! Why not you?'

I read the article again and I realise I don't feel anything. I don't understand why. My dream has been crushed, my future destroyed, and all I'm thinking about is Beardy.

I refresh my Google search and see that *The Herald* has just reported this: 'Sheriff Ruth Oliphant has been asked to take leave for an unspecified period, the Lord President's office confirmed today.' Is 'leave' a euphemism? I haven't jeopardised her career, have I? The idea makes me nauseous. I can handle the destruction of my own reputation and life, but not hers, not Dad's, not Leah's. I have only just allowed myself to acknowledge that I am an interloper, but I am far worse than that. I am a destroyer. Whose fault is that? I want to point a finger and I'm torn about where to aim it.

There's my birth mother, who abandoned me.

Leah, who resented and taunted me.

Scotland, which made me feel other.

Or did I come out this way? Perhaps the nurse had said to

my birth mother: 'Congratulations, you've given birth to a healthy slut!'

Rubbish, it's all Xano's fault.

I'm dizzy. I might faint. I should lower my head, let the blood reach it. But I can't take my eyes off the screen. I refresh my Google search again.

James has commented in the local paper. 'I don't know her very well. I met her at a debate.'

The bar owner is quoted in the *Guardian*: 'I didn't make her do it. Why should I apologise?'

#shagaluf is trending worldwide on Twitter.

If you type the word slut into Google, I am the first news item to appear. I honestly didn't know that the word slut was an okay one to say out loud, or to write online. I thought it was up there with Chinky as a forbidden term. Just shows how sheltered I've been, living with a feminist mother and a new-man dad. There you have it, slut slut slut. People feel they are doing a necessary and just thing, which they call slutshaming (its hashtag is trending in Scotland). I am on a wooden platform in the town square. My head and arms are in the pillory. And the people are throwing tweets at me.

A feeble few tweet for mercy: *Why is she the slut? What about the men?* But they are drowned out.

I should stop. I should go back to my room.

I refresh, scan page one, page two, three.

And there is a journalist's headshot of Beardy. He looks so serious there! As well as writing for the *Rough Guide*, he obviously also sells articles to newspapers. His latest, posted two hours ago, is about me:

Till now I've been cool, calm, collected Su. I've been hiding in a bad hotel till my blowing blows over. I've been patient and I planned to be patient for as long as it took. I had a life and I intended to return to it.

I should have realised this sooner, but it's clear now: I have no life. It's broken.

'I was transformed into a porn star' says Magaluf sex tape girl. Beardy is as comfortable with the word slut as the rest of the population. He regurgitates mostly, but does offer some new morsels: my virginity and the fact that I'd planned to lose it that night; my head-hitting (and I feel the urge as I read). 'She admitted to harming herself since the incident. *My family are better off without me. They would always have been better off without me.'*

There's a photo of Pension Paula in Beardy's article as well as the address (his name's Derek Brayshner. Derek. I'd keep that name a secret too). I race out of the café to get my things from the hotel but can see from the pavement that it's too late. A man is taking a photo of the sign above the front window and the foyer is crammed with people.

I left my room earlier with nothing but a twenty-euro note. After my salad and computer use I have seven euros and eighty cents left. I consider the risks for a moment and decide I can't face going back to the hotel. I have lost my mother her job and her dream of being the mother of a Nobel Prize-winner.

The man taking the photo outside has spotted me. I think he follows as I run along the street, turn the corner, and head into the market, criss-crossing as carefully as my high speed will allow. 'Sorry . . . sorry,' I say, as I bash the arms of shoppers and corners of tables. 'Sorry.'

I probably could stop running, I've been running a long time, but I've reached the beach, where there are no obstacles, and I'm in my stride, and I can keep going, so I do.

Chapter Nine

Ruth tried not to stare at the man's beer but she found it very difficult. He had to drink the whole thing for her to be sure this would work, and he'd only finished half. More worrying, he was eyeing a far younger cleavage. Still perched beside her, but with his back now leaning against the bar, he stared at a girl who was twerking thin air on the dance floor. She was no older than eighteen, and wearing cut-off denim shorts that did not cover her ample and dimpled bottom. Ruth wracked her brain for ways to regain the man's attention, trying to recall the tricks she'd used during her university years in the pubs of Glasgow's West End. But she hadn't needed tricks or twerking or even cut-off shorts back then. If she fancied taking someone back to her flat in Hillhead, she simply approached the person and began a conversation long enough for her to establish that he (and on one occasion, *she*) wasn't a psychopath or – worse – an idiot or – much worse – looking for a relationship. If satisfied, she would then suggest the person walk her home. That approach wasn't necessary or suitable with this man.

She hadn't planned to nab Bernie. They'd walked the same trail in Yosemite; and after two days overtaking each other sharing initially polite and increasingly entertaining exchanges, they found themselves walking the last five days together. They had both decided to do the trail solo in order to get head space, peace and quiet, but ended up talking non-stop. Bernie wasn't a psychopath or an idiot and he wasn't looking for a relationship. Funny that. Tears came to her heavily made-up eyes at the memory.

Perhaps she could she drop something, and bend over in front of him so he would see her (far superior, not a dimple to be found) bottom. No, this monster had seen enough of her already. 'Why don't you go ask her for a dance?' Ruth's question had the desired effect – he turned back to face her and the half-finished drink on the bar.

'Nah, she's a slag.' He gulped the rest of the beer.

She tried not to smile. Step one, tick. He really didn't recognise her still? In a minute she'd put his arm around her shoulder and tell him that they were leaving. He'd need to have his arm around her to stay standing, and he wouldn't be inclined or able to decline.

No more than a minute. She put her hand on his and counted the seconds in her head, gently rubbing the black ring on his middle finger. 57, 56, 55, 54, 53, 52 . . .

Yosemite, she thought, not caring if tears ruined her make-up this time. I first held Bernie's hand in Yosemite.

45, 44, 43 . . .

And she last held it . . . When was the last time she held Bernie's hand? She couldn't remember. Was it before this man met their daughter in this bar? She hoped not, God she hoped she hadn't neglected him the whole time. They always held hands, she and Bernie. It embarrassed Leah that they did so in public.

33, 32, 31 . . . 'How would you define a *slag*?' she asked.

His eyes were wetter than hers now, but not for the same

reason. (23 all the way down to 16 – he took a long while to attempt an answer.) 'A slag, slag, she's—' He couldn't finish his explanation, and slumped onto the bar stool.

'10, 9, 8.' Ruth now felt confident enough to count out loud.

She might have held Bernie's hand after the video was filmed in this bar. Had she? She needed to remember! Was it after Merilyn Davies from the university phoned? She'd cycled to MacDonald's, then home, locked the bike in the shed, and gone inside to get the car keys.

'Three, two, one.' Ruth draped the man's arm around her shoulders as planned. 'How about I take you home?'

Still able to stand, but just, and already unable to form ideas of his own, including the notion of resistance, the man shuffled across the dance floor, helped by Ruth. He was no drunker-looking than most people in the bar and his poor walking skills went unnoticed. They stumbled outside into the warm Magaluf air. Her anger hadn't dissipated, as she feared it might, but was intensifying with each exhausting step. She opened the back door and pushed him inside and then she suddenly remembered.

It was in their bedroom. She'd found Bernie huddled on the floor, sobbing, and she'd sat down beside him and held his hand. He'd flicked it away, that's right, that's what happened. For the first time ever he did not squeeze her hand, stroke it with his thumb. But she had held his hand for a second. She had touched it. Yes, that was the last time she had held Bernie's hand.

*

104

Ruth had been in a hurry and felt irritated that she could not find the car keys. By the time she'd cycled home from MacDonald's house, he'd already texted with Jim Docherty's home address in Glasgow. 'He got out of Bar L 6 wks ago,' he wrote. She messaged back, asking him to meet her there in an hour.

'Why? We agreed it's v unlikely to be him,' MacDonald replied.

'Process of elimination.' Right now, it was the only lead she had, although she knew it was more of a weak notion than a proper lead, and probably a foolish one. But it would also be foolish not to investigate it before erasing and moving on. The keys weren't on the key rack by the vestibule. 'Bernie?' Why could Bernie and Leah not comply with simple instructions? Key rack, for keys, she'd told them separately and together on at least twenty occasions. They weren't on the table, or in Bernie's jacket, which was hanging in the hall, on Su's coat hook and not on his coat hook. She and Su always put the keys on the key rack, and had no trouble at all remembering to hang their own coats on their designated coat hook. The disorganised and thoughtless habits of her husband and biological daughter made her furious almost every day, but today more than usual. 'Bernie? Bernard, where are you?' She heard noises upstairs, and as she neared their bedroom door she identified the noises as Bernie crying. He didn't have that manly need to suppress tears, Bernie. He'd cried when he read his vows, when they first laid eyes on Su, when Su was taken from them, when Leah was born, when they heard that Su would be returned to them, when she finally was, when Ruth's dad died, and when he and Leah watched mopey films like *The Notebook* together. Ruth usually appreciated the way he expressed his emotion, but not now. Their daughter was missing, even if the Spanish and UK police didn't see it that way; and every aspect of their lives was being ripped apart. They had too much to do to waste time and energy crying. She would have said exactly this to Bernie, no doubt in her intensely irritating 'My Lady' tone, had she not opened the bedroom door to find him in the foetal position with his phone in his hand, sobbing uncontrollably.

She sat on the carpet beside him and put her hand on his. 'Darling, are you all right?'

He flicked her hand away, and pounced to a standing position so abruptly that she cowered. 'Of course I'm not!'

'What? What is it?'

'Su bolted off from a hotel in Barcelona with no money, no passport, no cash card and no phone or clothes and –' he tapped his phone and read from it – 'she told some guy that she's self-harmed since it happened and that her family would be better off without her.'

'What? What do you mean?'

'Some bastard in Barcelona took her out for a drink and she spilled her guts and now she's definitely missing and possibly suicidal. And I've just spoken to Leah, who committed theft because you asked her to.'

'You think she's suicidal?'

'No. I don't know, I don't think she'd ever, no – did you even hear what I said about Leah? You sent a seventeen-year-old girl to Spain – on her own – and told her to break the law.'

'Did she get caught?'

'That's not the point. The point is we have two daughters, and as usual you're only thinking about one.'

Ruth exhaled loudly: this was a discussion they'd had many times and she did not feel like having it now. Usually Bernie would approach the subject softly-softly. *Do you think you're being a little hard on her, honey? Why not spend some time with her, take her shopping for the prom?* Ruth wasn't completely lacking in self-awareness. She knew she was impatient with Leah, that a disapproving tone often made its way into her voice when she was talking to (or okay, often *at*) her. Whenever Bernie confronted Ruth about her relationship with Leah, she'd listen. His motives were good, his concerns justified, and his solutions usually worked, if only momentarily. In May, she took Leah shopping for the prom as he'd advised, and she managed to suppress her irritation at the ridiculous heels she bought to match the too-tight dress she bought to match the vintage bag she'd hunted down in a charity shop. When they got home that night, Leah turned the hall into a runway. She lit candles, poured her parents a glass of champagne and Su a glass of mineral water, turned repetitive tinny music up loud enough to annoy Frieda next door, and modelled her outfit with more strut and pout than Naomi Campbell. Leah was so intoxicating in that moment that Ruth resolved to spend one-on-one time with her as often as possible.

Alas, an hour later, Ruth went outside to put the champagne bottle in the recycling bin and caught Leah smoking on the tyre swing. 'You're smoking? Is that . . .' Ruth sniffed 'Cannabis!' She looked towards the adjacent gardens to make sure no one had heard her, or could smell the skunk. 'Put that out and get inside. Did you hear me? Put that out and come inside!'

Leah didn't budge.

'Do as you're told!'

Leah kicked the ground to get the swing moving, joint defiantly in hand.

'You're grounded! You're not going to the prom!'

Leah propelled the swing with her legs and took a long drag, holding in the smoke in as she mimicked her mother: 'You're grounded! You're not going to the prom!' Swing at full flight now, Leah put her head back, blew the smoke to the sky and laughed.

Like all things that intoxicate, Leah did so fleetingly, and caused a bad hangover the rest of the time.

Ruth felt that Bernie's criticism was unnecessary and unhelpful. 'Well of course it's Su I'm worried about. Listen I've hired a lawyer – MacDonald, the one in *Pirates of Penzance*, remember? – and we've got some leads on the guy who took the video. Nothing concrete, but—'

'Stop! Let me talk. Leah just told me she convinced a bar tender to help her steal a stack of tapes. That doesn't worry you?'

'I don't know, Bernard. I'm spoilt for things to worry about right now.'

*

As the lights of Magaluf merged into a haze behind her, Ruth tried to remember the last thing Bernie had said to her. Was it when they were still yelling at each other in the bedroom? *This is not about you! Why do you make everything about you?* Or: *Get off your highfalutin bench and think like a mother for once! A mother to both girls!* Or: *Why don't you admit that you work harder at loving Su because you find Su harder to love?*

Ruth couldn't look him in the eye with a response to this last reproach, and turned away, resting her hands on the dresser. 'How can you say that?' She stared at her face in the mirror for a long moment before finishing. 'Why would you ask me to admit that?'

No, that wasn't his parting slur either, because Ruth remembered following him down the stairs afterwards and him saying: *I'll drink coffee if I want to drink coffee!* And then back up again because he wanted to pack: *I'm going to Barcelona to get Su. You're going to Magaluf to get Leah. Get your things. We can get the same flight to Puerto Pollensa.*

Bernie wasn't a seasoned planner, and this one was unsurprisingly ill-thought-out. 'Leah's in Magaluf and isn't in danger and Su's sensible and fit enough to run. I take on board that I shouldn't have sent Leah off alone, led her to think she should steal anything – I never told her to do that! – but maybe you should have said so at the time. And if you want to go and help her find Su, then good, you can go.'

'I didn't ask for your permission. I asked for you to focus on your daughters.'

'What do you think I'm doing?'

'I'm really not sure. You went to work this morning! Why on earth would you do that? Then you hired Michael MacDonald because – why – what matters is finding someone – other than you and yours – to blame, so you can punish them with your special little hammer? And you wouldn't even listen to my idea this morning.'

'What idea, Bernard, that Su should be chatting on Facebook right now?'

'It's already starting to work. I've enlisted Gregor and Val and they're working on it free of charge unlike your handsome lawyer. Our friends want to help, and we need help. It could be the only way to get our lives back.'

'You enlisted Gregor and Val to do what?'

'Gregor's blogging. Val's on Facebook, Twitter and the other social media sites. All banal, happy stuff. It's working. If you Google Su now, one of the stories on the first page is about the debate she won at school and it's peppered on the pages after that. People are sharing that one of me playing to the girls when they were babies – remember how cute they were, laughing like crazy? The Dux award is on page three and so on, and my advert for private tuition is dotted around because we've tagged all our names in every post. If we all work hard at it, we dilute the poison.'

'I told you not to do that.' Ruth was furious. She did not want Gregor, who Bernie befriended at the gates when the girls started school, publishing articles about her family. She found him insipid and thoughtless, always phoning Bernie before dinner time and talking for half an hour about the latest Green party meeting or how to get more customers to buy the golfing crap he sold online from his garden shed so he'd get out of helping his poor wife feed their four unruly boys. As for Val – who worked in the office at the Conservatoire – Ruth was certain she'd always had a thing for Bernie. Thirty-four and chronically single, Val blushed and stuttered around him as if he was Beethoven and never once looked Ruth in the eye. Ruth laughed about Val's crush with her husband, but secretly made a vow to keep her at arm's length.

'You told me, *told* me! You do that when you're stressed – treat me like your clerk of court. I'm your partner and I'm Su and Leah's father and I'm not the type to make hasty decisions based on fear.'

'You're talking about Saskia's bar? You've found it in you to be honest with me after all these years?' Ruth had repeatedly asked Bernie if he blamed her for what happened with the social workers – for going into that bar, having that drink, leaving Su on that pavement – but he always comforted her, saying: 'No, darling, of course not.' Perhaps he'd only responded like that because she was a quivering guilt-ridden mess. 'That's cruel. Why are you being cruel?'

'I didn't mean to be, I'm sorry. I don't want to upset you. I just don't think you should be making all the decisions right now and I want you to trust me.'

'You know what, Bernard, why don't you try making a decision then? Be a concert violinist. Stay in the United States of God Bless America. Don't have children. Let Su grow up in care. Go on, try it out. I'm waiting. I want to witness the first time you actually make a decision.'

The taxi driver outside tooted his horn and Bernie zipped his bag. 'Fuck you.'

*

Fuck you.

Ruth screeched to a halt at the side of the road and wound down the window to get some air. She wasn't feeling well.

The man in the back seat hadn't made a noise since they drove off from the Coconut Lounge. She turned to check on him. His torso had fallen sideways onto the seat. His eyes were open and aimed at hers. She waited for him to blink.

She wondered if the taxi driver had stared at Bernie for a while, waiting for him to blink, when he turned around to collect his fare.

Chapter Ten

This town is nothing like Magaluf and this bar is nothing like the Coconut Lounge. It's a village rather than a town, only a few streets, only one bar. All five customers look at least fifty, or maybe they're all at least seventy but look twenty years younger because they haven't spent their lives eating chips in the rain. None of the drinks are named after sexual acts, responses or positions, and customers wear clothing on their tops and bottoms at all times. No one is drunk and no one is dancing and no one is taking photos or videos because no one has a mobile phone and no one is doing anything worth recording anyway. I ran for a long time but I'm not sure exactly how far. I ran along a beach, along busy roads, then quiet roads. I stopped when I saw this bar. Now I'm wondering how to say: 'I am looking for work, out of sight if possible, dishes for example?'

'Do you speak English?' I ask the woman behind the bar. She shrugs her shoulders. I say the same thing again but louder. One of the five customers says something to me in Spanish and I realise I'm going to need Google Translate, or an old-fashioned dictionary made of paper. 'Gracias,' I say, and leave to find one of the above.

There are no internet cafés in this village and no bookshops. I take a drink from the village tap, spot a walkable hill, and head up it. I need to think things through.

~

To be clear, despite my ill-advised outpouring to Beardy, I'm not one of those emotionally tortured adoptees. Since I was twelve, I've tried not to think about my birth mother and it hasn't been too hard. Just before my thirteenth birthday I broached the subject of searching for her. I practised how best to say it, and noted several versions of my opening statement in my diary.

I'd love to find out more about myself. What do you think?

Woojin registered with an agency and guess what, he's got a brother!

Or

I wonder if there's a history of cervical cancer in my family? No, not 'family' – *in my genes,* I rewrote.

The last option was a winner, I decided. Mum would never argue with science.

Friday night was a good time, as they always celebrated the end of the week with one of Dad's slap-up meals, and a bottle or two of decent wine (before Dad gave up the booze, that is). They'd chat at the table for ages after eating, feeling relaxed and a little tipsy. Leah would scarper out to a friend's still chewing the last mouthful, and I'd usually head upstairs and leave them to it, but this time I hung back, eventually gathering the courage to say: *I wonder if there's a history of cervical cancer in my family.*

Ach, I'd used the word family.

Mum put her glass down shakily, one side resting on top of a spoon. Dad and I looked at each other, and then at her, waiting for her to speak. Her expression was that of a devoted wife whose husband has just told her he's in love with someone else. 'You're not worried about your health are you?'

I decided to nip the whole idea in the bud immediately. 'No, I'm fit as a fiddle. I just started thinking about it because we had the immunisation last week. What a breakthrough, hey! Soon we'll have jabs for all cancers. You finished with the cheese?' And with that, I lifted the cheeseboard, and waltzed out of the room with the cheerful nonchalance of a girl who does not have a burning, aching question, not one, just a cheeseboard.

Upstairs in my room, I ripped out the practice conversations in my diary and threw them in the bin. I took one last look at the online forums I'd been stalking. There was the endless register of teenage boys and girls like me posting all the information they had: *My mother was this age. I was left at this place on this date. Please help me find her.*

There was the one where an American was thinking about adopting, and a fourteen-year-old had responded with: 'PLEASE PLEASE DON'T! You will cause PAIN! You will rob this child of their culture, language, heritage! You will make them feel and act white but they are not! DON'T DO IT PLEASE!!'

Enough, I told myself that night. I wasn't in pain. I didn't need to find my mother as I had a selfless, clever, and generous one already. I deleted the forums from my favourites list and decided never to look at them again.

Three years later, when I was fifteen, Woojin and I bagged Ben Lomond together. His brother, who'd never been adopted and had remained in state care until he was organised enough to run away and not get caught, turned out to be a lying drunk apparently; kept asking for money for college and spending it on Soju. Woojin had moved on, and said it was probably a good thing that I'd never pursued it. He suggested

I think of myself as a recovering addict. 'You'll always want to find her – it's a bubbling ever-present urge. Suppress it, one day at a time, and call me if you're struggling. Think of me as your AA buddy!'

I called him once or twice and he managed to talk me out of posting on forums or emailing the orphanage. But last year, when I found out I got into Medicine, I persuaded him to do some digging on the sly. I wanted my birth mother to know how happy and successful I was. I wanted her to be proud of me. I imagined she might send me a lovely letter once Wooojin told her about my achievements and showed her pictures of me – *I've thought about you every day, Su-Jin. Every 2 July I've posted you a card, with no address on it – 'To Su-Jin, Happy birthday my darling baby. Please, please, know that I love you and that I'm sorry.' And now I have seen your face! And you are more beautiful, and far brighter than I could ever have imagined! Please come to me, daughter. Come home to your mother.* The letter would be stained with tears, I imagined, as would all the birthday cards she'd posted into the ether.

Two weeks before I left for Magaluf, Woojin turned up at my house. He was just back from his brother's funeral (he choked on his own vomit in a squat in a seedy area of Seoul). After the funeral, Woojin went to Myeong-dong police station. He's very charming, and he managed to track down several police officers who'd worked there eighteen years ago. After days of detective work, he finally found Moon Jihoo. Now retired, this kind-looking officer remembered the wicker basket all too well. He'd been heading into the station for a night shift when he saw a woman crouched over it at the doorstep. He called to her as he walked across the road towards the door. She looked up at him, startled, and then ran off apparently, leaving the wicker basket behind. Woojin asked why the officer remembered this incident, because surely it wouldn't stand out after all those years in the police. He told Woojin he remembered it because he knew who she was. Excited to be so close, Woojin pressed and pressed, but the officer refused to give him her name. 'He'd have told me if I paid him, but I thought I should talk to you first.'

Woojin had done all the groundwork for me. If I wanted to find her now, all I had to do was pay Moon Jihoo. It kept me awake for two weeks. I pictured my mother looking up at the officer and then running off. Perhaps if he hadn't caught her in the act, she'd have changed her mind and taken me home. I wondered if he recognised her because she was known to the local police. She might have been homeless, or a beggar. She may have lived in a squat similar to the one Woojin's brother was found in. Perhaps she was a care-in-the-community case, with mental health problems, a history of depression, of attempted suicide.

Compared to the Munros at home, this isn't much of a hill. More of an undulation. There's no precipice to leap off, and only one decent-sized tree about fifty metres down, which has two sizeable boughs. From here it looks like the lower one is sturdy enough to hold my weight. If I removed this ridiculous crop top, perhaps I could tear at the seam with my teeth, and rip the material in a straight line, very carefully, round and round, as if peeling an apple without breaking the skin.

Perhaps my mother contemplated suicide when she discovered her unwanted pregnancy, or after she'd left me in that wicker basket. Perhaps my mother was sex-addicted, slept with men all the time, abandoned babies all the time, #slut.

Is thinking about suicide suicidal? Is it the first step? I don't think so. I'm picturing it in the same way as I might imagine parachuting and I'd never jump out of a plane unless it was going to crash. Su Oliphant-Brotheridge from Doon is not the kind of person to embrace despair, even if she silently grieves the loss of the dash and the Jin which are the only things other than her skin to truly define her. Even if she disgraced herself on holiday, Su Oliphant-Brotheridge from Doon would never make plans involving tree boughs and makeshift nooses.

But if it's in my mind (albeit in a non-suicidal way) then it might be in Mum and Dad's minds. I need to let them know I'm not going to tear at my shirt and hang myself on that tree. If anyone should die, it's Xano (*Suck it, whore. Take it all the way, dirty bitch*). My death-penalty debate must have made an impact, because I picture him dangling from the tree; I conjure his eyes as he dies and it makes me feel really good. He deserves to be gone.

As much as I'd love to ruin, maim or kill Xano, I can't. Mum wouldn't approve. She's a believer in the law. Hell, she is the law. The last thing she'd want is for her perfect turned slut daughter to turn vigilante and fugitive daughter. Shame that, but I can't.

My family needs to know I'm not going to let a drunken night in Magaluf end my life, or ruin the lives of the people I care about. I run down the hill, go into the bar, and exchange my five-euro note for coins. At the ancient payphone in the main street, I dial Leah's mobile. She doesn't answer, so I try again ten minutes later, then ten minutes after that.

'Su? Su! Are you okay? Where are you?'

'I'm okay,' I tell her. 'I'm absolutely fine. Tell Mum and Dad not to worry about me.'

'I'm in Barcelona. Meet me somewhere. Let me take you home. Su?'

'I don't want to come home yet. I'm okay, though. I need to be alone. Are Mum and Dad all right? Tell them I'm sorry.'

'Where are you?'

'I'm just taking some time out. I'm fine, I promise.'

'But what are you going to do?'

'I'm going now, Leah. I love you. Tell Mum and Dad I love them and I'm really sorry. I'll be in touch soon.'

I don't plan what I do next. I have five euros and eighty cents left and use four-fifty of it to buy a nasty-looking bottle of red wine at the bar. As I head back towards the hill which I now consider to be mine it's not because I have decided to get drunk enough to hang myself from a sizeable bough. The wine buying and tree-setting are not conscious steps, no. I have nipped all thoughts about suicide in the bud. I'm good at nipping heavy stuff in the bud. I'm just drinking under this tree because I feel like getting drunk and I really like this tree.

'Su! Su!'

When I open my eyes, it's the red of the sunset I notice first, then the empty wine bottle I'm clutching like a proper Jakey, then Leah scrambling up the hill towards me.

'Su! Thank God. Are you okay?'

I stay where I am, lying spread-eagled under the soon-to-be stars. 'I'm airing out my body. I've never aired it. Why have I never aired my body?' My speech is slurry, and no wonder, as I swilled that whole bottle down in four long gulps.

'Thank God, oh thank God.' Leah kneels on the ground beside me and hugs me. She's crying and keeps thanking God. I try to push her away because I don't like her hugging me and also because I suddenly realise that I'm sick and tired of everything about Leah. She won't go away and my brain can't instruct my body to move so I can't go away either.

I've never thought of Leah as being anything like Mum, but she's quite the determined and organised detective. After I called, she kept ringing the number of the phone booth, which to her surprise had registered on her mobile.

'It took ages, but eventually a man answered. But he didn't speak English so I had to find someone who could. By the time I did, the man had hung up, but luckily he answered again straight away, and that's how I found out where you rang from.' Since arriving half an hour ago, she'd scoured the town showing people my photo. The woman in the bar pointed her in the direction of this almost-hill.

She sits me up against the tree and takes her phone out of her backpack. It's the same as the one I have – a top-of-the-range Ri7 (Christmas presents. I got the white, she got the black, she wanted the white, so did I, I swapped because I was pathetic, had been for years). I snatch it from her before she can use it.

'Su, give it back. Please, I need to let them both know. They're so worried. They just want you to be safe. They don't care about that stupid video. Please?'

She can't prise the phone from my hand and gives up.

'Here, drink some water.' She holds the bottle to my lips but I refuse to open my mouth. 'Please have some, please.' I'm pursing my lips shut like a toddler. She's frustrated and helpless and I like that she's feeling this way. 'I don't blame you for hating me. I'm so sorry. I should never have let you get so off your face. I should have looked out for you. I was so drunk. I was tripping, I'm sorry.'

I remove the back from the mobile phone.

'Please drink some water.' She stares at the phone in my hand, but is too intimidated to question my reasons for dismantling it. I love that I'm scaring Leah. She should know how it feels. I open her backpack and take a look. My wallet's in there. 'I got them from the man at the hotel.'

I check that my Thomas Cook cash card and passport are in my wallet, then I check what's in hers – five hundred euros, Mum's Nationwide card, and my Santander debit card. I put my cards and all her cash in my wallet. 'Tell Mum I'll transfer what I've spent into her account. You said you were drunk *and* tripping?'

She bites her lip. 'I bought pills, remember? I asked if you wanted one and you said no.'

'Did I?'

She starts crying again, covers her face with her hands, and starts making noises which are mostly moans but I can detect two words: *drink* and *sorry*.

'I can't hear you and I don't care anyway. I just want you to go away.'

Hands still covering her face, she takes a moment to compose herself and speaks clearly: 'I put one in your drink. I'm so sorry. I'm *so* sorry.'

She freezes while I take this in, then tentatively removes her hands to check my reaction. I'm not giving her one, not yet. I'm staring blankly into her blue eyes like a robot, an ice queen.

'Say something, please! Su! I'm sorry. I put a pill in your drink and I'm not even sure what it was.'

I'm almost certain my face is giving nothing away, but I am feeling a great deal on the inside. Mostly, a strong impulse to smash her skull in with the empty wine bottle. 'You gave me the same pill you guys had?' Or perhaps I could finish fashioning the crop top into long thin stretch of fabric, strangle her with it, hang her from the tree and attach a note: *It's all my fault. I spiked Su's drink. I'm sorry.*

Leah nods slowly, as if a hasty one may provoke me.

'You bought four of the same pills and we had one each?'

'I bought six.'

'All the same?'

'Yeah. Natasha and I had two each. Millie had one. I put one in your drink while you were nose-dancing.'

'And you don't know what they were?'

'The PR guy said eccy and it felt like it. Made me love everyone and think everything was really beautiful. When I first noticed you were doing that thing, I thought it was liberating and I wanted that for you. I wanted to liberate you. I wanted you to have fun and I felt like you were. I remember thinking how good your new haircut looked and all I remember after that is the song they were playing in the back section of the bar and that I just had to dance.'

'Were they white or yellow?'

'White.'

'With a thumb or a butterfly?'

'Thumb. How do you know that?'

'So you and Natasha took twice what I took?'

'Yeah.'

'And Millie had the same as me.'

'Yes.'

'But you all knew you were taking it.'

'Yes, I'm sorry! Millie and Natasha don't know what I did to you, still don't. I've been too scared to say. It's all my fault. I've ruined everything. I'm such a fucking arsehole.'

'So that means you gave twenty-four blow jobs that night?'

'What?'

'And Natasha, twenty-four as well?'

She shakes her head.

'Did Millie suck twelve?' Leah's now seeing my point, and is lapping it up as it's conciliatory.

'So the pills weren't those magic ones that turn girls into public penis gobblers?'

She's giving me a little smile, increasing my urge to smash her with the wine bottle.

'It's not your fault. Can I have some of that water?'

'Thank God, you don't hate me. I couldn't stand it if you hated me.'

She's too busy being relieved to hand me the water, so I lean across her and take it. I then remove the tiny SIM card from her phone, pop it in my mouth, and wash it down with a solid swig. I can feel my brain rehydrating.

'What did you do? Why'd you do that?'

'I dunno, hunger.'

'Can we please go into town and ring Mum?'

'I'm not going anywhere with you. I've spent years pussy-footing around you and all you've done is treat me like dirt. Did you spike my drink because your friends started liking me, Leah? Were you mad about that? You feel left out, that the order of the universe was shaken? Did you shout "go, go go" because you wanted me back in my place, because it was such a blast to watch me ruin myself? Whatever. I've had an epiphany, seen the light. I want and need to be away from you. To not be anywhere near you! To not care if you like me, or if your friends like me, to not worry that I'm embarrassing, a geek, a Chinky, you idiot. I don't want to be your play thing, or your friend, or your relative, or your pupil. You have nothing to teach me. This tree here, this tree is as much my sister as you are but I prefer the company of the tree. I took one of those pills the day before, no biggie, so forget about that. I said it's not your fault, Leah, and I mean it. I didn't say I don't hate you. Scram.'

I'm as surprised by this speech as Leah is but I don't regret it. I feel elated. I've wasted the last six years of my life begging for her love. And what do I get in exchange? She thought it was beautiful and liberating and she just had to dance! No-go Su doesn't keep this kind of person in her life. I'm starting to enjoy being her. I'm going with it.

Leah's standing now, and whiter than usual.

'I said scram!'

'I can't. I can't leave without you. Mum'll kill me. She hates me, now more than ever! I promised her I'd bring you home. And you're scaring me. What are you planning to do? I will not go home without you. It's my restoration justice.'

'Restorative.'

'I have to make it up to you. And she doesn't even know about the pill. Will you tell her about the pill? Please don't tell her! I have no right to ask you that.'

Wailing, wailing, how to stop this wailing. 'I know how you can make it up to me.' I stand up and face her. 'Tell Mum you found me here and that I'm fine. Tell her I know about Edinburgh Uni and I've decided to take a gap year and apply to other Uni's for next year and that Edinburgh can go to hell. Tell her I have it all sussed out and there is absolutely nothing to worry about. I just need time on my own.'

'But you don't understand. If I don't take you back with me—'

'Tell Mum I snuck off in the middle of the night.'

'She'll say I should've stayed awake to make sure that didn't happen. I'm dead meat, Su, please help me with this.'

I guess I always knew that Leah was weird about Mum, but I never knew she was scared of her. What a family, hey? I'm scared of Leah and Leah's scared of Mum and Mum's scared of me and round and round the oestrogen goes. 'Okay then, tell her we had a room above that bar in town and that it was too late to get a flight and you stayed up to keep watch over me. Say you were getting drowsy and I took advantage and tried to leave but you caught me just as I was opening the door. Tell her you tried to stop me and I punched you so hard in the face that you lost consciousness. Say you woke some time later with a broken nose and with me gone.'

'She'll never believe that!'

I punch Leah quite hard and she stumbles back against

the tree. Nose and consciousness intact, she's too shocked to realise that she should defend herself against a second blow.

I lean down to check nose and eyes – yes, it's done the trick.

Chapter Eleven

As Ruth watched the taxi turn and disappear at the end of her street, she had many bad thoughts about her husband. She saw his 'Fuck you' and raised him a 'No – fuck you, you imbecilic lump of American lard.' The bad thoughts intensified as she searched for the car keys, which she eventually found on the nest of tables in the living room.

Jim Docherty's latest address was a cottage flat in rejuvenated Castlemilk. MacDonald was parked outside when she arrived. They walked around to the side entrance and peered in the kitchen window. There was drug-taking paraphernalia on the table – papers, a glass bowl filled to the brim with weed, tobacco, a bong. MacDonald knocked on the white PVC door and a moment later a girl answered. She looked much younger than Su and Leah, fifteen perhaps. Dressed in a bathrobe, she chewed on a clump of wet hair in an attempt to cover the blue bruise on her cheek.

'Is Jim in?' MacDonald asked.

'He doesn't have to be in till 7.'

'We're not police, nothing like that. What's your name, love?'

'Bethany.'

'How old are you?'

'None of your business. Eighteen.'

'That looks sore. Did he hit you?'

'Naw!' Her teeth lost grip of the hair she'd been nibbling, unveiling the bruise in its fist-shaped entirety. 'I fell. You social work or something? He already met his this morning and mine's coming tomorrow, it's on my calendar.'

'I'm his lawyer. Tell him Michael MacDonald's here will you?' MacDonald barged inside and sat at the kitchen table in front of the stash of grass. 'We'll wait for him here, Bethany. What did you say your last name was again?'

Bethany was too stupid not to answer. 'Mathieson.'

'You live here with Jim, Bethany?'

'Kind of.'

'You got a dog?'

'No.'

'You like dogs?'

'Aye, naw, I dunno, why the fuck?'

'Don't get a dog.'

'Okay then!' Her teenage snarl was just like Leah's.

'You hear me? Don't let Jim Docherty anywhere near a dog.'

'All right, whatever, no dog, fuckssake.'

When the girl left the kitchen to wake her man, Ruth took a photo of the drugs on the table, and quickly returned her phone to her bag. She wondered what MacDonald would've done if the girl did have a dog. He'd have taken it from the house without permission or hesitation, probably, and fair enough. But if so, should he not forcefully remove the battered female human before she's set on fire?

Jim Docherty yawned as he entered the kitchen, dressed only in floral shorts. Holiday shorts, Ruth wondered? 'Micky, what you doin' here?' He tossed a tea towel over the bowl of grass, then put it in the fridge, not overly concerned. He hadn't recognised Ruth yet.

'Just wanted to ask what you've been doing since you got out. This is Sheriff Oliphant by the way. You do remember Sheriff Oliphant?'

Confusion and panic spread across his face as he looked at Ruth, at the bong on the table, at the fridge, back at Ruth, MacDonald. 'What the fuck is this?'

'We want to know if you were in Magaluf this week,' Ruth said. 'We can find out elsewhere, but it's quicker to ask direct.'

'Ha!' Docherty smiled as he made the connection. 'Shagaluf! How many was it, seventeen?'

He was wearing his 8-ball ring. Ruth cocked her head to get a side view. 'Twelve.' From this angle, did it look the same as the one in the video?

'You think I had something to do with that? Why?'

'Nine months in B Hall perhaps.' He wasn't wearing a red fabric bracelet, but there was a tan mark on his left wrist. Perhaps it wasn't a foolish notion. Perhaps it was him.

'We expected at least two years, didn't we, Micky! Got out in nine, piece of piss. Needed a lie-down – life gets hectic you know.'

'Do you recall threatening me after I sentenced you? *I know where you live! I'll get you for this, bitch!?*'

'I was upset! Listen, no hard feelings about that, none at all, hand on heart. You've got your job and I've got mine, well . . . not a job, but I keep busy. And I've changed and I've learned all sorts of shite and man do I regret meeting Veronica. I was having a mental breakdown at the time and I made wrong decisions and stuff, and I'm filled with that thing – what do you say in court, Micky, what's the word you use that I have?'

'Remorse.'

'Aye, that. Remorse. I have tons of that shit. Look, you must be upset about that film I suppose . . .' He put his hands up. 'Nothing to do with me, man.' Docherty scratched his balls and gestured to his child-lover. 'Put the kettle on, eh? You want tea? You Micky?'

MacDonald shook his head.

'My Lady?'

'I don't want tea. I want to know if you were you in Magaluf yesterday and the day before.' Ruth was wondering how to proceed if this was her man. She'd phone the police immediately. They'd do him for the drugs and the underage girl and her bruised cheek, definitely enough for him to be recalled to prison.

'I'm on curfew, seven till seven. Ask down the road, I've been a good boy. They've visited every fuckin' night so they have.'

'So you weren't in Spain?'

'I wish.'

'And you didn't go to the Coconut Lounge on the strip in Magaluf?'

'I was in this flat, ask the pigs at Dougrie Road.'

'So if I check they'll confirm that?' MacDonald was already dialling the local police station. He went outside to talk.

Ruth eyed the tan mark on his left wrist. 'You usually wear jewellery?'

He seemed to skirt the question. 'I've been here for six weeks, honest, Lady, My Lady, watching telly, been to the Co-op for my messages couple of times a week, down the

Bru or else you'll get sanctioned the fuck out of. What else? Seen Colin with the red bit in his fringe once a week for that Supervised Release thing you said I had to do after getting out. Done the stupid homework he makes me do. Talked about animals and how they have rights and shite and how no one should burn even a fuckin' rat. Drawn ripples and trees and role-played as a bird and all sorts of fuckin' bullshit honestly, you would not believe it.'

Ruth couldn't help but share Docherty's attitude to his social worker. 'As part of your Supervised Release Order you had to pretend you could fly?'

'Nah, ha, not a bird with wings, a fanny hahaha.'

She'd been too hasty to judge. 'What do you wear on your wrist?'

Docherty took a silver Armani watch from the top of the fridge and handed it to Ruth. It had a blue face, looked very expensive. 'I didn't steal it but it was a steal – £163. I gave up smoking for a bit, saved.'

Ruth rested the watch beside his tan mark. The shape was a perfect match, round bit and all.

'Gets me to the court on time! I know I've done wrong, but my head's down now and I'm turning things round. I'm in love! Check her out. She could give your daughter a lesson or two in the head department, I tell you she's a fucking star she is, so you are, baby.'

MacDonald got back inside just in time to grab Ruth's arm and stop her lunging at the cretin. She took a breath, contained herself.

'He's telling the truth,' MacDonald said. 'They've done a check here every night since he got out. And she is eighteen.

Where did you buy the ring?'

'This? Govanhill. Beauty, eh?'

'In a jewellery shop?'

'Nah, pool hall. Some dude – Kev, no Matt or Bob. No . . . Kevin, yeah – Kevin at the pool place makes them as a wee sideline. Allison Street.'

On the way home, Ruth's stomach felt leaden, and she wanted to cry. She hadn't felt this way since Leah was a baby. If she did have postnatal depression back then, she was too busy and too angry to acknowledge it. She would fight rather than wallow this time too. But with her only lead – however flimsy – out of the picture, she wasn't sure who to fight with.

Four missed calls from Bernie. He must be at the gate by now, she thought, feeling guilty, wanting to say sorry and make things right. Before returning his call, Ruth made herself a camomile tea. She was still feeling upset that she'd wasted so much time today – and she was still angry with Bernie for making her feel like a bad mother. How dare he? She was an A-star mother, all the evidence supported this. She needed to calm down before returning his call, or she might say bad things to do with weight and America. He was right, after all (there, she was calmer already), she shouldn't have sent Leah off alone, and she shouldn't have gone to work, and she shouldn't be prioritising finding and punishing the perpetrator over finding and supporting the victim, their beautiful and terrified daughter. She still wasn't happy about Gregor and Val publishing personal information about her family, but she would explain why and put a stop to it. How lucky she was to know Bernie so well, to know that he'd be desperate for her to answer so he could say some or all of the following: *I'm sorry. I was out of order. I was upset. I love you so much, my darling, and you are a fabulous mother. I'll be home tomorrow with Leah and hopefully with Su. If Su's not ready to come home yet, let's give her space till she is. We know how strong she is, we know she's safe, and we know she loves us. She knows we love her unconditionally. It was just one out of control night in a bar. We won't let that ruin our lives.*

She took the last sip of her tea, smiled, and pressed redial. Bernie wasn't useless or lazy. As she pressed redial, she knew he'd say something like all of the above; that he'd melt the lead in her tummy, that he'd contain her urge to storm into battle. As the phone rang, and rang, she became more and more desperate to hear his soothing and sensible words.

'Hello?' A female voice. Perhaps he'd lost his phone.

'Who's that?'

'My name's Katherine Hempenstall. Can I ask who I'm speaking to?'

'Why are you using my husband's phone?'

Pause. 'Is that you, Mrs Brotheridge?'

'I'm Ms and have my own surname but I am married to Mr Brotheridge. Can you answer my question please?'

'I'm Nurse Hempenstall from the A&E at the Southern General. I'm so sorry, I have very bad news.'

Ruth made her first recording in the A&E department. She didn't realise a plan might be formulating in her mind at the time, and still couldn't be sure if that's when the winning idea first sprouted. She'd waited for Katherine Hempenstall to leave her alone to say goodbye, drawn the curtains, taken out her phone, and pressed record. She filmed his face first, moving over it carefully so that every detail was documented. She filmed his dead lips and his dead eyelids. She opened the lids and filmed his dead eyes. She filmed his dead neck and his dead shoulders all the way down to his dead feet, only stopping when the nurse knocked to ask if she was okay.

She hid the phone and took Bernie's hand to look like a normal person. 'I'm fine, come in. Actually I need to ask you something.'

'Of course.'

Katherine Hempenstall seemed to be the kindest woman Ruth had ever met. She'd feel bonded to her for ever. Hundreds probably felt this way about Nurse Hempenstall, because hundreds had probably held a dead hand in her presence. She was about the same age as Ruth, but happier about it; her grey allowed to be grey, her arms allowed to be fat.

'My daughter's all over the internet at the moment, but you probably know that already.'

Katherine didn't flinch. She knew.

'She's okay, but she won't come home and I'm having difficulty tracking her down. Our other daughter's in Spain looking for her. I don't want them to find out about this online or in the newspapers. I don't want anyone to know their dad's dead before they do. Is there anything you can do to keep it quiet till I've told them?'

The nurse didn't say anything for a long time and Ruth felt stupid for asking. How could a bottom-of-the-rung nurse stop this news from spreading? But Ruth had underestimated Katherine Hempenstall, who eventually stopped staring into space and said: 'The taxi driver and the two paramedics know. Dr Kirkpatrick knows. Viv who's on with me – she's a good friend – knows. And crazy overdose guy next door did know, but he had a bad seizure an hour ago and lost consciousness and he seems in no hurry to regain it – and if he does I doubt he'll remember. If I take your husband downstairs now, then no one else will find out except the people I've mentioned. I'll talk to the Doc and Viv and Pete in the mortuary and the paramedics – great guys by the way, Billy and Andreas, they tried really hard, *really* hard. And the taxi driver wanted to say sorry – poor guy, he had his music on, and feels awful that he didn't notice, but there's nothing he could have done, you know that, right? If we both repeat exactly what you just said to me, what decent person would call the newspapers?'

Ruth was comforted by the nurse's plan – she didn't have a better one – but did not share her confidence in human decency. She put her bony hand on the nurse's bulging one: 'Thank you. You're very, very good at your job.'

There was a loud moan from the bed next door. Crazy overdose guy was awake again. 'Not always. Look, I should hurry and take him now. And you should leave the back way. The Nurse took a folded cotton sheet from the trolley and held it at the end of the bed. 'Are you ready?' She put the sheet on Bernie's feet and unfolded a layer until it covered up to his knees.

'Wait! I wasn't! I wasn't ready, sorry. Can you start again from when you were holding the sheet up at the end of the bed? It's weird, forgive me, but could you do that for me please?' Ruth fumbled for her phone. It shook with her hand as she filmed the gentle covering-over of her lover, husband, partner, co-parent, friend.

'Bernie,' she sobbed, 'Bernie.' And with brakes unlocked, the two kindest people Ruth had ever known left the room.

*

To Ruth's relief, the man lying on the back seat finally blinked. She'd made an unplanned stop at the side of this quiet road, and it wasn't a particularly safe place to be. Her hazards illuminated a huge advertisement-board on long stilts and it scared her when she saw the man in the poster light up the first time. She watched the ten-foot-face brighten then fade into the darkness, on and off, on and off. It was a movie poster, George Clooney. His face took up most of the space. His eyes were familiar. Bernie? George Clooney's eyes were just like Bernie's eyes.

Am I mad, Bernie? she said out loud.

Were his eyes encouraging and guiding her? *Of course you're not mad, my darling, don't doubt yourself. It's a great plan!*

Or were they disapproving, getting more so with each flash of red light? *Stop and look at yourself! You are making a poor decision based on fear and anger!*

It was an ad, just an ad. She switched the hazards off, turned to check on the man before resuming the drive, and saw that his bladder was giving way. She switched on the internal lights, pointed her Ri6 at the small wet patch on the left pocket of his lime green skinny jeans and filmed as the urine spread to dampen half his thigh. He farted loudly, and Ruth opened her window, her phone now aimed at his face in case a headshot might seem essential in the editing room later. He looked like a happy drunk, quite relaxed there on the back seat. He'd probably be smiling if he could work his lips. He farted again and it sounded wet. Ruth grimaced, pushed the button to open the passenger window, and kept filming. The man managed to close his eyes. His face tensed a little. His cheeks reddened. He was defecating. When he finished, Ruth opened the back door and rolled him onto his stomach. It was important to get the lump on camera, and the wet brownness on those ludicrous trousers. It also seemed important to push at the lump till it squelched up his lower back and out the top of his jeans, and to film this as well.

Ruth drove faster than she would choose to in the dark and on the right-hand side of the road. She kept the front windows down, and breathed through her mouth. Bernie had been looking over her when she was parked at the side of the road, she decided, and he approved, so much so that he magicked the opening scene she'd just shot. It wasn't the scene she had drafted in her mind, but perhaps it would work better if she built the piece slowly.

Was that the same advertisement on the flyover ahead? Ruth put her lights on full beam and there was Bernie again: *It works much better! It's drama, my darling! Don't start with the bang, earn it.*

Chapter Twelve

I check Leah's breathing, put her in the recovery position, and head down the hill. My hand's throbbing and swollen by the time I reach the town store. The old lady at the checkout scans my purchases slowly. Bread, ham, water, apples, two bottles of sangria, a pair of large pink underpants, a pair of long white socks, a T-shirt that says 'I ❤ Barcelona', toothbrush and paste, soap, and a bandage for my hand. It comes to sixty-five euros. 'Do you have any bikes?'

The old woman yells and a chirpy girl of around eight pounces in through the back door. 'She doesn't speak any English but I do because my mum's from Manchester – but we don't mention her round here any more.'

'I want to buy a bike. Do you know where I can get one?'

The girl asks her grandmother, who shakes her head.

'Whose is that?' I point at the bike with the large basket leaning by the front door.

'That's my grandmother's.'

'How much would she sell it for?'

'She said it's not for sale,' the little girl translates. 'She said how would she get to Claudia's?'

'100 euros?'

The little girl relays the offer to her grandmother, who shakes her head, no deal.

'120? . . . 130?'

No. And nup, all the way to 150. I should walk to the next town and wait for the buses to start again, but the situation has become competitive and I'm in deep. 'Okay, so say to your grandmother that I'll give you 200 for the groceries, the bike, plus a little favour.'

The girl refuses to pass the offer on. 'It's no use, she doesn't want to sell the bike because she has precious feelings about it and Claudia's house is two miles from here.'

'Okay, Jeez, tell her I only have 400 euros, that's all, and she can have it all in exchange for the groceries, the bike and the favour.'

The girl sighs, then translates. Her gran, who hasn't been informed of any progress since we were at 150, screams with joy, laughs, and jumps up and down. She scoops up the little girl and twirls her, freezing when she remembers I'm still here. She says something which sounds very grave but translates as: 'My grandmother says it's an excellent bike, top quality.'

I count out the 400 and almost give it to her. 'The favour.'

The grandmother looks terrified when the word is translated. She thinks I'm going to ask her to murder someone for me. 'There's a teenage girl under the tree up the hill across from the bar. You know the hill? There's a tree about halfway up? She's unconscious and bleeding. Would you go and make sure she's okay, or ask someone else to? She might need a hand walking back now it's dark.'

The old lady looks at me as if I *have* asked her to murder someone. After a long wait, she eventually nudges her granddaughter and whispers at least ten agitated and very lengthy sentences. What seems like half an hour later, she concludes with a sign of the cross.

The little girl folds her arms: 'She said okay, that's 400 euros please.' Arms still folded, the little girl forces a smile, and stops still.

I put the cash on the counter and wait for the grandmother to pick it up, but she's as stiff as her granddaughter, and has the same unmoving smile. I lean towards the girl: 'She said a lot more than that.'

The girl maintains her pose until I wave another fifty-euro note over the counter, at which point she looks sideways at her grandmother, who then says something through her teeth.

'My grandmother says I shouldn't tell you what she said, not even for 150.'

I shake my head and put the fifty-euro note in the pocket of my shorts. This is silly, I should leave. But Grandma unfreezes and begins to yell and gesticulate.

'Okay, fifty, my grandmother says fifty, thank you.'

The old woman adds the fifty to her pile and nods at the little girl, who keeps her arms tightly folded as she talks. 'When you told us about the favour, my grandmother said . . .' She takes a deep breath: 'Why didn't you say about the girl on the hill first? You must be a psychopath not mentioning that straight away, browsing round our shop buying ham and wine and she said your eyes are scaring her and she can't look at them any more they're so dark, dark as where Marco went – that's my grandfather. He's dead. Then she said, Curse the mother of God, did you *stab* the girl at the tree? Is that why your hand's injured and why she's unconscious and bleeding and why you paid – she did some sums – 335 euros for a rusty getaway vehicle worth twenty euros, if that, and she said: Be very polite, Mariella, don't encourage the conversation but don't provoke her, whatever you do, oh oh, I looked at the eyes, I shit in the milk, we're in danger, Mariella, stay still and keep smiling and hopefully she'll just leave on the bike and ride away and never come back – tell me your father fixed that puncture, tell me he did, Mariella, but not out loud! Fold your arms if your dad fixed the puncture like I asked. Keep them at your side if he didn't. Understand? Fold now if the bike works.'

Before pedalling into the darkness, I give Mariella and her gran my last fifty. They deserve it.

After ten minutes on the road (and several on the gravel avoiding scary lorries with flashing lights and beeping horns) a sign says it's nine kilometres to Barcelona. I stop, irritated, because I thought I was heading away from civilisation, not back into it – but then I notice that there's a picture of an aeroplane on the list of destinations. I stare at the wee plane and wonder if the supernatural exists for the first time since Michael O'Hare's mother's statue of the Madonna winked at me. Perhaps this is a *sign*, not a sign.

I continue in the same direction because I have just made a snap and inspired decision. I'd planned to hide out a while longer. I'd hoped that time would dilute my desire to hurt the man who filmed me; that time and space would stop me disappointing Mum all over again by breaking the law, by breaking his neck, by slitting his throat, by poisoning him with drain cleaner. The picture of the aeroplane has cleared my head. I'm going to the airport. This is the perfect, and possibly the only, time. I'll call them once I land in Seoul. I'll explain that some good has come out of all this. I'll be assertive and tell them this is something I've needed to do for a long time. I think they might understand now. I think they'll be relieved that I'm out of sight for a while.

The plan gathers detail as I gain speed. When I arrive, I'll buy a smart trouser suit and I'll book into a hotel and I'll scrub myself clean. I'll go and visit retired officer Moon Jihoo and I'll pay him to tell me what he knows. Then I'll go to the squat my mother smokes crystal methamphetamine in, or to the street she begs on, or to the dark alley where she grasps her near-empty bottle of Soju, or to the prison or mental institution where she repeatedly cuts at a designated portion of her upper left thigh. I'll go to her and I'll tell her who I am. She won't have seen the sex tape, no way. She probably doesn't even have the internet.

A fine notion, in fact. People existed without the internet for centuries and survived. Poor people, like my birth mother, still do. I, too, can live without it. I decide to declare it out loud. 'I hereby swear that I will never go online again.' The oath brings on the desire to make others, which I yell as I pedal. 'I hereby swear that I will never go to Magaluf again. I hereby swear that I will never perform sex acts in public again. And . . .' I stop at the side of the road, take out the two bottles of sangria I bought at the village shop, and toss them over the fence into a field, 'I hereby swear that I will never drink or take anything that results in the handing over of my faculties ever again!' Pedalling faster now due to the onset of an unparalleled excitement, and perhaps because I'm minus the weight of the wine, I picture my birth mother's face when I tell her who I am. It'll crumple! And then she'll spurt tears of agonised guilt. I feel like I can actually see her – not her face exactly, but the shape of her, and her response – she's begging for my forgiveness, she's saying she knows it's no excuse, and she doesn't deserve or expect me to forgive her, but she had no choice, you see (You are so beautiful!), because she was destitute and still is (doesn't even have the internet), and she was all alone, with no family, and still is, and she had and still has at least two other serious health problems that made/make motherhood impossible (she's blind and a paraplegic, for instance).

After she's said all this and is on her knees with her hands pressed together as if in prayer, I will look down on her with Dalai Lama-serenity and this is what I will say: 'I forgive you.'

Her tears of guilt will recede and pride will surface. Her face will redden and her heartbeat will quicken. She'll manage to stand and start talking with speed, confidence, but mostly gratitude: *You forgive me, really? Su-Jin, you are good, so good. And I am not, because I put you in a basket and I abandoned you. I should have fought for you but I couldn't – for so many excellent reasons like the paraplegia (oh, need to edit the scene 'cause she wouldn't be able to kneel or stand up) – for so many excellent reasons like the blindness – (oh, she wouldn't have said 'You're so beautiful' because she wouldn't have been able to see me) – reasons like the leprosy! Su-Jin, you grew inside me, inside this hopeless and undernourished outcast.* She'll put her hands on my shoulders: *It's a myth that it's contagious, just prejudice, but I see you know that already because you are highly educated, exceptionally clever and know everything there is to know about all the medical conditions in the universe.* And she'll stretch her arms straight to hold me there and absorb from a comfortable distance, because she simply. Can. Not. Get. Over. That the incredible woman standing in front of her is Su-Jin.

I go by Su, I'll say, and she'll ask if she can use the Jin and I'll say no, because I make my own decisions, me, and I'm Su. I'm Su of forty-eight hours ago. Su, who's 100 per cent sane, not even .015 per cent crazy, who's respectable and purposeful and who will study Medicine somewhere more prestigious than Edinburgh and who'll go on to win a Nobel Prize for curing something highly horrible, but not leprosy because someone did that already (and you will have the treatment now that I've found you, birth mother. I will take you to the hospital immediately and I will pay Western money to rid you of this affliction which – strangely and thankfully – has caused no scabby lesions that I can see). Um, where was I? I'm the Su who's going to win the Nobel Prize for curing – dementia! – so when you start forgetting things that you would never, ever forget, like where you left the Soju, I'm the Su who won the prize for discovering the meds that mean you remember where it is – it's in the 'garage at the side of your villa', otherwise known as the side pocket of your walk-and-rest tri-wheel shopping trolley.

I'm smiling, haven't done that for a while. My success will ease the suffering my birth mother has endured due to poverty/homelessness/mental illness/addiction (delete as appropriate), because I am proof that her genes are from Waitrose, it's just her luck that's Co-op.

I can't stop smiling. Comforting her will comfort me. Easing her guilt will restore my virtue.

Airport, 5k. This is happening, at last. I'm on my way.

Chapter Thirteen

Ruth didn't turn the lights on when she arrived home from the hospital. Once inside, she sat in the dark with her back against the front door, and dialled Leah's mobile again and again. She'd been sitting there a while – she had no idea how long – when the house phone rang. She pounced and checked the caller ID on the screen before answering – *international*. It was Leah. She stifled the need to howl with grief when she heard her voice.

'I'm in a shop in a village outside Barcelona. Su rode off on a bike. I'll find her again, Mum, I promise. I'll follow her.'

'You saw her? Was she okay?'

'She was furious. She hates me. Mum, there's something I have to tell you.'

Furious, good, Ruth thought, *furious survives*. 'Don't worry about any of that now. Is there a hotel or a B&B you can stay in tonight?'

'I'm going to follow her. I can get a lift, I can catch up with her.'

'Honey, no, I don't want you to do that now. I'll hire a professional to look for her. Ask the person in the shop if there's a hotel in town.'

'I don't want to. I want to go after her.'

'Do as I say, Leah. Now, no arguments. I need you to come home.'

Leah paused, sighed, and then spoke to someone in the background. Ruth could hear a little girl speaking in English, translating for a woman by the sounds of it.

'I can stay in a room at Claudia's, but—'

'But nothing. Get some sleep. I'll book a taxi to take you to Barcelona airport at 4.45 a.m. There's a flight to Glasgow, leaving at 7.50. I'll organise for you to collect the ticket at the KLM desk. When you arrive in Glasgow, get a taxi straight home from the airport, *straight* home.'

'No! I can't come back without her.'

'You have to. Leah, do as I say. I should never have sent you there alone. I am telling you to come home. Now put the girl who speaks English on. I need the address and phone number.'

After hanging up, Ruth crawled up the stairs and into Leah's bed. There were things she had to do. *What were they?* She had to arrange Leah's ticket. She had to ring Michael MacDonald and ask him to hire someone to find Su. Instead of doing either of these things, she covered herself with Leah's duvet, and tried to make herself small: head buried into knees, arms encasing legs. She was still too large. She had to organise a taxi to Barcelona airport. Ruth curled her toes inwards. She clenched her fists. She shut her eyes tightly. It was no use, she still existed. Loosening the grip she had on herself, she swiped her phone on. She could do the essentials listed above without coming out.

A crack of light entered her cocoon. It took a moment to see that Leah had lifted the corner of the duvet. Grief must have sapped the hours away, just as sleep does. Ruth could now hear journalists talking outside and she could see from Leah's face that one of them had told her. Without saying a word, Leah crawled into the bed, and put the cover over the two of them.

They stayed huddled there for hours with their mobiles and the landline handset. They cried and held each other without saying a word. They ignored the doorbell. They checked caller ID when one of the phones rang but none of the calls were from Su or MacDonald. They took no notice of the journalists banging on windows and yelling for interviews. The sunlight filtered through the duvet in pastel pink. In Leah, Ruth could see Bernie's kind blue-grey eyes and his full wide mouth. He was so beautiful, Bernie, and here he was, in his daughter.

Why had Ruth always agonised about her relationship with Leah? Why had she always focused on Leah's negative qualities – the rudeness, ingratitude and laziness typical of a girl of her age? There were times when Bernie had conceded that Ruth was right to agonise and that she should make changes, because sometimes she was impatient, judgemental and harsh. And at times she did appear to favour the placid and self-contained Su. But most of the time, Bernie reassured her that there was no need for the self-flagellation. 'You're just very, very close. Can't you see that? When she's older, you two'll be inseparable, watch.'

She felt intensely close to Leah now. When MacDonald finally phoned, they dragged themselves out of bed. Ruth took hold of her daughter's hand and never wanted to let go. She gripped it tightly as she spoke to MacDonald. Last night, he said, Su had made three withdrawals at Barcelona airport: 300 euros from her Thomas Cook cash card, and two lots of 300 from her Santander: one late last night, and one in the early hours of this morning. She had bought an open-ended return flight to Seoul, a journey which left at 9.30 this morning and would take thirteen hours and fifty minutes, with one change in Frankfurt. MacDonald had contacted Lufthansa staff in Spain, Frankfurt and Seoul, and asked them to pass on the urgent message that Su should contact her mother immediately.

Ruth and Bernie had expected – and even hoped for – this moment for years. They often worried that Su had never seemed interested in discovering more about her roots. The language lessons and the Korean banquets and the picnics with Woojin all seemed to make Su irritable and withdrawn. Eventually they stopped forcing these things on her, and decided to wait till she was ready. The only time she'd ever broached the subject was several years ago, after Woojin found his brother. *I wonder if there's a history of cervical cancer in my family?*, she'd said casually, but then receded immediately. Ruth scolded herself after Su left the room and talked it over with Bernie. She should not have responded by asking Su if she was worried about her health. She should have said: 'Maybe we should find out. We think it's important too. We support you. We'll help you.' They deliberated about going upstairs to say these things, but decided to leave it. They might have misread the intent behind Su's question. Perhaps she wasn't broaching the subject, but simply wanting to talk about the immunisation she and Leah had a week earlier at school. No, they'd leave it till she was ready.

Sure, it made Ruth and Bernie nervous. If Su found

nothing, it might depress her, or obsess her and sap her energy. And if she found something – her mother – she risked rejection a second time.

There was also the possibility, of course, that Su would find and adore her biological mother/father/brother/half-brother etc., that she would want to be with them, and that she would become resentful and hostile towards Ruth and Bernie. She might start to think of them as selfish and naïve and even racist. Her adoptive parents believed, she might conclude, that they had saved her from the otherness of South Korea, and given her the gift of a place in their white (superior) world, a world where she would always be 'other'. The possibility had long loomed that the social workers were right after all.

Ruth understood why Su had decided to ask questions now. She was too ashamed to come back. She wanted to hide. She was scared. But most of all, she would be wondering who the hell the girl in that video is.

If Bernie was alive, he'd probably be relieved that Su was on her way to Seoul. He'd often worried that she was repressed – too self-contained, too well behaved. He worried that she never did broach the subject again, and that questions and resentments might be eating away at her insides. He hoped one day she would set them free. He'd be relieved that the day had arrived.

If Bernie were here, Ruth would also welcome Su's quest. But not now. Su would be alone in an unfamiliar land when she found out that her dad was gone. And she'd blame herself. She'd need her mum and her sister. They'd comfort her, alleviate any guilt. Nausea rose from Ruth's stomach as she contemplated Su's situation. 'Don't panic,' Leah said. 'Being over there won't necessarily make this worse for her. We just need to talk to her, make sure she knows it's not her fault and that we love her.'

'Are you sure?'

'I am, completely. We just need to talk to her, that's all. It's a good thing that she decided to go. It means she's moved on already. I knew she would, because she's Su-Jin. Yesterday, she yelled and screamed at me, Mum, she was so angry, and it scared the shit out of me, but on the way home I started thinking Magaluf happened for a reason. She's saying "Fuck you, world!" – at last, no? Don't panic, take another sip of water, here, good. Su-Jin won't wallow. She's a survivor and a fighter. She's amazing. She's you! Another sip, well done. Now,' Leah began dialling a number, 'Cherry and Bud should hear first,' and she handed the phone to her mother.

Ruth spoke to Bernie's mum, Cherry, then to her own mother. She called her sisters, Bernie's friend Jamie from Berklee days, Frank from the Oregon orchestra, Will who he'd known since he was four, the school he was supposed to be teaching at today. She phoned his mate Paul from the quiz night, three neighbours he was close to, Norine from the corner shop who worshipped him and always gave him a home-made treat with his morning newspaper. Gregor cried so hard that Ruth didn't have the heart to tell him to stop the daft blogging. Leah called Val, who either hung up or fainted, as the phone went dead.

Calls complete, Leah set about making tea and toast.

'His last words to me were *Fuck you.*'

'No, really? Don't think about it, don't. Those are only two of the millions of words he's said to you. You had an argument, no big deal. You two are normal, you argue. Who wouldn't have lost it in this situation? He adores you. You have fun together. His favourite place in the world is here with you, with us: this house, this garden, that cherry blossom he planted! He's a really happy guy. Was. You were a very happy couple. Are. Were. Shit.'

Ruth wondered if Bernie's spirit had taken possession of Leah. Bernie would have said what she'd just said, and with exactly the same tone. And when Leah had hugged her earlier, it was a Bernie hug: one arm under, one arm over, as if the hug might transform into a dance. Ruth couldn't remember the last time Leah lifted an arm or even a hand in return when she hugged her – must be years. Bernie had possessed her. It wasn't just the hug that made her think this, but also how she behaved while Ruth endured those lengthy conversations on the phone, each of which forced her to relive events – dead . . . taxi . . . attack . . . sudden . . . Leah remained calm throughout, stroking her hand when her composure wavered, giving her the strength she needed to make the next call. *Jamie? It's Ruth Oliphant. I have very bad news . . . dead*, and so on.

When they braved the die-hard hacks out the front to go to the Funeral Director's, Leah maintained control just as her father would have, taking her place on the easy-exit stage she had picked out, and making a brief statement: 'We are devastated by this loss and we ask that you please respect our privacy.'

At the funeral place, Leah made all the decisions because Ruth was crying too violently to talk. The cremation would be for immediate family only, in a small room with a discreet entrance, in the nicely distant Clydebank crematorium. There would be no flowers, no announcements and strictly no press. They would bring music, one of the CDs of Bernie playing in the Oregon Symphony Orchestra. It would be miserable but they'd find another time and place to applaud him. It would be at 9.30 a.m., in three days. If they hadn't talked to Su by this time tomorrow, they could change to Saturday at 1, but the slot could only be held as backup till 12.30 tomorrow.

Leah made decisions as efficiently and as calmly as Bernie had for Ruth's dad's service. Why had Ruth always thought of herself as the decision maker in the marriage? All day every day, Bernie had quietly made almost all the small ones, and thinking about it now, he drove at least half the biggies.

Of course Bernie's spirit hadn't possessed Leah. But if she'd always been so like her father – as kind and as clever and as loving – then for some reason, Ruth had never noticed before.

*

Ruth turned off the main road and put her lights on full beam. It was difficult to see the small sign to the villa, so she drove slowly, with her eyes peeled. A mile and a half later, she headed up the long, steep driveway, and parked by the pool.

Blame hadn't always played a central role in Ruth's life. She blamed right-on social workers for its entrance to centre stage. And she blamed criminal law for keeping it there. That's the job, after all. Find out who's at fault, and punish. And now you may relax – righteous ones – safe once more, because the guilty rot in cells that stink of sweat and semen. In the two days that followed the posting of Su's video, Ruth's desire for blame and punishment had risen to an all-time high. It evaporated in the days between Bernie's death and funeral.

But then it came back. Oh boy, did it come back.

Chapter Fourteen

Get lost, I say to myself when the air steward passes on the message. I'm not even in Frankfurt, and they've tracked me down. 'Thank you,' I say instead when he's finished showing me how to use the in-flight phone that I will not use. I put the phone on my lap. I've made a plan and it's a good one. I'll call when I'm standing on Korean soil. I believe the soil of my homeland will strengthen me, that I'll cope better with the conversation once I'm on it. Most of all, though, I don't want to be talked out of this. I don't want Mum to hurl guilt my way like she did at the table that time, as if I'm leaving her for someone else. I'm sticking to the plan, which is restoring me already. Since it came to me last night on that dark Spanish road, I haven't hit myself on the head once, not once. *Seven million three hundred thousand four hundred and eleven*? So what? Xavier from the pool has seen it? Big deal and whoop-dee-doo. Jessica, Kelly-Marie, Jason, Tim and Emily have seen it? I do a raspberry. I check if any of the passengers heard because I can't be sure how loud the raspberry was. If they did hear it, they're not letting on. Who cares if Cherry and Bud walked miles from their hippy dope-filled commune to watch their granddaughter suck penises on some unenlightened consumer's computer? I don't. I don't care. I don't care about Xano. I won't waste energy thinking about strangling him with paddle wire.

I'm on the aisle seat beside a couple in their twenties. She has her head on his shoulder and he's got his hand on her leg. He started moving his fingers ever so gently about a minute ago, a loving rub that's made her twitch with anticipation and pleasure. Her movement has encouraged him and he's putting an airline-issue blanket over their laps. I'm not moving my head sideways at all, but can almost smell what's going on. There's sex in row 12, seats A and B. Sex, and I feel the heaviness again and I welcome it this time. My knees part a little and the phone falls between my legs. Tomorrow, I might find myself a nice Korean boy. I unwrap my airline blanket and cover my lap and a wriggle lodges the phone in place. The Korean boy might rub me and touch me between the legs. I try to picture it. And that will be my first experience, the seed that ignites my sexuality, that determines what will arouse me henceforth. My first boyfriend, touching me.

Begone, Magaluf.

My boyfriend, touching me, down there.

I close my eyes – *begone!* – and – *focus!*

I soak in my new first time. The Korean boy is called Ji. He's a man not a boy, and tall for a Korean.

I said get out of my fantasy, Coconut Lounge.

He's gorgeous, everyone wants him, but it's me he's touching, mm.

It's very difficult to banish Magaluf from this scenario. I banish, it intrudes, and in the end I let Ji into the Coconut Lounge.

I feel that all three of us in row 12, seats A, B and C, are fidgeting in sync with each other and with some welcome turbulence.

Go go go, Ji!

The tall Korean man in the Coconut Lounge is so stirred by me that he has no trouble getting and staying hard and: 'Yes, yes,' he's saying through the spasms, 'I'm, I'm, I . . .'

When I open my eyes, the couple next to me are giggling and trying not to look at me. I must have made an inappropriate noise.

I unbuckle and race to the loo so I can giggle too.

When I get back to row 12, the lovebirds are staring at the phone which dangles before my seat like a used condom.

They think I should be embarrassed about making an inappropriate noise?

I click the phone into place with confidence and take my seat.

Ha.

This room is on the fifth floor of a modern four-star hotel in Myeong-dong. It has a large and comfortable super-king-size bed with cabinets either side (hairdryer in one, Bible in the other). A wood panel lines the bottom half of the rectangular space. Above it, white walls, no pictures. Opposite the bed is a built-in bench. On it, a flat-screen TV with three English-speaking, twenty-four-hour news channels that I'm too scared to watch, a kettle and a remote control for the aircon, which I need because it's an impenetrably humid thirty-one degrees outside. Like the bedroom area, the en-suite could be in any modern hotel in any country in the world. I've been in this room for a long time. I wonder how agoraphobia develops, and whether it might be taking root in me.

After I landed, I took a taxi to Myeong-dong police station and hovered at the doorstep for a while. My plan still seemed an excellent one at that point. The heat and noise and colour in the street both energised and relaxed me.

After a lifetime among the pale, it was bizarre and wonderful to be surrounded by people with skin like mine. Initially, I felt conspicuous, the odd one out, but I caught no one's attention. Not one passer-by glanced at me a second time, their thoughts written on their faces – Where's she from? Wonder what she's doing here?

As I knew from Google Earth, there was a rectangle of lighter-coloured concrete at the entrance to the police station, encased by the slightly darker concrete of the pavement. The arched double doors were made of glass and I could see a few folk sitting on seats inside, and two police officers behind the counter.

No one was giving me a second look!

I felt so inconspicuous that I bent down to touch the ground. I imagined my birth mother must have left me within the confines of this rectangle of light concrete, as I'd be an obstruction to those entering and exiting, and more likely to be noticed and dealt with. I imagined the basket, the bundle inside, the note. As I touched the concrete, I thought: *I was on this spot here and she was standing where I am now. Or I was on this spot here, she there . . . Or maybe here, like so . . . Me here, her leaning over like this.*

An officer opened the glass door and nearly hit me on the head. He shouted at me in Korean.

'I'm sorry, but I do not understand,' I said, thankful this was one of the four sentences Rosetta Stone had left me with.

The officer waved his hands, 'Shoo, shoo!'

I scurried off, terrified and embarrassed. The confidence I'd found on the bike and carried on the plane was wavering. I'd been in the country for one hour and had already made a fool of myself. Perhaps Magaluf was only the beginning, and my life hereon would be a snowball of shame. In a nearby lane, I hit myself on the head, and then talked out loud: 'I hereby swear that that I will not hit myself on the head again.'

I glanced around me – no one was in the lane to witness the whack or hear my first sign of crazy.

I bought myself some amazing-looking street food, and when I bit into a portion I realised it was fried blood sausage – you can take the girl outa Scotland. I bought a smart trouser suit, shoes, shorts that fitted me, a top, a new battery and SIM for my phone, make-up and toiletries.

I booked into this hotel. I waited an hour till there was enough charge on my phone, another hour to go over the exact words I'd use when I finally dialled, a whole night to try and get some sleep because I wasn't feeling ready and perhaps sleep would help, and many more hours the next day writing and rewriting what I'd say to Mum and Dad on hotel note-pads. By the time I finally did the deed – yesterday afternoon – it was too late to get home in time.

It's 10 a.m. in Scotland now. My dad, Bernard Adam Brotheridge, is in a coffin.

I'm looking at a video Leah emailed me. It's from eight years ago. Dad's in the living room doing a concert for us. He's extraordinary. He looks jubilant.

It's 10.18. He's disappearing through a curtain.

10.40, burning in a furnace.

I'm crying as hard as Mum and Leah. I'm as sad and as empty as they are.

But I'm sorrier. I'm so, so sorry.

I've talked to Mum and Leah constantly since yesterday – must be costing a fortune – and they've said the same thing over and over. It's not my fault. Ticking bomb. Would it help if I saw the report?

Yes please, yes it would. Mum messaged it immediately. Okay, so his heart had had it, and okay, so it seems this would have happened soon, regardless. We have all read the report and we have all said it over and over – not Su's fault, not Su's fault.

None of us believe it.

We discussed postponing it – there was a place in Falkirk with availability on Monday, and a flight that'd get me home late Sunday. In the end, I persuaded them that it was actually better this way. What would it be like if I was there? Journalists would swarm around our house. They'd follow us to the funeral. I'd disguise myself with hat and glasses and sneak out the back door and jump over the back fence and into a car and I'd lie down on the back seat all the way to Falkirk. They'd scream at me as I walked into the crematorium: 'Do you blame yourself for this? Is it your fault?' and we'd all be thinking yes. Once inside, I'd hide behind a curtain or under a table. Yes, it is my fault. He died because of me, and now I have completely ruined his send-off. I convinced Mum and Leah that Dad would never want me to be in that situation. He'd want me to stay where I am, in the safety of a nice hotel, and say goodbye in my own time and in my own way. 'I'll get a flight the day after,' I told them.

The idiotic sense I talked. I should be there. I need to be there.

I'm heading into wallowing territory again, but Mum's calling just in time to stop me again. 'We're driving home,' she says. 'It was fine. Two journalists found it somehow, but they must've been disappointed because they were gone when we came out. You were right, Su. If you'd come, it would have been awful for you. So yeah, it was okay, but like we discussed, the crematorium bit was practical, it wouldn't have mattered to him. What would've mattered to him is that we're safe and that we love each other and that we'll always love and remember him. The three of us will celebrate his life properly when the time's right. Now, remember what I said?'

Mum's said a lot of things since yesterday, all of them amazing and lovely, but I do know what she's referring to. She'd put forward a second argument for me staying in Seoul. 'You've taken the first step,' she'd said. 'Don't chicken out now.'

Who'd have thought my parents wanted me to do this? I thought I was insightful and I'm not, although realising this might mean I am a tiny bit.

'I should be saying there's no hurry, that your dad just died, that you need to lock yourself away – here or there – and cry for weeks like people do, but bollocks to that. You're there, and now is the time. Your dad would want you to.' Leah says something in the background. 'Leah wants you to too. Take your grief and your anger and your fear and roll it into one humungous sun-sized ball of energy and use it, Su. Use it to

161

get the job done. That's what I'm going to do. That's *exactly* what I'm going to do.'

I'm so comforted by Mum's words that I don't think to ask what job she feels compelled to do. I wish I had.

Chapter Fifteen

After the girls had settled into Primary One, Ruth went to work with Gills and Skelton: Defence Lawyers. To congratulate and encourage her, Bernie organised for builders to convert the attic into a home office. Stairs led from what was once a hall cupboard on the first floor to an enormous carpeted room with three dormer windows in its pitched walls, and a door that locked on the small landing. When Ruth shut herself away, her family knew to leave well alone. They understood the importance of her work, and that she needed to concentrate. When Oliphant was added to the Gills and Skelton firm name, Bernie bought the antique cherry wood desk she was sitting at now. The ornate mirror on the wall opposite the desk was the present he gave her when she became Sheriff.

She had checked herself regularly since the funeral, looking up from her desk and into the mirror: *Answer these questions honestly, Ruth. Are you doing anything that would get you into trouble? Are you going mad? Have you lost control?*

She'd bought some very expensive software, and had been teaching herself how to use it for hours. On her computer screen, she examined the first experimental scene she'd managed to put together – pic of man laughing, overlaid with the soundtrack of a man laughing, *ha ha ha*. It was a tiny scene, and she'd probably change it, may even toss it to the cutting-room floor, but it was proof that she was getting the hang of this. She was even enjoying it! She lifted her arms into a self-congratulatory stretch. And then she looked into the mirror: *Are you doing anything that would get you into trouble? Are you going mad? Have you lost control?*

No, no. And no.

Hang on, perhaps it was a little crazy that she was dressed in her first-ever wig and robe set, which she'd kept for sentimental reasons. She walked over to the mirror for a second interrogation. She removed the wig and let the gown slip to the carpet. The woman standing before her was five-foot-five. She was toned, not an ounce of fat, but would no longer be described as athletic: thin probably, gaunt possibly. She wore black yoga trousers, a silver sports top, and Asics trainers. Her skin did not seem to fit her hands, which were trembling. Thick blue veins bubbled between her wrists and knuckles. Her dyed-brown hair had lost its bounce and shape, and the roots needed attention. Tributaries of blood vessels wound outwards from her nose. Her eyes were red, the bags under them heavy and dark. Her lips were pale, cracked and dry, and a cold sore fizzed and blistered at one corner. Ruth couldn't get the wig and the gown back on quickly enough.

She sat at her chair, and banged her fist on the desk. No. And no.

Ruth had genuinely meant everything she'd said to Su. The service was merely a practical piece of business. She felt confident that Su's absence was the right decision when she walked into the discreet back room they'd booked, and when she took her place on the head-griever's grey plastic chair and switched on her phone to film the service.

'The hearse is delayed in traffic,' the minister whispered

a moment later, 'but won't be too long.' He had breath like warm pus. To improve the vibe, he put on the CD Leah had brought, and turned the volume down low. What you could hear of Bernie's violin sounded tinny on the portable player, and it got stuck like an old-fashioned record about a minute in.

Leah turned it off, thank God, and then returned to Number-Two's seat to hold Number-One's hand. 'Why are you filming this?' she asked her mum.

'I'm not really sure.'

The coffin appeared ten minutes late, which meant they were only left with ten minutes for the service.

'Sorry, but the room is booked solidly all day.' The minister assaulted her with his breath again before going through the motions. He'd never met Bernie, and read from the notes Leah had given him with a fake solemnity that made Ruth want to spit at him.

The hearse was late and the chairs were plastic and the carpet was threadbare and the wallpaper was peeling and the 1980s CD player was broken and Su was not here. There were only five other people in the room – Ruth's mum, sister and husband, sister and partner. They had decided not to invite his friends for fear of media harassment, but she now regretted it. This was the funeral of an outcast: of a child-molester; of a 101-year-old with no remaining relatives or friends who care staff had no interest in sending off after a decade of dementia-induced biting.

As the coffin groaned its way along the conveyor belt and through the faded purple velvet curtains, Ruth heard someone's phone ping. She wondered how many people outside the building were watching the video right now. Kids in class, call centre staff, a Japanese businessman on a Tokyo train, Bernie's cousin Gemma in San Francisco. Perhaps even inside this building someone was watching it – a bored teenager at his gran's funeral in the larger room next door, perhaps.

The video was their family legacy.

You remember Bernie Brotheridge?

Yeah, his daughter's the one in that sex tape, ha!

The mechanism to the conveyor belt shuddered to a halt as soon as the coffin disappeared behind the curtains, which surprised Ruth because she assumed the belt would convey her husband all the way to a grand, foreboding furnace. She could hear someone whispering behind the curtain. A loud clunk, then another. Employees in oversized council fleeces, probably, moving him onto a trolley like airport luggage, then wheeling him through the grotty bowels of the building and depositing him in an uninspired and drama-less oven door as if he was dinner.

Someone sobbed behind her – probably her little sister Marie. Leah took Ruth's hand, but for the first time in days she didn't want to hold it. The minister checked his watch, picked up the framed photo they'd placed on the table by the coffin and handed it to her with the I-feel-your-pain smile he'd perfected. Ruth looked at the picture, which Su had taken on Bernie's birthday last November. He had a party hat on, and was beaming before the huge chocolate birthday cake Leah had baked. He looked so happy in this shot that Ruth caught a tinge of it and found herself smiling back at him.

Who's he again?

The one who brought up that Asian whore.

Her smile receded.

'I was wondering if I could go and see Millie and Natasha?' Leah said, a mile before Doon. 'Will you be all right if I spend some time with my friends?'

'Sure, that's a good idea.' Little twits that they were, but Ruth wanted to be alone with her rage, which had intensified to a worrying degree since calling Su and had fired up the rash on her neck again. Of course it made sense for Su to stay in Seoul and begin the search Ruth and Bernie had long anticipated. Ruth had meant everything she'd said. But as soon as she hung up, she felt an overwhelming urge to be violent. Right now, she wanted to break Millie's legs with a brick. She wanted to stab Natasha in the neck with a kitchen knife. If she had a gun, she'd shoot the girl walking along the main street, laughing at something (Ruth knew what) on her phone. She needed time and space to calm down.

There were a lot of rooms in their house – four on the ground floor, five on the first – and she had paced around each of them two or three times already. Instead of calming her, the rooms made her angrier – that's where the happy family ate the birthday cake, that's a pic of Ruth in her very first wig, one of the four of them on the beach in Viareggio last year (best holiday ever), that's the South Korean flag, that's Su's award for being Dux, that's where Bernie attempted to grow a lettuce in a jar of water. Ruth paused in the living room and a memory overwhelmed her. She closed her eyes and breathed it in. When the girls were babies, Bernie used to play to them all the time. Lullabies at bedtime, cheerful songs at playtime. When Su was eighteen months, and Leah nine months, Ruth recorded them watching as their dad performed the modern Scottish folk ballad, 'Caledonia'. They were both tired and moany after a car journey. Bernie had placed them side by side in their car seats on the living-room floor, and began playing. Su was impossibly gorgeous at eighteen months, and almost twice the size of her little sister. At this age, they were different generations. Both girls calmed down as he began, immediately transfixed by the beauty of the piece. As the emotion of the song reached a high, Bernie did a deliberate bum-note, briefly scolding himself with an 'Aw!!' before resuming – a routine he'd learned from the famous old comedy duo, Morecambe and Wise. The bum note and the 'Aw!' caused Su to break into laughter, arms and legs flailing with hysteria. Her toddler chuckle was infectious, and baby-faced Leah soon joined in, limbs and all. The babies guffawed at the bum notes all the way through. Towards the end, Ruth noticed that they'd taken hold of each other's hand at some point; she'd honed in on the hand-hold. It was the cutest and funniest thing she'd ever seen.

Leah had emailed the film to her and Su before the funeral. Laptop in hand, Ruth pondered. She should watch it now. It would make her laugh. It would make her feel better. She couldn't. Instead, she walked out into the garden. That was his favourite rose, where he barbecued the ribs, the cherry blossom he planted, now twenty foot tall, the bench he'd built underneath, where he'd read, and think – his favourite spot in the world. She went back inside and vaulted two steps at a time all the way to the attic. She retrieved her precious wig and robe from the built-in wardrobe, put them on, and sat at her desk.

She played the Magaluf video on her laptop and took

notes. How did the incident make her feel?

You fucking cow. Suck it, whore . . .

Violent.

Second, she noted the facts so far. What is known to have happened?

Su had been sexually assaulted by twelve men in Magaluf. A man had filmed her without consent and shared the incident with the world. As a result, Su's future was ruined and she was looking for a better mother in South Korea, Ruth's career was screwed, Leah was probably smoking dope with the two ignorant bitches who'd colluded and cheered as the incident took place, and Bernie was dead.

Okay, so which laws are alleged to have been broken?

None.

Ruth couldn't move on to her third pre-trial step – What questions haven't been asked? What questions remain un-answered? – because it was as clear as ever that no law had been broken, not one, so there would be no trial.

Ruth spotted her reflection – she looked ludicrous. Why was she wearing her old wig and gown? She sprung from her desk, removed the offending mirror from its sturdy hook and slid it across the carpet and into the built-in wardrobe. Without the mirror, the wall opposite her desk was a bare expanse of white.

No trial?

Yes there would be.

The pausing and zooming calmed her. Ruth printed what was visible of each offender onto A4 sheets and separated them into piles on her desk.

She ran downstairs for hammer and tacks, relieved that

Leah hadn't returned home to see her dressed like this. She locked the attic door, and picked up the top sheet from the largest pile. It was a photo of Leah in the bar that night: one of the crowd who watched Su, all of whom were guilty of witnessing, encouraging and failing to report a gang sexual assault. Leah was at the top of this pile because she should have been the first to try and stop it. Next were Millie and Natasha. Ruth pondered the snapshot of Leah. She was floppy and bent, and barely able to grip the bottle of beer in her hand. Her pupils were pin-sized. She was dribbling. But even if she hadn't been completely off her face, Ruth still wouldn't punish her. With trademark logic and consistency (and not a trace of madness – Should she check? Where was the mirror?), she tossed the photo of Leah, and the photos of Millie, Natasha, and the other goaders, whoever they were, in the bin.

Guilty, yes. But admonished. The crime was on their records, but no further action had been taken.

The second pile was much smaller. She took the first sheet, placed it at the bottom left of the white wall, and hammered it in with a loud bang. The printed picture showed the bottom half of a man. He had white, trainer-style shoes, with white laces threaded through black eyelets. His shorts were white and folded, and pulled down to his ankles. His boxer shorts were grey. Half a centimetre of flaccid pink poked out from the gap between his boxer's buttons. Above the picture, Ruth used black marker pen to write: Euan Grier.

Back at the bench, she concluded out loud: '*Euan Grier, you are guilty of being a misogynistic prick, possibly brought on and/or exacerbated by the fact that your penis is well below*

British standard size and you can't get it up. You are guilty of being intoxicated and stupid enough to pull down your shorts in public. Euan Grier, this court finds you guilty of sexual assault.'

Less than an hour later, the wall was decorated with a triangle of the guilty. The twelve men who had thrust their penises into Su's mouth lined the base of the triangle, all but Euan Grier's devoid of useful detail. The only other lead she had was that one of the penises was very long and thin from what she could see (she could hardly put out a search for the man using this as his profile). In the middle were two A3-sized photos – one of the bare-chested PR guy who apparently had bird tattoos, and beside him, a photo of the bar owner, Gary Smythe, which she'd printed off from the recent *Guardian* article.

PR guy with bird tattoos who offers 'Free drinks, ladies? Jäger bomb, ladies?', and Gary Smythe who does not feel the need to apologise, you have been found guilty of being women-hating pieces of shit. In relation to the charge of supplying Class A drugs: I find you both guilty. Supplying alcohol to minors: guilty. Organising and encouraging the sexual assault of my daughter and probably many girls before her, and possibly some since: guilty.

The top half of the wall was all for Xano. Ruth used several sheets of paper to hammer in the details she knew before the 'trial' commenced – the photo of his arm around the white T-shirted woman in the Coconut Lounge, a close-up of his red bracelet and ring, a transcript of the words he'd muttered while filming (West of Scotland accent, she also noted on this sheet). She then added details she had just discovered – the name of his very own YouTube Channel

(The!Next!Stanley!), his profile (UK Film Director), and the titles and opening shots of the seven other videos he'd 'directed' and uploaded, all of which involved a middle-aged woman with huge breasts who was dressed like Dolly Parton. In these videos – which were called 'Talented Marmie' 1 to 7 – the woman stood on a nasty black coffee table, microphone in hand, and sang soppy Dolly songs to camera (very well actually, almost as well as Ms Parton). She was in her living room, by the looks of it, and it was a depressing little space. The coffee table and the red leather corner sofa and the huge vulgar television and the ugly blue wallpaper with complementing borders and the tiny windows with an all-sky view screamed high-rise housing estate. Talented Marmie, Xano's mother perhaps, lived in a high-rise council flat somewhere near Glasgow.

Xano, you have been found guilty of filming the sexual assault of my daughter. You have been found guilty of sharing abusive images. You have been found guilty of sharing lewd images without consent. You have been found guilty of destroying the life of Su Brotheridge-Oliphant. Guilty of destroying her self-image, her confidence, her friendships, her past and future relationships, her sexual well-being, her career, and her entire future. In relation to destroying my career: guilty. My life, everything I've worked for, fought for, and loved: guilty. And last, on the count of the murder of Bernard Brotheridge: guilty.

Trials complete, Ruth calmed her breathing, removed the mirror she'd hidden in the wardrobe, and leant it against the desk. *Are you doing anything that would get you into trouble? Are you going mad? Have you lost control?*

Satisfied that she was still composed enough to ask these questions, and that the answers were still no, no and no, Ruth put the mirror back in the cupboard, and sat at her bench to consider the sentencing options.

She'd been at her desk for hours when Leah knocked. 'Are you in there, Mum? Mum, are you okay? Mum?'

She was very busy, and probably didn't give a reassuring enough answer, because Leah returned a few minutes later. 'Can I get you something?'

'No thanks, darling. I'm just working.'

Ten minutes or so later: 'Come downstairs, I've made soup.'

At least an hour after that: 'Open up, I've got soup.'

Leah was starting to annoy her, making her lose focus. 'Great, thanks honey, just leave it there. I'll get it in a sec. Hang on, are you still there? I'm on Facebook now. Will you friend me?'

Leah's 'Sure' was a tentative one.

'Ask Millie and Natasha to as well?'

'Okay, but why? And why can't I come in? Let me in!'

Ruth dragged herself from the computer and opened the door a couple of inches. 'I'm fine. Are you? Is it lonely downstairs?'

'Millie and Natasha are here.'

Ruth's jaw tightened. She should recover the pictures of those girls from her bin and nail them to the wall. 'Can you ask them to friend me straight away?'

Leah was holding a tray with soup, buttered bread and orange juice. Her eyes were red raw from crying. 'Only if you let me in.' She pushed the door open with her elbow, walked inside, and put the tray on the desk. 'You hate Facebook. What are you up to?'

From her extensive experience of dealing with liars, Ruth knew it was best to stick closely to the truth, but not to tell all of it. 'I'm making a video. I've bought this amazing software. Thanks for the soup.'

Leah had noticed the hammered sheets on the wall. 'What's all this? Jeez, can't you just forget about Magaluf?'

Forget Magaluf? No, she would not lose her temper with Leah, never again. 'It's my job to see that the law keeps up with the times.'

'Since when do Sheriffs go on Facebook and make internet videos?'

'I've decided it's the best way in this case.'

'How? What kind of video?'

'Viral.'

Leah smirked. 'Oh, a *viral* one.'

'Fine, smart arse, tell me then: how do I make it go viral?'

'I'm not telling you unless I know what it is.'

'Okay, it's about pornography and the law.'

Leah sighed, obviously relieved it wouldn't embarrass her, and headed for the door. 'If it's helping, I'll leave you to it.'

'Hang on, you have to answer my question.'

'It's not easy. A lot is luck and timing. Okay, so a video might go viral if it's gross, embarrassing, hilarious – like the one of that cute kid off his face after the dentist, or just too awful – nothing beats a good beheading. Basically, they have to be about someone who's done a bad thing. If you can get someone major talking about it – tipping-point types like Kim Kardashian or Perez Hilton – then you're in there, defo.

Tulisa from *X Factor* did one after her ex released a sex tape. Don't think it went crazy though, sounds a bit 'yawn', and sorry, but so does yours. If you want more hits, you could hire a social media guru, probably won't help though – no one's gonna share a law lecture vid, unless Keira Knightley's giving it naked.'

Door locked again, Ruth looked over the snippet she'd been working on, a small scene with her voice laid over (she was a genius at this!). The perfect punishment had light-bulbed soon after the wall-hammering. She'd phoned MacDonald with a list of urgent tasks, and had sentenced Euan Grier to this video.

Voiceover: This is Euan Grier. He went to Woodvale High School. He's eighteen and is taking a gap year! Euan is funny . . .

Pic of Euan laughing (copied from the many pics on his naïvely public Facebook page), overlaid with the soundtrack of a man laughing, ha ha ha.

Voiceover: He's into fitness . . .

Pic of Euan doing weights.

Voiceover: Enjoys getting an Indian, jamming with Andrew Ingis and Will Frederickson, and drinking anything over 35 per cent . . .

Moving image, Coconut Lounge, frantic intercutting of Euan downing a pint, another pint, something red, something blue, a shot, another, another.

(Really, she should be a film director, like Xano.)

Voiceover: You won't believe this, but Euan Grier is single.

Applause. Screen-grab of Euan's Facebook relationship status.

Voiceover: These are his trainers . . .

Shot of Euan's white trainers, white laces through black eyelets, shorts undone and at his ankles.

Voiceover: And this is his willy . . .

Close-up of Euan's willy.

Voiceover: Sorry, we'll zoom in . . .

Zoom.

Voiceover: Euan also enjoys air guitar . . .

Pic of Euan air-guitaring with mates mentioned above, their names tagged in bubbles. Sitcom laughter track, which starts to fade.

Voiceover: And sexually assaulting women!

Laughter track fades out. Close-up of Euan taking a handful of hair and pushing a head down to his crotch.

Voiceover: This is Euan sexually assaulting one now.

Zoom in on the softness he's jabbing at someone's mouth. (You don't see Su. You will never see Su.)

Voiceover: He can't get it up, bless, which is very frustrating for a sex offender.

As Euan thrusts, his face is angry, as if he's bludgeoning Freddy Krueger to death.

Voiceover: Euan Grier is single, ladies, single!

The closing titles scroll over Euan's tiny dick again, which wriggles in sync with the track of a man's laughter, ha ha ha. The title reads:

Euan Grier

18

Woodvale High

Cheetham Hill

Likes to get an Indian

Do. Not. Miss.
Out ladies!
Message NOW:
facebook.com/euan.grier
09738 285286

As the first of two practice shorts before the feature, it wasn't half bad. There was more squirm than chuckle, but it ticked the embarrassing box with confidence. Ruth was heftily impressed with her debut, and hadn't even come close to breaking the law. She wasn't bothered in the slightest if people judged her after opening it on Twitter or hearing about it on Radio Scotland or seeing it on the Channel 4 News. Being despised and/or feared was a small price to pay for getting the world to see. She posted it to the YouTube channel she'd created, on the Twitter account she'd opened, and on her new Facebook page. Great, all three girls had already friended her. She put it on their timelines with a ☺ *please share lol.* They'd be too terrified to disobey. They might even find it funny and enjoy passing it on. It was just a tester, she'd wait and see if it spread, learn from it, so the next one would be better.

While she waited for the numbers to come in, she'd figure out a way to reach one of those tipping-point types Leah mentioned. Kim someone or other? Not her, Ruth had no idea who she was or what she did and she needed a woman who was world famous, massive. She'd do the research, and select the right celeb to target. Maybe she'd also hire one of those gurus. There was so much to do! For a while there, she'd almost forgotten that Bernie wasn't downstairs and that Su was someone else's daughter.

Hours later, Ruth was so absorbed with her second film that she didn't want to stop and answer the phone. It was on the desk, in front of her, but she had to find the right picture for this scene. The ringing stopped. She'd moved on to the bar owner, the only other perpetrator she had any information about. With his name, Gary Smythe, and his place of work, Coconut Lounge, she found some intel on the guy. He was thirty-nine, married with two kids, grew up in Yorkshire, has a recently deceased twin sister, Sally, manages his asthma. There were three photos of him online, all boring headshots. Nothing juicy. She needed juicy.

She answered the phone immediately the second time it rang. It was MacDonald. 'What did you get on Smythe?'

'Hi, Ruth, actually I was thinking of coming over.'

'No, don't do that. What have you got, quick? I'm in the zone here.'

'He's forty-two, separated. His ex has two kids from her previous. He did grow up in Yorkshire, but he's an only child, the dead twin story is bollocks, no idea why. He has three convictions over the last five years, two for possession, um, diamorphine, diamorphine, and one for intent to supply amphetamines. The wife went back to the ex two months into his stint of five at Barlinnie and his dad died three weeks later, left him a fortune. When he got out in March, he moved to Majorca, bought the bar. He manages his asthma. I had a word with Leah about the CCTV footage she sent me. She didn't steal any tapes. She convinced a female member of staff to download them and the footage was emailed to her later. This woman hated her job, and was packing it in and heading home to Amsterdam the following day. She was more than happy to oblige for free. She'd have done anything to screw over that arsehole boss of hers. Anyway, thanks to your clever daughter, the tapes confirm that Smythe and the PR guy sell drugs there. I found Xano by the way.'

'What did you say?' So dramatic, MacDonald, sneaking up to the climax like that.

The CCTV footage Leah had been sent made it a simple task to find Xano, apparently. All footage on the night of the event, as Ruth now called it, had either been deleted or taped over, but it didn't matter. Three days beforehand, the camera showed a man sitting at the bar. It was 2 p.m., there were no other customers, and he sat there by himself for ninety minutes, sipping his first beer so slowly that he only finished it at 3. He wore a thick ring made of shiny black plastic. There was no 8-ball, just a bulbous thickening of black plastic. He wore a red cotton bracelet on his left arm. At around 3.20, he ordered a second beer and chatted with the bartender, a square-jawed twenty-something who seemed too handsome and polite to be working in that place. MacDonald had emailed the footage and a snapshot of Xano's face to a private detective in Majorca, who located the bartender an hour later, and Xano an hour after that.

'Xano's name is John Martin. He's thirty-two. He bought a black ring from Kevin Meechan at the pool hall in Allison Street in November 2014 but didn't want a number on it. His mum is alive. He's an only child and a mummy's boy. His mum lives in a Maryhill high-rise and is into karaoke. He caused no trouble at school, passed his Highers, just, completed a forklift driving course in Ibrox, a three-year joinery apprenticeship without incident, was employed by KL Joinery in Glasgow for thirteen years and got a decent, though vague, reference. He's never been married. He has no kids. Single. No previous convictions.'

Disappointment overwhelmed Ruth. Xano wasn't what she imagined – a screwed-up kid turned total prick. She'd hoped for a bastard, like the guy behind the 8-ball. It'd be pleasant and good for the world to punish a man like that. But this John Martin, with his ordinary name and his ordinary life, was upsetting her.

The notion that Xano could be every boy and every man had crossed her mind more than once. Would a nice boy like Su's James have filmed the scene in the Coconut Lounge? Would a good boy like Frieda's son Eric have said 'You fucking cow. Suck it, whore'? Would the boy next door, literally, Barry, have uploaded it? It was too sickening to dwell on, but perhaps Xano's behaviour did not set him apart from his peers.

'Have I lost you?'

That's right, MacDonald was still on the phone.

'I've been building to the good stuff. Four years ago, a woman complained to the Maryhill police. He'd built shelving or something at hers, apparently. Couldn't get the details of her allegation, but it went no further than a talking to. Not long after, he flew to Magaluf, landed a handyman job at the five-star Sol Adela, and has hopped from hotel to hotel since. He's well known about town for being promiscuous and not much of a talker. He frequents the VD clinic, was questioned in June about a Rohypnol rape, but no charge was ever brought, and has a cocaine habit. The only bar in town that'll let him in is the Coconut Lounge, maybe 'cos he's Gary Smythe's best customer, buys £80 of coke from him, every day.'

At some point in the last minute, Ruth had stood up. She said it out loud: 'John Martin.' Now that MacDonald had given her the second half of his biography, his name didn't seem ordinary at all.

Chapter Sixteen

John here says he'll shag you.

My muscles spasm and I open my eyes with an overwhelming feeling of anger. Must have been on the verge of falling asleep. This room is so hot in spite of the aircon. I'm drenched. My T-shirt is stained with sweat, just like it was that night, which is perhaps why a scene has just played out in my mind. I take off my T-shirt, wipe the liquid from my body, and shake myself out, hoping the details will hush, shhh, go back to sleep. But it's no use. Lord, the heat is as intense as the anger. I don't want to remember.

I remember.

A hangover was threatening to overtake drunkenness. The music was hurting my brain and self-hate was now head to head with hate for this place and everyone in it. The girls had been introducing me to men all night and not one of them wanted to have sex with me. Not surprising, I now realise, considering the breast sweat and the hate-vibe.

I clung to the bar as Natasha hauled over yet another.

'Your friend just said you're dead set on losing your virginity tonight?'

'That's right.' Actually, all I wanted now was to go home, but the only way I'd ever be allowed is if I took a man with me. This one looked okay. Why not? 'I'm Su.'

He shook my hand, which seemed absurd in this place. 'Nathan. Shall I get you a drink? Water, maybe?'

The offer was judgey – I must have looked really pissed. But if it was going to happen tonight, maybe with Nathan, I needed to keep drinking. 'I'll get my own, ta.'

'Good idea. Don't let guys buy you drinks here. I've heard stories.'

I ordered a Jäger bomb, which was four euros. At some point, they'd stopped being free. I handed over my last five, skulled the drink, and gave Nathan a smile which I hoped was sexy but feared was not, because he was also about to reject me.

'Your first should be special, don't you think? Not like this.' He shook my hand again. 'It was nice to meet you, Su. Tell your friends to stop blabbing about you. It's personal, no one's business but yours.' With that, he left, to get some sleep I imagined. Nathan seemed the type to value a good eight hours.

Millie and Natasha were high on pills by this time, dancing like crazy, tongue-kissing each other to entice random males, and then kissing the random males. At one point, Natasha disappeared for a few minutes.

'She had sex with him in the gents'!' Leah told me after.

In three minutes? Blimey.

The girls kept asking if I wanted a pill, as did the PR guy who had plenty, a tenner each. I didn't need it, because that last Jäger bomb had rekindled my party mood. I started to feel quite sexy, in fact. I'd run out of money, but Natasha and Millie kept the drinks coming, as well as the men.

'Not into Asians,' said one. A few minutes later, I saw the

same guy snogging a woman at a table in the corner. She had her nice white hand down his trousers, and her elbow was bobbing.

'What's the time?' asked another. It was 2.30 a.m. He considered the offer, and perused the bar, which was still teeming with un-pulled women. 'I'll keep you on reserve.' And he headed over to a girl with one boob hanging out of her dress.

'Yeah, she has nice eyes,' said the next in response to Natasha's pitch. 'But I wouldn't say she's the *most* beautiful-looking girl I've ever seen.'

'No?' Natasha raised an eyebrow at the man – no, boy. 'Who is then?' Natasha and the boy joined heads and wrestled tongues within a millimetre of my nose.

What was wrong with me? I needed another drink, and tapped the bar. 'Jäger bomb, please!'

When the drink slid to my open hand a moment later, I realised I only had fifty cents. God, I wasn't even sexy enough to convince the bartender to give me a discount, and he sold the drink to someone else.

I might have headed home, I reckon, had Millie not pounced on me. 'John here says he'll shag you.'

Millie bounded back to the dance floor to watch the latest organised entertainment. The PR guy was in the centre with three women and one man, giving instructions for the next game.

'Drink first?' John asked.

He wasn't ugly. Yeah, he could buy me a drink.

The game involved one man being blindfolded and three women removing their bras.

'Thanks, John.' I downed the drink he'd bought.

'Shuffle yourselves!' the PR guy yelled. 'Move around, move around.' He then positioned the guy in the blindfold in front of the women. 'Guess one right and you win one free drink. Two right, free drinks all night. Three correct answers, you win free drinks for a week!'

The blindfolded guy fondled the first set of breasts and pondered – hmmm – 'C'. He groped the woman's back, shoulders, then squeezed her breasts again. '36C.'

'36C?' The PR guy shouted. 'Your final answer is 36C?'

'36C!' the guy yelled with a grin, and the crowd cheered as he moved on to question 2, a too-thin girl with bulbous fakies.

I wished I hadn't skulled that last drink so quickly, my goodness, her fake nipples were staring at me!

John wasn't talkative, hadn't said anything till now. 'Let's get out of here.' He twirled my bar stool round and wedged himself between my knees. 'I want some of that tight pussy.'

Woah, some air, air would be good. I put my hands on his chest to ease him away. 'Yuck!'

He pressed himself even closer this time, rubbed his crotch against me. 'C'mon, let's go.' His arms were around me and he was slurping at my neck, tonguing my ear. His hand was on my inner thigh, then tugging at the button on my shorts.

Swirling, everything was swirling. The crowd cheered because the blindfolded guy had guessed two out of three correctly and would receive free drinks for the rest of the night.

'I hear you want to suck cock tonight. Let's get outa here, hmm. Then I'll push it in your tight virgin cunt.'

I was feeling too many things. I was seeing too many colours. I'd let a stranger buy me a drink. 'No. In your what?

Did you put something in my drink?'

He giggled into my ear, grabbed my hand so hard that it hurt, and pressed it against his erection. 'This'll be all yours soon.'

'Gross, get off me!' I pushed him away and he stumbled back and hit a table. Some glasses smashed.

He took a moment to right himself. 'What the fuck, you frigid Chink!' He yelled this louder than he meant to, and the bar quietened.

This fuzzy, lovely, coloury bar! The room span round and round as I made my way to the dance floor, a glorious haze of moving rainbow, and I was Su Oliphant-Brotheridge from Doon, and people were parting to clear a path for me – me! – and I was sexy, the sexiest woman in the bar, if not the world, and if only Leah could see me now – where was she? 'Leah! Leah!' If Millie and Natasha could see me now – woah, almost fell over, ha – I'd kill for another drink.

Ooh, he'd followed me. He was right there, with a very serious grievance to pronounce. 'Your friend said you'd suck my cock.'

By now, every single person in the room was looking at me. Haha! I had a silent pulsing audience to address: 'For a free Jäger bomb,' I declared, twirling to include all the fans in the circle surrounding me, 'I'd suck every cock in this room.' My twirl ended face to face with the scumbag, who had a puffed-up chest that I deflated with my finger: 'Except yours.'

Chapter Seventeen

This room is so hot that there's steam in it, probably from the gallons of tears I've cried. Su, that was Su on that dance floor. Me, I'm someone else. I'm not sure who yet, but by ordering a taxi I'm one step closer to finding out.

I'm too nervous to notice anything but traffic. Cars just like those at home, four-lane motorways like those at home. I'm shaking when we arrive at a high-rise apartment building, which is as depressing as the ones in Glasgow, and take a clunking lift to the fourteenth floor.

Moon Jihoo is as kind-looking as Woojin described, and answers the door with a welcoming smile.

'My name is Su-Jin.' Thanks again, Rosetta. He waits for me to say something else. I point at my chest, 'English', and show him the Google Translate screen on my phone with the introduction I'd typed on the way:

'My friend Woojin visited you a few weeks ago. I was left in a wicker basket at Myeong-dong station eighteen years ago. You saw my mother. You know who she is. Please tell me. I will pay you 350,000 won.'

£200, a decent starting point. I have the won equivalent of £900 on me, having withdrawn three lots of £300 these past few days.

He takes ages to read it and I wonder if the translated hangul lettering imparts any of the above information.

Perhaps I should re-word it.

He looks really confused. He's been staring at the screen, then at me, for minutes now. I can see into his apartment. It's tiny. A woman is calling for him from inside. Without shutting the door, he goes in and disappears into a room. I stay put. He has my phone, and it's very expensive. Also, he'd have shut the door if he wanted me to leave. A moment later, he wheels a very frail elderly woman across the hall and into another room. They have a conversation in Korean. He returns to the door, shakes his head, and hands me my phone.

I sigh. Is that it? My only lead gone with a shake of the head? I wonder what to type next, how to persuade him, and I realise he's not going anywhere. He's not shut the door. I look at my phone – he's come back with a Google translation of his own.

3,500,000.

£2,000, cheeky bugger. He's staring at me, waiting.

I shake my head and show him my counter-offer. 1,000,000. And he shows me his. 3,000,000.

The phone switches hands seven more times before it's settled. 2,100,000 won, which is £1,200.

I type my intention to go to a bank and return immediately, but he wants to come too, and we walk the two blocks together. He waits by the machine as I withdraw the rest. I can hardly breathe. I want to know now, on this street, outside this bank, but he's walking at high speed back to the apartment, hurrying me along with his hands. I guess this is a transaction he'd like to conclude in private.

Who is she? Why did he recognise her? She must have done a load of shoplifting for a local plod to know her. Who is she? Who am I?

He doesn't want me to come in, but he gestures for me to stay at the door, and checks on the invalid watching TV. Back at the door, he holds out his hand, and I hesitate. I don't want to hand over the cash before he's given me the name. I shake my head and hold out my hands – you first.

He shakes his head, holds out his.

I type 'Name first then money' into Translate and hand him the phone.

He jabs at the top of my phone with his fingernail, says: 'Sue me.'

I'm confused. He's going to sue me?

He jabs at it again, frustrated. 'Sue me. Sue me.' He holds it an inch from my eyes, points his finger at the top of the phone. Finally, he sighs, types into Google Translate and hands it over again. 'Your mother name Su-Mi.'

My mother's name is Su-Mi. She gave me a little something of herself, a wee Su. I feel like crying.

He taps at the phone again and hands it back. On screen is the Wikipedia page for a Korean woman named Kim Su-Mi. She's beautiful. She's thirty-five. She's worth . . . $1.3 billion, the third richest woman in Korea.

Moon Jihoo notices that I need to sit down, and gestures to the step. He watches as I take it in. Now I understand his relentless jabbing at the top of my phone. My mother's family own Ri, the largest business conglomerate in South Korea, one of the largest companies in the world, into everything: retail, hotels, medicine, technology, construction.

Moon Jihoo jabs at the Ri logo, one of the most familiar worldwide logos there is. He's thrilled for me. My family's royalty. I'm royalty. I ask him why he's never told anyone.

'She begged me never tell,' he types.

(*Kind man*)

'And paid me 500,000 won.'

(*Greedy man*)

But he wouldn't have betrayed her secret anyway. Why ruin her life? Now, though, he feels more strongly about my life, feels I have the right to know.

(*Kind*)

The old lady hollers from inside. He has to go. I give him the 2,100,000 won.

(*My arse*)

I stay on the step with my Ri7, which is one of the 200 million the family shipped this year. My family tree's in *Forbes Magazine*, with the headshots of my nearest if not dearest.

My mother has a Masters in Maths and Business Administration from the women's university in Seoul. She's married to a man who would have been on the rich list if he hadn't married into the family, but is way closer to the top as a result. She has two girls, six and eight. The youngest has eyes and lips like mine. The other, a nose a bit like mine. My mother's everything is like mine. She's my double, which is odd, because she's incredibly beautiful and I'm so disgusting I can't even pull in Magaluf.

Chapter Eighteen

And it's a wrap. Ruth was pleased with her second video, but not as elated as she was with the first, perhaps because she was anxious to move on to John Martin. She entered the title: 'Coconut Lounge Promo Video', and watched it one last time before uploading.

She'd viewed several other nightclub promotional videos, and copied the format. Ruth had found all the images she needed online and from the CCTV footage Leah had acquired. There was no voiceover this time, just captions.

A dance track builds slowly from the beginning, reaching a frenzied crescendo just before the end title.

We open with the lights and sounds of the Magaluf strip, and hone in on the fluorescent lettering – *The Coconut Lounge*.

Inside, vibrant happy cocktails line the slick bar.

Cocktails!

An inordinately handsome bartender hands a stunning woman a red drink with an umbrella poking out of it.

Dancing!

Close-up of the DJ's deck. The volume of the music increases. The dance floor is crowded with people jumping, dancing, laughing, having a ball.

Games!

Cut to the PR guy overseeing one of his games. A man throws paint at a naked woman. People cheer.

Drinking!

Four women down a shot at the bar, then one more, then one more. Two men with funnels in their mouths drown in the beer their mates are pouring. A teenage girl falls drunkenly to her knees and puts her head in a bucket of green alcohol. An even drunker boy downs half a bottle of vodka, glug glug glug.

Sex!

The CCTV shot is a little blurry, but it's not hard to make out the couple having sex outside the ladies'. A bare bum thrusts into a wobbling woman who'd fall over if she wasn't pinned against the wall.

Drugs!

The PR guy's face is clear as could be. He hands a girl two pills, and takes twenty euros from her. She puts the pills in her mouth.

Fights!

A woman pulls another woman's hair at the bar. The woman retaliates with a punch to the chin. The hair-puller falls to the ground, but she's still holding onto the hair, so the other woman falls with her. They lay into each other on the sticky floor. The crowd yell 'fight fight fight!'

Sex!

A snippet from Su's film. A man pushes a woman's head onto a very long thin penis.

More drugs!

The PR guy hands a wad of notes to the bar owner, who then passes him a handful of pills to sell sell sell.

The Coconut Lounge.

The film ends with a woman lying in her own pee and

vomit in the entrance. The street's quiet – it's morning. The bar owner kicks her foot out of the way so he can close the doors and lock up. She's unconscious, or close to it. Her shorts and pants are at her ankles. She's on display, but Ruth has blurred out the detail. She must have been taking a pee before she threw up and fainted.

The place to be in Magaluf.

It was good enough. At the least, it should get the two of them charged with dealing. Ruth uploaded it to YouTube.

Oops, she was supposed to learn from the first before finishing the second. She'd been so engrossed she had forgotten to check how it was doing.

The number of hits for the Euan Grier YouTube video? Thirteen. Shit, really?

She checked Twitter. No replies. No followers. No retweets. No favourites. She needed advice about Twitter. Should she have followed some people first? How does the stupid thing work?

She'd emailed the agents of a selection of celebrities, ranging from Angelina Jolie and Jennifer Lawrence, to Germaine Greer and the biggest soap star in Scotland who lived round the corner. The only reply in her email was from the latter, Glenda, better known as Jenny in Clyde Street.

'I understand your anger,' she wrote, 'but I'm afraid I'm just not comfortable with being involved. Have you phoned Victim Support? They're very helpful. 0141 735 975.'

Her Facebook page was desolate. Millie and Natasha must have unfriended her. No one had shared the video. The only activity was several messages from Leah: 'Mum, I've been knocking and ringing and knocking. Let me in. Answer. That video! You're scaring me.'

A wave of grief swept over Ruth. Bernie had turned to ash today. The videos had distracted her, but they'd achieved nothing. Should she give the whole idea up? Should she accept that her family was ruined and move on to live that ruined life?

No. She had to find a way to get those two films seen. More importantly, she had to get to work on her finale, a thriller starring John Martin.

An hour or so later, Ruth had all the information she needed, thanks to MacDonald and her secretary, Anne. It had taken a bit of persuading – and a slight bending of the truth – but Anne had sent the transcripts and reports that she'd requested. She was Googling social media experts when she heard Leah knocking.

'Thank God. I wondered if you were dead in there. Don't lock it again. I'm taking the key. The police are here, Mum.' Leah removed Ruth's wig and robe and put them on the desk. 'Campbell and the other one, same as last time. Come.' She took her hand and led her down.

Last time Campbell and Brown were here, they'd chosen to sit on an armchair each, opposite the sofa where Bernie had held Ruth's hand. This time, they chose the kitchen table, just as the social workers had after the whisky incident. Ruth was in trouble.

Campbell didn't bother to say hello, let alone mention Bernie's death. 'We've had a complaint about you.'

Ruth had decided she wouldn't sit down. She put the kettle on, scooped Lavazza into the plunger.

'Perhaps you should take a seat?'

'Thanks for offering me one of my seats, but no thank you, unless you have a standing-prevention order.'

'A Mrs Grier from Cheetham has complained that you uploaded a video to YouTube accusing her son of sexual assault.'

Ruth smiled – hoorah – someone had seen it. His mother, excellent. Of course she'd complain to the police – most mothers would – but she'd probably also beat him with a rolling pin, the little shit. Ruth poured boiling water into the glass plunger and heated some milk in the microwave. 'She's wrong.'

Campbell nodded to his female colleague – Brown, if she recalled correctly – who fiddled with her police-issue iPad and held it up.

Voiceover: Euan also enjoys air guitar . . .

Pic of Euan air-guitaring with mates mentioned above, their names tagged in bubbles. Sitcom laughter track, which starts to fade . . .

Voiceover: And sexually assaulting women!

Ruth smiled at her work – it really was very good. She finished making her coffee, leant on the kitchen bench, and took a sip.

Brown gave Campbell a questioning look, which he was too powerful and professional to return. He fidgeted, though, jiggled his knee.

Brown had muted the video and put the iPad on the table, but it was still playing. Ruth looked at the screen, took another sip of her coffee. 'Can you pause it there? Good, thank you. Now could you please turn it up, play?'

Voiceover: This is Euan sexually assaulting one now.

Zoom in on the softness he's jabbing at someone's mouth.

'Stop it there, thanks so much. Do you have a first name, or is it Brown you go by at work?'

'Um, Mary.'

'Thanks Mary.' Mm, the coffee was excellent. 'I didn't *accuse* Euan Grier of sexual assault. I simply showed publicly available footage of him *committing* sexual assault.'

Ruth wasn't quite sure why she was the enemy here. Campbell hated her guts. He was digging his fingernails into his thighs under the table. 'Mrs Grier wants to press charges.'

Another slow sip. 'Oh? What charge is she thinking of pressing, exactly?'

Brown wasn't very good at this cop job. She was bamboozled, had no idea what to say or who to look at. At the moment, she was saying nothing and looking at her hand.

'Consider this a warning, Mrs Oliphant,' Campbell said.

Coffee finished, Ruth rinsed the mug and set about warming milk for a second. 'If there's nothing else, I have another coffee to drink.'

After Leah had escorted them to the door, she returned to the kitchen, leant against the bench, and let out a worried sigh. 'Jesus!'

'One day, when you're a mother, you'll look back on what I'm doing and think of me as a hero.'

'His dad has cancer, Mum.'

'Whose dad?'

'Euan's.'

'Well I'm sorry about that, but what does that have to do with anything? I know plenty of people with cancer and as far as I'm aware none of their children sexually assault women as a result.'

'But he didn't even . . .'

'He did, Leah, so did the others. In the scheme of things, they're the minor offenders, but they still need to be dealt with. I'm working from the bottom up. In case you're panicking, I've decided not to take action against the crowd.'

Leah sighed again, and slumped onto a stool. 'Euan's not bad. He was just *there*. We were all just there.'

'So any boy would do what Euan did, then?'

'Probably.'

'Would any boy have filmed it, like Xano?'

'Probably.'

'And say: "whore, dirty bitch?"'

'Probably! I'm just, I don't know, embarrassed, concerned, tired. You always go on the rampage. I only wish you'd find another way, for now anyway, with Dad – his funeral was yesterday! And Su's thousands of miles away meeting her birth mother.'

'What, have you spoken to Su?'

'She called before the cops arrived. If you'd answered the phone or let me in when I knocked, then you could have spoken to her.'

'She's seen her mother?'

'Not yet, I don't think so anyway. She's hoping to find out more today.'

'Have you got a cigarette? I need a cigarette.'

'What? No! I don't have any. I don't . . . *you* don't smoke.'

'I'll go and buy some then.'

'Hang on, hang on. Stay, I'll roll you one.'

The first drag helped. She could form words now: 'Who is she?' She sucked harder the second time, drew the smoke in deeper.

'I don't know – Su didn't have details.'

Ruth put out her cigarette in the unfinished cup of coffee. 'Will you be okay if I go out? I need to go out.'

'Sure, get some air. Good idea. Take your phone, though. Don't go far.'

'I won't.' Keys in hand, Ruth stormed out to the car, and drove to 8-ball's house.

Chapter Nineteen

Ruth kept her eye on the speedometer as she drove along the M77 towards Glasgow. At sixty-three miles per hour, she was three miles over the limit, almost certainly not enough to be booked, but she was breaking the law, and it felt good. Every day and every night of Ruth's life had been spent not breaking the law. Take any ordinary day – Monday, three weeks ago, for instance. Her routine on that Monday had included not stabbing the postman, not throwing boiling milk at her daughter over breakfast, not buying heroin in Saltcoats on the way to work, not smoking it on the beach, not shooting a cycle-phobic driver on the A89, not beating a yawning clerk with her hammer, not bribing a witness, not robbing the Clydesdale Bank and not littering or jaywalking to the not stolen getaway car which would not be driven well over the speed limit while drunk. Like most people, she had always abided by an unfathomably thick rulebook. It was easy, natural. Amazing, when you think about it.

Sixty-three miles per hour. Her first intentional violation ever, but as she turned off the motorway towards Castlemilk, she knew it would not be her last.

She understood that this was no longer about Su. Su had a new mother now, or an old one: the original, the real-deal. After eighteen years, Ruth had finally lost. There was no need to fight any more. But she wanted to, more than ever. *Why?* she asked herself as she turned onto the A726 to Castlemilk. And she finally realised the answer. *For me. Me!* Perhaps all her battles had been for her. She was the victim of the social workers. She was the victim of the video. For the second time in her life, she felt powerless, and now understood that powerlessness was contradictory, that it had a power of its own because it enticed a fury which demanded a release. She wanted to drive at eighty-five miles an hour. She wanted to kill John Martin. She wouldn't do any of those things, because she was thinking clearly. She couldn't go to prison. She had Leah to look after. She had a job to return to. And her attempts at viral videos had failed. What she would do instead is seek restorative justice. To achieve this goal, she needed to break the law a little, but she wouldn't harm anyone in the process and she'd get away with it, just as she was getting away with driving three miles in excess of the speed limit now.

8-ball answered the door this time. Once again, he was dressed only in floral holiday shorts. Once again, drug paraphernalia littered the kitchen table. He didn't manage to whisk it away before Ruth snapped a photo of him at the door, the huge fruit bowl filled with green in view behind him.

'What the fuck, Jeez? It's just weed.'

'It's enough to be recalled. Let me in, Jim. I'll delete it and the one I took last time if you do me a favour.'

She stepped inside and took a seat at the table, fingering the marijuana as she spoke. 'Is Bethany here?'

'Nah, she was a fuckin' nutjob, man.' He removed the bowl from the table and put it in the fridge. 'Delete the photos and we'll talk.'

'Get me two Rohypnol, no three, and I will.'

'Rohypnol? What the fuck you up to? Why do you think I'd have that?'

'I think you'll find a way. I'll wait here till you have, then I'll delete the photos, and you won't go back to B Hall.'

*

Ruth removed the items in the carrier bag on the passenger seat. She knew she might have been a little unstable the first time she donned the wig and gown out of context, and it had worried her a smidgeon at the time. She removed the pink bob she'd bought in a shop in Puerto Pollensa, replaced it with the stern grey hairpiece, and twisted the rear-view mirror to take a look. *You doing anything that'd get you in trouble?* So far so good. She'd disguised herself well, and had been careful to avoid the CCTV camera in the Coconut Lounge, so no one would've noticed her slip the pill into his drink. *You mad?* Not in a mental health way, no. *Lost control?* Ruth Oliphant? Absolutely not.

She pushed the mirror away.

The villa she'd rented was a rare find on this crowded island: well away from the main road, impossible to see from the closest minor one, on top of a hill, and with a panoramic view in every direction so she'd have plenty of warning if anyone approached. Ruth unlocked the front door, checked everything was as she'd left it, then took a glass of water out to the car.

'Hey!' She poured the whole glass over his head. 'Wakey wakey. You fell asleep Mister! Can you stand? That's good, good. Let's go in. Let's get inside.'

She'd set the living room up before heading to the bar earlier that evening. Two armchairs, a two-seater sofa and a tripod were arranged in a circle in the large space. His chair was in front of the tripod. Behind the chair: a bare, white, nondescript wall. Before she deposited him there, he needed a wash.

He was able to walk with her assistance, but found it impossible to stay standing in the shower cubicle. Ruth sprayed him with the shower head until the last of the excrement vanished down the drain. The cold water brought him round a little.

'What the fuck? Who are you?'

'You pulled, remember? But you had an accident on the way here. Too much coke maybe?' Ruth had emptied the contents of his money belt onto the bathroom cabinet – phone, house key, 430 euros, seventy cents, a small plastic bag filled with white powder, silver foil with five tablets just like the three that 8-ball had bought for her from the guy upstairs, a photo of his mum, a tube of medical cream.

He slipped twice before managing to stand. He turned the lever from cold to hot, put his hands on the tiled walls to balance himself, and relaxed under the steaming shower. 'What the fuck are you wearing?'

'Just a change of wig. I'll explain soon. Here, dry yourself off.' Ruth turned the shower off, and held out a fresh towel. 'I'll put your jeans and boxers in the wash, hey? It's on your T-shirt too, better pop that in as well. They'll be done by the time we're finished.'

After Ruth had put the washing on, she found Xano sitting on the sofa, towel over his knees and crotch, money belt refilled and clipped around his waist, snorting a line of coke on the coffee table. 'So what's with all the wigs?'

'I like to dress up. Tonight I'm a judge.'

'If you're into the S and M, old lady, you should know I'm gonna be the S not the M. Got anything to drink?'

'Sure, what would you like? I've got vodka, tonic, lemonade, one beer – Heineken, I think.'

'Beer.'

She opened a bottle, handed it to him, and swiped his Ri7 on. 'So, what are you into, Xano?'

'What? What did you call me? Is that my phone?' He unzipped his money belt to check if he'd put it back in. 'Give me my phone.'

'You been working on anything new?' She clicked through his video files, opening one of a topless woman sunbathing on the beach, obviously unaware she was being filmed. 'Hmm, she's cute!'

'Why would I have picked you out, you're old! Give me my phone.'

'I picked *you* out, Xano.'

'Xano? How do you . . . Xano?'

'Come on, you are talented! I recognised you as soon as I saw you at the bar. I've been following your career. Surely I'm not your only fan! Will you film us? I'd love it if you made a movie with me in it. I'm into film-making too. I made an intro already.' She was referring to the video she'd made so far – of Bernie's dead face in the hospital cubicle, newspaper clippings about Su being missing, Ruth being asked to take leave from the court, Su losing her place at medical school. She clicked Xano's phone into place on the tripod. 'You've got a live stream app already, cool. It'll be horny, no, us, live?'

'I'm not in the mood, grandma.' He skulled the last of his beer and snorted another line of coke.

'Okay, fine. But we'll need to wait for your clothes. I'll drive you home soon as they're done.' Ruth poured two vodka and tonics, adding ice to both. She cut the second of her three Rohypnol tablets in half, popped one half into his drink, and stirred.

He sat with his legs open and turned on the television with the remote control. Ruth leant in and shifted the towel to cover him up. She didn't want to spot anything stomach-churning. She sat on the chair opposite him and watched him as he sipped the vodka and tonic. 'Your mum's impressive. Such a talented family!'

Only two channels worked on the television and both were in Spanish. Xano switched it off. 'How long does the washing machine take?'

'Half an hour, same for the dryer. Relax. What's the hurry? Has she ever thought about going on the *X Factor*? She could win, really.'

His thus-far dull eyes brightened. 'I know! I've told her the same. It's never too late, but she says it is. Too old, she says. Get me another drink. It's making you more attractive.'

'Good!' Ruth poured another vodka and tonic for Xano and put it in his hand, which was becoming nicely unsteady. 'Tell me about your mum.'

Perhaps it was the third line of coke that got him going; that combined with the half Rohypnol. He was uninhibited, surprisingly animated. 'She brought me up all on her own. She was in the Maryhill Youth Theatre, you know, when she was nine. The boss from Neville or Newmark or New something Productions in London spotted her and wanted her to be Annie in the West End. She would've gone all the way to Broadway and got record deals but she was pregnant.' The glass slipped from his hand and his knees spread open further – ook, Ruth almost got a glimpse, and put the towel back in place.

'I doubt she was pregnant at the age of nine.'

'Ha! No, daft, not nine, not Annie. It was Maria in *The Sound of Music*. Fifteen. Newmains it was, Newmains Productions. She woulda been like Kylie or Madonna and had houses in LA and on like her own island and married Brad Pitt or something but she had me.' His lip quivered and he dribbled a little.

'She shouldn't blame you. It wasn't your fault. Are you okay there? You feeling okay?'

'It's funny, I don't usually talk and here I am, blurting, blah-de . . . dum.' He took the bag of coke out of his money belt, tipped some out onto the table, and straightened it into two lines. 'God. The thingamajig guy at the place said I should talk more, that it'd be good – healing, he said. Always thought he was just a quack bullshit fuck, but yeah . . . Poor Mum. You want a line? It's crisp, nice. You sure?' He snorted both. 'Ahh . . . crispety crunch. I never knew my dad and Mum said that was good and that she wished she never met him either, not that she "met" him exactly, bumped into more like on the way back from panto rehearsals. He was into coke, too, must be a genetic whatsit, dispossession! He died in Shotts prison when I was thirteen months old. I was cute, me! Hair was blonde as a wean, curly like, and I had really chubby cheeks. I like talking, but maybe just to you 'cos you're old, mature I mean – no offence attended! – or 'cos that wig is a magician's! What the fuck is that all about? But no, don't take it off, there's something about it, it's making me open and I need to be open, so says that bullshit guy my boss made me go to or he wouldn't give me a reference after all those fucking years working like a dog. Don't take the wig off or the gown 'cos there's something about it makes me feel – woo-hoo! – good, like talking and talking and I never talk, not even to Mum but I think she's okay with that 'cos she says when I do talk it's always shite comes out and if she ever catches me using coke again she'll fucking kill me. What did you say your name is, what is it you're called?'

'I didn't.' Ruth propped a pillow behind his head. 'Why was your dad in jail?'

'Um.' His lips began to quiver. 'Poor Mum, she should have had number one hits at Christmas and then he comes up behind her in the Sainsbury's car park, although it was Safeways then and it shut at five, and it was just before Christmas and she had a breakthrough role as Elf number 12 at the Citz. It was dark, yeah, so no one saw his face 'cept her, and she still sees it she says, all the fuckin' time – *get that fuckin' face away*! – cos it's mine, see, my face. I don't believe he killed himself. You can't kill yourself eating a Bible.'

While Ruth suspected that a level of dysfunction might exist between Xano and his mother, she was shocked by the extent of it. John Martin had been rejected by his mother for a real and significant reason. The fact that single parenthood prevented her and Brad Pitt from buying an island with a house on it faded in comparison. Ruth didn't want to feel sorry for him, but she reminded herself that restorative justice required some understanding of the perpetrator's background, disadvantages and complexities. Without understanding these things and helping him address them, how would he ever change his behaviour?

'Who referred you to a psychiatrist, John? You said your boss made you go or you wouldn't get a reference? Was that KL Joinery in Glasgow? Why did he make you go?'

'Och – hey, can I wear the wig?'

'No.'

'The gown?'

'No. What happened that you had to leave your job in Glasgow? Why did your boss ask you to see a psychiatrist?'

'But that's not fair. If we're doing dress-ups, I should get to wear something. How about that other wig, the pink one? Can I have that?'

If the towel hadn't opened fully to reveal John Martin's penis, Ruth would have said no to this too. She tried not to grimace at the average-sized appendage before her, covered from tip to base in above-average-sized genital warts. 'Sure, let me put it on you.'

The pink bob offset his naked frame (bar money belt) and wart-covered knob to perfection. 'What happened in Glasgow?'

'Och, it was daft. Some bitch accused me of coming on to her when she was the one making coffees and home-made shortbread and brownies all the time and a steak pie that particular Wednesday dressed in this tiny, slinky nightie that was see-through, I kid you not, and she sat me at the kitchen table and leant over all like, mmm, you enjoying that, John? And it's me loses a fucking job when I'd worked like a fucking slave thirteen years, me who won't get a reference or any job ever again unless I go to this Billsworth mental place and sit for an hour while some wank says nothing, not a thing. I wouldn't mind a wee nap now.'

'You take too much coke, John. It's bad for you. Does your mother know you still have a habit?' She didn't want him to lose consciousness, and was worried that the half tablet was a bad idea combined with the cocaine and the alcohol. 'How did that make you feel, losing your job because of the woman in the see-through nightie?'

'Like moving to Spain. Right now, I feel really chilled. Do you?'

'I do. I'm glad you do too.'

His eyes were drooping. Ruth gave him another glass of water. 'Hey Mr, no snoozing. We're talking! We're chilled, don't waste it by sleeping. All's good, yeah?' She sprinkled some water on his face and patted it gently. 'Stay with me. You okay?'

He roused again. 'Cool, yeah, yeah, I'm good, all's good in the world that ends well.'

'Do you like yourself, John? Do you like John Martin?'

He evoked a Rambo movie: 'I am John Martin!'

Good. He was able to talk. He was able to think, probably as clearly as he was ever able. He was settled, with no intention of doing a runner, and she had successfully built up a rapport with him. It was time to get on with this. Ruth sat on the chair opposite him. 'John Martin, otherwise known as Xano, you have been found guilty of destroying everything that I care about. Do you understand?'

'Have I? But I like you. We're chilling, man, talking

yappety-yap, man, *wo-man*! I haven't talked like this to anyone ever. I would not destroy your stuff. I love your stuff. I
love your wigs!'

'Your most successful film to date is of my daughter in the
Coconut Lounge.'

'No. What? Which? No no, that was a Chinky!' He laughed.

'You mean Su Oliphant-Brotheridge? My daughter.'

'Holy shit, but you're not slanty-eyed, haha. This is weird
man. Is this real? Freaky! Shit, I love talking to you! I never
want to go. Don't ever make me go.'

'I'm glad you like talking to me because I want us to talk
some more. If you look around you'll see I've placed the chairs
and the tripod into what's called a restorative justice circle.'

'Cool!'

'It is cool, yes. Restorative justice is a creative response to
the trauma of crime. It's a way to recognise that victims have
needs which are not met in the criminal justice system; to seek
solutions when the laws and the courts have failed. It involves
the offender – you, John Martin, otherwise known as Xano.
The victim – me, Sheriff Ruth Oliphant. And the community.' Ruth gestured to the phone attached to the tripod. 'In
a moment, I'll press the record button on your phone and we
will live-stream to the internet, the community.'

He giggled. 'Woah man, fucking weird, cool! You remind
me of my mum more and more! She's always finding me
guilty of shit. Sorry, don't think I can fuck you after all. It'd
be incest like! Also, I feel a bit sick.'

'What I want is for you to understand the harm you've
done. What this process will do, is give us both a voice, so we
can heal and move on. Are you following me?'

'Um, I do, I so do, honey. Show me your tits.'

'I'm not going to show you my tits, John. Concentrate now.' Ruth repeated her instructions and he focused on her mouth like a terrified schoolboy. 'Now, are you following me?'

'Yes, Miss.'

'Yes, *My Lady*.'

'Yes, My Lady. But hey, if you're a sheriffy with a wig and stuff and I have to call you "My Lady" like in court, then this is court, not that circle thingme.'

'John Martin, you're right. Indeed you are.' Ruth removed her wig and gown and placed them on the arm of the sofa. 'You really have been following, haven't you? You do under-stand. Thank you. I appreciate your keen attention to detail and your feedback.'

'Can I have another drink?'

'Sure.' Ruth poured him a large glass of water. She wanted him to straighten up, just a little. She looked through the cut-lery drawers for a suitable implement for the next stage of her intervention. The metal egg whisk was too comedic somehow; the rolling pin too phallic. Under the sink was a toolbox. She picked up a hammer and pondered. John Martin was a sad, lost little boy who viewed her as a kinder, better version of his mother. Right now, she did not feel at risk in the slightest, and handing it over would demonstrate a high level of trust which would further cement his bond to her. Ruth took it with her to the bathroom – she needed a pee – and was thankful for the unplanned minute alone. Giving this man a hammer was a naïve and dangerous idea. When she'd washed her hands, she took her hairbrush from the cabinet under the sink, left the hammer in its place, and returned to the living room with the brush and the glass of water. 'Drink it down, go on, good boy. Now, this hairbrush will be our talking piece. The person holding the talking piece is the only person who can speak, who has the floor.'

'That was water! I wanted a drink!'

'Sure.' He was sufficiently compos mentis, so Ruth poured him another vodka and tonic. 'I'm going to go first.' Hairbrush in hand, she began the speech she'd rehearsed. 'By filming my daughter and uploading it to your YouTube channel, you harmed me in the following ways: you lost me the respect of my peers and may have lost me my job. You lost me my daughter and all the plans and hopes I had for her. And you caused my husband to suffer so much stress that he died of a heart attack.

'Now I'm going to press record on your phone. I'm going to hand you the hairbrush and you're going to tell me and the community why you did it, and how you feel about what you did. The film will stream live until I feel your apology is genuine. I need to know, and the community needs to know, that you are sorry, repentant, and that you will never behave in this way again. Does that make sense, John?'

'It's like you're her! Just like Mum. Don't hit me with it.'

'I'm not going to hit you. I'm going to hand it to you, see – it's our talking piece – and you're going to say why you filmed my daughter that night, why you called her a whore and a slut and why you uploaded the video to YouTube. Then you'll say sorry and mean it and tell us what you're going to do to change your behaviour. Okay? I'm not going to say another word. That's all you have to do, then I'll take you home. I've written the subjects you must cover on these sheets – I'll hold them up for you so you don't lose track.'

'Can I go to the bathroom first, please? I feel a bit sick.'

'I'll get a bucket.'

'No, I need to take a leak. I'll do the talking piece thingy, promise, soon as.'

'You're going to talk now, John, or I'll phone your mum and tell her all about the cocaine you're using – £80 a day purchased from Gary Smythe, yes?' Ruth handed him the hairbrush, and pressed record on his phone. She stood behind the camera and held up the first of the A4 sheets she'd prepared. On it she had written in thick black pen: *Explain what you did in the Coconut Lounge the night my daughter was there.*

He was still reasonably chilled, but a little more fidgety than before. He didn't seem at all aware or worried that his deformed penis was being streamed live on the internet. His fidgeting was bladder related, she realised. He wanted to get this over with so he could do a pee. 'This Chink was off her face and sucking everyone's cock and I filmed it.'

Ruth bit her lip. Do not lose it. Do not lose control. She held up the second sheet. *Why did you upload it?*

'I uploaded it 'cos I thought it was funny, so funny – one after the other, shit!' He laughed, but when he looked at Ruth, he stopped. 'But it's not funny?' His response was a genuine question.

Ruth gritted her teeth. She'd obsessed about Xano's possible reasons since the event: he wanted revenge on Ruth, he was a psychopath, a serial rapist, a serial killer. But he did it for a laugh. She held up her third A4 sheet. *How do you feel now you know the harm you caused?*

He crossed his legs tightly, winced, and rocked back and forth. He was going to burst.

'I feel really bad. I'm sorry.'

Ruth scribbled angrily and held an impromptu sheet that said: *What for?*

Still rocking, he thought hard, then said: 'I ruined jobs and hopes and futures and caused a heart attack.'

Ruth scrawled another sheet. *Are you sorry? Are you really sorry, John? Or shall I call your mother?*

He spoke as fast as he rocked. 'I feel terrible. I will never forgive myself. I'm going to make sure I never harm anyone again.' He couldn't stand it any more, tossed the brush to the floor, pounced from the sofa, and ran towards the loo.

Ruth pressed stop on the phone. Standing outside the bathroom door, she felt bereft. So far, the experience had achieved nothing but to make her feel incredibly low. He was sad and pathetic and the thought of bludgeoning him to death no longer soothed her. His apology was even more pathetic than his life. When he came out of the bathroom, Ruth realised she'd have to let him go. She'd have to dry his clothes, help him get dressed, and drive him home to his flat in Magaluf. Nothing had been restored. And as for justice – what was that? She wanted to cry. She wanted to hide under Leah's duvet and cry. 'Open the door, John.' She could hear him vomiting. 'You all right in there? Open the door.' She heard the shower door opening, then the water running. A bang, another loud retch. 'John! John?' She knocked furiously, yelled again and again: 'John, hey John, let me in. Are you okay?' But he didn't answer. All she could hear was the sound of the shower running. Was he dead? Had she killed him? 'John!' She ran into the kitchen, grabbed a chisel, and returned to the bathroom door. 'John, I'm going to try and lever the door open.' She wedged the flat metal edge into the crack beside the lock, but before she could attempt to lever it, the door opened. John Martin, naked and dripping wet, no longer looked sad and lost and pathetic. 'What the fuck have you been doing to me? You fucking bitch!'

She had made a sensible decision re the talking piece, but a bad one leaving the hammer in the cabinet under the sink. Her jaw cracked as it connected, and again when she hit the tiled floor.

Chapter Twenty

By the time I finally leave Moon Jihoo's step, I have my mother's home address in Seoul, her main office address, her favourite restaurant, and the name and email address of her personal assistant. I know everything I need to know, thanks to Woojin's groundwork, and to the Kim family who are plastered all over the internet (just like me). I know she heads up Ri's technology department with her husband and that he's not my father (they met when she was at Uni). I know the two of them are first in line to take over the $200 billion business when her dad dies. I know she 'travelled' after school, which translates as 'hid in the city somewhere and had a baby which she then dumped'. I know she's sharp and ambitious and some say formidable. She's a swimmer and a runner. She's not a good cook. Her city pad is a penthouse in Falleria Foret, a complex with two forty-five-storey buildings near the Seoul forest. I decide to go there first.

I'm sitting on a bench outside the building now, pretending to read something on my – her – phone. I can see into the bare glass and marble foyer. I wonder if the concierge will let me walk past and take the elevator, or if I'd be stopped – 'Stop that woman!' – ach, mortifying. I need to plan this. I need to take my time.

Most of all, I need to rethink my approach. Since I was six, I've imagined the words I'd say and the facial expression

I'd don. In all these scenarios, my mother has been shorter than me, pathetic-looking, and living in squalor. My words have shaken and moved her, my forgiveness has surprised and relieved her. I have been the one with the power.

She's five-seven, an inch taller than me. My father must've been a midget, probably because he was poor, from the under-nourished side of town, and hence an unimaginable choice. Her beauty is formidable. And she lives here, on the forty-fifth floor, with a roof garden and a lap pool that has a current so you swim but don't get anywhere.

I sit outside for three hours, trying not to be too obvious as I scrutinise the faces of those who walk in and out, and the cars that enter and exit the basement car park. Now mid-morning, I wonder if she might be at the office, and hail a taxi to Ri headquarters. As we drive off, I change my mind and ask the driver to drop me at the Jusaran Orphanage. On my phone, I read the latest news about Pastor Lee Jong-rak's baby box. The government's trying to close it down, arguing it makes it all too easy, that it encourages sex before marriage. The state is refusing to take these babies on, according to the latest article, a move that's packed the small orphanage with infants who will not be looked after by the government. I get out of the taxi at the end of the small lane. On the ram-shackle wall is a metal door, like a safe. I wonder if there's a baby inside now. I stand behind a bin at the end of the lane and wait. I want to see a woman walk along the lane with a bundle hidden in her bag or basket. I need to see her tremble as she looks around to make sure no one can see her. I want to watch her kiss the forehead of her child, open the door, and place it inside. Most of all, I need to see the woman sob, so overtaken with grief that she can hardly walk away. I want to see her walk back again, try to open the box, collapse before it in a withering heap. I want to watch her disappear into a life of regret. I want to feel sorry for her.

No one comes. It's daytime. No one will. I take a taxi to the international business district. The family building is not the tallest in the cluster of mirrored skyscrapers, but it's the thickest. To my relief, the security guards don't bat an eyelid as I head to the elevator – must be the trouser suit I bought. I don't take the first two because I want to be alone inside. Three doors open before I'm the only taker. I step in, and press 67, top floor. To my dismay, it stops on the fiftieth and a suited man in his forties steps in. He sees that 67 has been pressed, looks at me suspiciously, and says something in Korean.

'Sorry but I do not understand.'

'You're English?' Bugger, his is perfect. He doesn't take his eyes off me as we catapult skywards at dizzying speed. 'Where is your pass?'

'I have an appointment with Kim Su-Mi.'

'No you don't.'

'Yes I do. I'm a bit late, in fact.'

'You don't. She's not in today. Where's your pass?'

'Of course! She's at home today. I was supposed to meet her there.' A risk, but one worth taking.

'She doesn't take meetings when she's working at home.'

'With me she does. I'm her niece.'

He examines me, and surely must be noticing the family resemblance. 'But she doesn't have a niece.'

Bummer. 'Well no, I know, but I've always called her Aunty. My mum and her mum are—'

'Enough.' He presses the button for the ground floor and stares at me with angry disbelief. His eyes stay on me all the way to the top, and all the way back down again.

'If I see you in here again I'll call the police. He watches me leave the foyer, and speaks to the security guard in Korean.

Today I have learned that I am not cut out to be a spy. I've learned that Kim Su-Mi is as closely guarded as the Queen. I've also learned that Mum's coping very badly.

'I think she's going a bit nuts,' Leah said when I called from Moon Jihoo's step. 'She's been locked in the attic for over twenty-four hours.'

I can't dilly dally. I need to get home, which means I have to be brazen.

It's 7.30 p.m. I've been hovering outside the apartment building for hours. I've changed activity and position about a hundred times to avoid suspicion – me on a bench reading a book on my phone, me strolling fifty metres along the forest path and back again, me doing tai chi, me texting, me staring, me stopping staring as someone has given me a look, me walking ten metres along the forest path, waiting, walking back, sitting at the bench and pretending to read something on my phone. I've been waiting to spot her, or to follow the right people inside. But there's been no sign of her or her husband or her pretty little girls. And no one has been quite right to follow. That woman, perhaps? She seems distracted. No, I need a group of at least three. Everyone who lives here seems to go home alone. Of the dozens I've watched enter the foyer and press the elevator buzzer, all have been solo bar two couples. I can't give up. She's up there. Developing the Ri8 or a wristwatch phone at her desk, or eating the meal her chef has prepared, or swimming to nowhere on the roof.

8.30. She's putting the girls to bed, or one of the nannies is informing her that *she* has. She's sipping a glass of £1,000-a-bottle wine with her suitable husband.

At last, four men in suits. Before they're in the door, I walk fast and tail them, hoping the concierge thinks I'm one of the gang.

Success. I'm in the elevator. The men stop the loud, serious chat as soon as the door closes, and one of them presses 12. I press 23 and join the silence, hoping they won't question me like in Ri head office. As it turns out, they probably wouldn't have had time to ask me anything. This elevator is so fast and smooth that the door has opened at the twelfth floor in less than five seconds.

Door closes. Deep breath. I press 45.

This room is so small. The walls and the ceiling are mirrored. There's no getting away from myself. I've moved between the forty-fourth and the forty-fifth floor three times now, pinging up, pinging down, too scared to knock on her door. I feel hot and seasick. Each time the door opens it's been the same empty space with its marble floor and oak-lined walls. I'm surprised there's no guard standing in front of the double penthouse doors. I could hardly breathe the first time it opened, expecting to see a man with a gun, who'd spot and accost me. Now I'm wishing there had been an armed guard. At least then I wouldn't be bobbing up and down in this tiny hall of mirrors.

When it opens again, she might be standing there. She might get in the elevator with me. We'll be in this room alone. And without hesitation, I will say this: 'My name is Su-Jin. I am eighteen. I have been very well looked after.' And even though she's not a homeless alcoholic with leprosy, she'll react the same way as the birth mother of my dreams, the same way any mother would. She'll crumple! She'll beg for my forgiveness. She'll say it's no excuse, and she doesn't deserve or expect me to forgive her, but she had no choice, you see (You are so beautiful!), because her father threatened to kill her if she didn't hide for the last three months of her pregnancy, if she didn't give birth in the flat they'd rented for that purpose, with the assistance of the doctor her father paid to keep schtum. She'll fall to her knees in this tiny space, hands pressed together as if in prayer, and beg. She won't care about shame and honour now. She's not scared of her father any more. She's an adult and she's sorry and she will now repent. She's suffered for so long! She'll beg and I will look down on her with Dalai Lama-serenity and this is what I will say: 'I forgive you.'

Perhaps if I'd eaten something today I wouldn't feel like throwing up. The meagre contents of my tummy sway with the movement of the elevator. I'm not sure I can hold it in for much longer. I should get out when it opens. I should step onto the marble and knock on the oak door. If an armed guard or a nanny or a butler or a chef or her husband or one of her little girls answers, I'll say: 'I'm here to see Kim Su-Mi.' If I'm met with resistance, which I'm certain I will be, I'll say: 'Tell her I'm here to return the wicker basket she lost in Myeong-dong a long time ago.' I'll say it loudly so she might overhear from her desk or dining table.

Ping. That sound. Will it ever go away? Will my mistake forever rain on the world in pings and toots and buzzes? But the sound is not from a device. It's the elevator.

Next time. I'm going to do it next time.

Down to 44 again. Agh, I can't be sick in here. And back up. I don't think I can hold it in. The door opens at 45, but I'm chickening out again. I'm thinking I should go back to the hotel, pay my bill, and get a taxi to the airport.

The close-button isn't working. The door gets stuck halfway because she's pressing *open* on the other side and is standing in front of me on the marble. I poke at the button fast, but she pokes at hers faster and better. The elevator door opens fully and she steps inside.

She's in running gear. She has one earphone in. She glances at me, a question on her face. She's probably wondering why I pressed 45, why I'm on her floor. She presses Ground. She's even more like me than in the photos I've seen. Same hair, same eyes, same mouth, same nose, same figure. The question doesn't bother her for long, her glance a fleeting one. She stands at the front of the lift with her back to me and puts her other earphone in. She fiddles with her phone, chooses a song. I can hear George Ezra's 'Budapest', one of my favourites, and am surprised that she's into it too. The elevator heads down and I panic. I only have a few seconds.

'Excuse me,' I say, leaning across to press a button, any button. 17's the one I get.

She looks at me with the kind of smile she'd give any stranger who leant across to press an elevator button, and lowers the volume on her phone.

Now is the moment. Say the words, Su, say them.

But a question has appeared on her face again and she turns around and looks at me. It's a far bigger question than 'Why did you take this elevator to my floor?' Big enough for her to remove the earphones and for her face to lighten to my wishy-washy shade and for her eyes and mouth to widen. Before I can begin my speech, she presses the emergency stop and we shudder to a halt.

Silence for a moment. She stands poised, her hands at her side, as if this is a duel.

'My name is Su-Jin,' My voice quavers, there's no power in it, and she doesn't let me finish, because she knows who I am.

'What do you want?'

I've imagined this more than a thousand times. Never once has she said this. I'm flustered. I've forgotten the speech. 'I've been very well looked after. I'm eighteen . . . Um, what? Nothing.'

The colour's back in her face already. She doesn't flinch. 'Then why are you here?'

I think about what to say – I'm here to overwhelm you with my fabulousness? I'm here so you know what you have missed? I'm here to see your sadness and your guilt? I'm here to see you beg for forgiveness? I'm here to forgive you so you can live with yourself? I'm here to forgive you so I can live with myself?

If she's feeling anything at all, she's very good at not showing it.

'I don't know,' I say.

A Korean man speaks over the intercom. My birth mother says something back into the speaker. She's assuring him there's no emergency, I assume, that everything's okay. By the rigidity of her face and frame, she lied to him. 'You do,' she says to me. Her hardness is chilling. I don't want to share her air.

But maybe she's even more scared than I am. Perhaps she only knows how to cope with the guilt by being defensive and closing herself off. I hadn't factored in her shell, and how hard it might be to crack. She had no warning, after all, so it's fair enough to wonder what motivated me to arrive here now. I should explain honestly, give her time to process. 'I wanted to meet you. I wanted you to know that I've done well.'

Either my mother's had botox, or she's never been able to move her face. I look very closely, but can't detect what's she's thinking or feeling. She deliberates for ages (I think. Who knows?) then comes back with: 'You're a very pretty girl.'

It's a disappointing response, but an improvement. I think we're heading in the right direction. 'I just wanted to see you in the flesh. You're beautiful.'

Stone face. 'Thank you.'

'I've thought about this moment for so long. Have you? Have you thought about me?'

'Of course I have.' Face of stone.

'Really! Have you tried to find me? Have you written me letters? Birthday cards?'

'For goodness sake, how much do you want?'

I'm so gobsmacked that I find myself laughing.

She shakes her head. I'm an alien with no boardroom skills. 'I suppose you've done your sums so I won't waste time. 200,000. Pounds, I assume, from your accent.'

All of a sudden, she's nothing like me. She's aggressive, disdainful and heartless. She holds her chin so high it must hurt her neck. She's used to looking and talking down. Her eyes reveal nothing – there's no wetness, no narrowing, no rapid blinking. I suspect her flawless silky bob won't move at all when she runs. She has make-up on, bright red lipstick – to go running! She smells of expensive perfume. Her perfectly contoured sportswear boasts the Prada label, twinkles in places, and is matchy matchy. I'm not sure I mean to say this out loud: 'Is this you? Is this what you're like?' I'm talking to a woman from a different generation, country, class and culture, a woman whose first language is not English, and who I only met five minutes ago. Stupid of me to expect an immediate chemistry, a connection. She's a complete stranger. And what I've learned about her these last minutes, I don't like.

'300.'

I'm incredulous. 'I don't believe this is what you're really like.'

'And what are you thinking, Su-Jin? 400,000 and my husband and children will never know what I'm really like? Make it five and the world will never know either?'

A great weight has lifted from me. I feel elated, freer than I've ever felt in my life. She's horrible! She's the worst person I've ever met. What luck to have escaped a life with her. What incredible, wonderful luck to have been chosen by Ruth and Bernie, my mum and dad. I'm suddenly aching to be home. I need to hold Mum and Leah. I need to cry with them. We need to say goodbye to Dad together.

'I won't go any higher than that,' she says.

What the hell, I'll let her go for it. I'm feeling power after all, just not the kind I expected. I pretend to ponder the offer. I'm interested to know how much I'm worth.

'500,000, last offer.'

I don't think this is as high as she'll go. 'You're terrified! The shame! What would happen if people discovered that you got pregnant at seventeen? Who was my father by the way?' The power is epic. I could never have imagined this encounter would feel so good.

'He was no one. I don't even remember his name.'

'I don't believe you.'

'I met him at a school dance. We had sex in the cloakroom. He was stupid. His father had a shop. If I knew his name that night, I forgot it straight after. I've never even thought about him, ever. I'm in a hurry, Su-Jin, and I see no benefit in sharing biographies and attempting to fast-track a bond. How much money will it take for you to keep quiet?'

'Hmm.' My finger's on my chin. 'You're in a hurry, are you? What's your schedule tonight?'

She speaks into the intercom again, presses 45, and the lift takes us back up. 'Wait here and don't move. Keep the doors open.'

'Aren't you worried what I might say if someone sees me?'

'They're abroad. Don't move.'

She opens the front door and leaves it ajar. She runs into an enormous, open-plan living area. City lights sprinkle the floor-to-ceiling glass. She comes back and stands just outside the elevator door. '650,000, but I need a guarantee that you will never disclose the event or make contact again.'

'The *event*, hilarious!' I've been holding the door open. I take my hand off to let it close.

She stops it, forces it open, puts her finger on the button outside and keeps it there. 'One million pounds.'

I smile, shake my head. 'No one ever tells you how expensive *events* are.'

She's flustered, losing it. I guess she and hubby are in deep trouble if this comes out; at the least they probably won't inherit the company. Wowee, I am worth a tonne.

'If you give me your account details, it'll be yours in a few minutes.'

'I'm in a hurry too, Su-Mi. I don't want your money. Remove your hand from the button. I need to go home to my mum.'

'Wait, wait.' She holds out a business card with her number written in pen on the blank side. 'If you ever feel the urge to make this public, call me first. Believe me, being rich is much better than dwelling on the past. Call me, don't be self-destructive and illogical. This is my private mobile. Don't call on any other number. And if it's not money you need, but something else—'

'Yeah, like what?' Is she the type to chop a horse in two? Am I Korean mafia? I don't take the card, and push her hand off the button. She tosses her card into the lift just before it closes and it lands at my feet. When I reach the ground floor, I look at it for a moment then pick it up.

In the taxi back to the hotel, I text her private number. 'Hiding your shame has ruined you, poor thing. You're so scared, so suspicious. All I wanted was for you to think I'm amazing, that's all. Take a look at this, please? Click on it, watch me and you'll see – your daughter is amazing.'

Is she opening it? Has she pressed play? Is she watching it? Is that the glorious ping of another hit I hear? Is that her 'event' in that bar?

Zzzz, I have a text. It's only one word, but from the little I know about her, it's carefully chosen and true to form:

Anything

Chapter Twenty-one

I cry for at least half of the ten-hour-and-fifteen-minute flight to Dubai. Quite loudly, I fear, because the young mother to my left, her toddler to hers, has only looked me in the eye once and it was with hate. The pocket on the seat in front of me is filled with the two packets of tissues the steward gave me when I asked, and the scrunched-up loo roll I resorted to when she refused to give me any more. When I get home, Dad won't be there to meet me. When I come in after a run, he won't ask me if I beat my best time and congratulate me if the answer's yes. After I've showered, he won't call me down because the lamb roast's ready. When I get ready for bed, I won't hear him playing his violin in the music room.

I spend the two-hour stop in Dubai airport wandering along the main shopping area, a frantic rectangle filled with gold bracelets and tired people who end up buying them because there's nowhere to sit. At last, I'm in the queue for the final leg. Glasgow, the board says, and the word makes me melt with a mixture of relief and devastation. Home, but no Bernie B.

I hope to sleep for the eight-hour flight, but I don't even manage a minute. I'm trying to imagine Mum without Dad and I can't. As strong as she is, she needs him, relies on him, and I'm not sure if she'd ever have seemed or been as strong on her own. I don't know how she'll get up in the morning without smelling the fresh coffee he's made to wake her; how she'll eat at night without the meal he's prepared; how she'll survive the stress of her job without the after-dinner de-briefs he always, always, has time for. They were in love, my parents. After all these years, they were still in love. I try to watch a few movies, but the earphones hurt my ears, the sound hurts my brain, and the films are stupid. I cry again, and decide I should try to change my technique because it is definitely noisy. The freckled boy beside me just asked me why I'm crying and if it'd be possible for me to stop because he's watching *Frozen* and he can't hear what Olaf is saying. I walk up and down the aisle a few times, and when I sit I wonder if anyone recognised me. I'd stared blankly into grief as I trod, so I didn't notice the other passengers. Anyway, who cares about any of that? Dad's dead.

We descend through the clouds and there it is, so green it seems fake. I can see Loch Lomond, and land breaking into mountains in the north. Underneath me now are neat, well-used fields; large sandstone houses; small concrete boxes. A few people clap when we land, and I would have too, if not for Dad. When the engines have finally been turned off, the plane tinkles with the unclipping of seatbelts, and the pinging and zzzing of phones as they're switched on. You have a new text, a voicemail, Laura has posted on your timeline. Have you seen this video? (Of course you have.)

Passport control is speedy. I walk past the baggage reclaim area with the small backpack I bought at Incheon airport and pause before the door that divides me and reality. No one knows I'm coming home now. I won't be confronted with an unrecognisably frail-looking mum or Leah's broken nose or flashing cameras. I turn around and face the people who are walking out. I want people to look at me before I exit. I want to know how it'll feel for me out there. The couple and their freckled *Frozen* fan walk towards me, trolley filled with neat black cases. The man catches my eye for a second, but – nope – he hasn't reacted and – no – he's not whispering to his wife 'Hey, that's the Magaluf slut, can't believe we sat next to the Magaluf slut, can't wait to tell Pete and Emma we practically know the Magaluf slut.' A woman of around eighty, dressed in colourful, casual, hippy-looking clothes, passes on her happy anticipatory smile to me. Nope, nothing. Two businessmen in suits chat to each other, skimming my arm as they pass, but not looking at me. I take a deep breath. It's over. Someone has done something worse, or at least more recently, than me. I don't need to hate myself. I don't need to blame anyone else. I don't need revenge. I turn and face the door, and walk out. It'll all be okay, or it would be okay, if Dad wasn't dead.

And if Leah wasn't standing at the front of the arrivals area with two cabin bags and a pale and desperate expression on her face. She runs towards me, hugs me, and we both burst into tears. Happy arrivals skirt around us to embrace their loved ones. 'How did you know I was on this flight?'

Leah disengages. 'This lawyer friend of Mum's, Michael MacDonald, he's like a right dodgy Sherlock Holmes or something. I think he might fancy her and I think I might fancy him.'

'Your nose is the same, not skew-whiff, thank God. I'm so sorry.'

'Ach, you didn't even break it, ya wimp. Did you meet her? Who is she? What's she like?'

I don't know if I'm going to keep Kim Su-Mi a secret for ever. All I know is that I have no interest in thinking about her or talking about her. I now wish I'd cut the Su from my name rather than the Jin, but it's too late to change who I am. I am Su with no dash and no Jin and no headshot in *Forbes Magazine*. 'I decided against it.'

'No! You should have gone through with it.'

'I have a mum. Why the bags?'

Leah looks at the departure board, grabs my hand, and leads me to a Costa table. 'Flat white?'

'Aye, ta, but tell me, is everything okay?'

'Yeah, yeah, let's get some caffeine into us. I've not slept since the night before last.' Leah returns with two coffees, takes a sip of her latte and looks around. 'See the woman over there?'

'Where?'

'WH Smiths, pretending to look at the newspapers on the stand at the front, scraggly brown hair, too long, split ends, middle part, smelly-looking T-shirt that's too tight, face that looks like its habitat is underwater.'

'Uh-huh.'

'Journalist. Will not leave us alone. Followed me here. Let's drink and walk. Good idea anyway, our flight leaves in an hour.'

'What flight?' Leah's almost running because the plane's boarding, apparently. I scramble behind her, rolling the cabin bag she handed me without knowing why, and start noticing the looks people are giving me. That guy's face is going red and he's now trying very hard to look anywhere else. That air hostess is smirking at me. The fat journalist with the bad hair is running behind me and yelling. 'Su? Su! How does it feel to be home? Su!'

Leah hands me a boarding pass, and we queue at the scanning machine.

'Su! Su, stop!' the journalist shrieks. She taps me on the shoulder several times with aggravating resolve. How dare she jab at my shoulder? She's doing it again. 'Do you blame yourself for your father's death, Su? Su, do you think it was your fault?'

Leah scans her pass and races towards the shortest security check queue, turning around to hurry me 'Quick! Come!'

But I want to answer the journalist's question. 'Of course I feel it's my fault, at times, because my actions caused him a great deal of stress, but it was the actions of others that caused him more stress, far more. My father died because a man filmed his daughter in a bar and uploaded the film and because others decided to share it. He died because he had a heart condition and because journalists decided to harass him and his family. The fact that I gave oral sex to more than one stranger in Magaluf is a factor, yes, and not an insignificant one, so of course I feel guilty and thank you for asking. In the scheme of things, however, it was one small factor among many. Sex acts in other countries rarely induce fatal heart attacks in this one.'

I scan my pass and race to the security queue. Surprising, I think as I remove my belt, I'm a celebrity, and I think I might be good at it.

Cabin bag on the belt, Leah finally explains why I have a cabin bag on the belt. 'She'd asked me how to make a video go viral and I told her what I knew without thinking – y'know make them outrageous, funny, cute, or horrendous like the chainsaw one, get a celebrity interested, that kind of thing – but I never thought she'd – shite, Su-Jin, I am so embarrassed. Take a look.' Leah swipes and hands me her phone. A video is paused on screen. 'And all it achieved was that she got herself into trouble with the cops. Not big trouble, a hand slap, but it pissed her off, boy oh boy. She disappeared for a few hours after the cops left. I looked all over for her and when I got home she'd left a note saying she'd be in Magaluf for a few days. MacDonald managed to get the address of the villa she rented, so that's where we're going. I'm really worried. I think she's going after the guy who filmed you.'

'She's going after John?' A warm feeling waves through me. Mum had been feeling the same way as me after all. I should have trusted myself, gone with my instincts.

'You know his name?'

'I remembered all of a sudden, can't even think what day it was – yesterday morning, dunno, but it came back, bang. I'm 90 per cent sure he spiked my drink just before it all took off. I let him buy me a drink, idiot that I am, and everything went so strange after that, not MDMA or alcohol strange, like pfff my lordy. He's horrible, yuk, does not deal with rejection, I tell you. But what's her plan?' While I'm panicking for Mum's sanity and safety, I can't help feeling a tinge of excitement as I watch the videos she made. I think they're pretty good to be honest – if more than three people had actually seen them. And I think John whatever-his-last-name-is should be punished for almost certainly spiking girls' drinks and definitely filming them when they're unable to stand, let alone consent.

~

The Jet2 flight to Magaluf is full of school leavers, most of whom are already drunk, which is probably why they don't recognise or even notice me. Four boys at the front chant something about being Kelvinsiders with huge cocks. About a dozen girls behind me sing something about Williamwood women wanting wood . . . *What do we want? Wood!* The Kelvinside boys reply that they have wood and are willing to give it. Half an hour in, one of the former and one of the latter have apparently joined the mile high club. I feel about a hundred years older than these former peers. I feel like standing and declaring: Mock me but know you may soon be me. Beware, chicken nuggets, beware the Jäger bomb! I don't. They won't listen. I fall asleep on Leah's shoulder and wake to the turning-on of phones. Forty-five minutes later, Kelvinside Academy and Williamwood High are being whipped up by PR reps on buses and Leah and I are in a taxi to the villa Mum rented.

'Why is Mum like this?' Leah asks.

'Like what?'

'Always fighting, you know, an Alpha or something. It's not because of her job. She was always the same.'

It's not a family trait. Gran's calm and content, Grandpa laughed all the time, Aunty Marie's soft and soppy, and Aunty Louise is a relaxed housewife. Nothing happened to Mum as a kid. No neighbour or gym teacher molested her, no one hit her, no one she loved died. Her childhood was idyllic. She wanted ours to be just like it, with family barbecues and music playing somewhere in the house and parents who enjoyed and respected each other and their children.

But even if everything is perfect – God (or whatever) creates a masterpiece of a person, parents and family nurture you, friends and schools cherish and cultivate you – even if you're on track to be blissfully happy and at peace, something can happen, a big traumatic event, boom! – and all those sturdy foundations are blown to dust and you're suddenly someone else altogether. I don't want to spell it out to Leah, but I've known Mum's event since I was twelve. Before approaching the subject of looking for my birth mother, I decided to rummage in the attic in case there was a secret file or something. I imagined a letter from the adoption agency, for example, with my biological mother's name and/or address or her height or hobbies or something. I didn't find anything like that, but I did find several huge cardboard files about Mum's fight to keep me after she got pregnant with Leah: the research she did, the cases she studied, newspaper clippings, social work reports, her letters of complaint (there were over seventy). Leah and I knew the basics: the surprise but 'miracle' pregnancy, that the social workers had taken me away, but neither of us knew the extent of Mum's battle.

Since I can remember, Mum has always referred to social workers as imbeciles and do-badders. She constantly rants about the disgraceful grammar and jargon in their court reports. Once at Brownies when I was about seven, one of the leaders, Mrs McSweeney, told Mum that Leah had used the F-word when told to be quiet and wondered if everything was all right at home. 'Everything's *fucking* wonderful,' Mum said, before dragging us out of the church hall never to return. That night, after Dad had finished some

Rosetta Stone with me, I asked him why Mum had used a bad word with the Brown Owl.

'Mrs McSweeney's a social worker,' Dad said, as if this was an adequate explanation.

'So you're allowed to swear at her?'

'No, Mum was just upset. She had a hard time with social workers when Leah came along.'

Till now, Leah has been holding my hand and stroking it with her thumb. It's felt more glorious than diving into cool water. She removes her hand, I hope not for long. 'I think Mum changed because of a big trauma, a hugely stressful life event: adopting me.'

Leah doesn't look at me as she comes back with: 'No, it was after getting pregnant with me. I was her trauma. I was the reason she lost you.'

'No! It was the situation. You know she adores you?'

'You're easier, your relationship is easier.'

'Because I never disappointed her,' I say. I never spat out cauliflower cheese, never swore at a Brown Owl, never smoked dope, never flunked classes, never arrived home drunk at 2 in the morning and said: *What are you gonna give me, My Lady, eighteen months?* I had the easiest and most unnatural relationship a girl has ever had with a mother because, until a week ago, I never disappointed her. Leah's not seen me like this in years. My lips have lost their place on my face and my nose is running. 'I never disappointed her. Well I made up for that, eh. She's always fought for me. Why would she do that now? How will she love me now?'

'She'll love you the same as always: big time!'

Leah's response is so reassuring it makes me whimper.

'She's always fought for me too, just in a different way. Do you know I've hidden dope in about twenty places in the house and she has found it every time and thrown it out? Even when I wrapped it in cling film then foil then two plastic bags and stuck it underneath the barbecue with masking tape! I think she's got a sniffer dog hidden in the garden shed. And I could never say "Hey, where's my skunk, bitch?" Tell you what: I'll stop beating myself up if you do. You saw the report – Dad should've been dead months or even years ago. The way I've been thinking about what happened with Dad is: he's in a cab on a mission, right – and he loved a mission – and the mission was motivated by love for the three of us, and boy did he love the three of us – then bang: dead. Overwhelmed with love and purpose one second, dead the next. I want to die that way.'

'Thank you for saying that! You're back, after all these years!'

'I never went anywhere, dickhead. You were just too uncomfortable to notice because of the stick up your arse.' Leah mimics something I said after we had an argument about coat hooks about a year ago (she'd used mine, again): '*Perhaps I'll win the Nobel Prize for curing Leah's personality!*'

I can't help laughing. I liked that line.

'I'm almost glad it happened – you needed bringing down a peg or two. Welcome to the world, Su-Jin, where members of a nuclear family hang their coats on any one of the four hooks on offer.'

I am tempted to point out (again) that when Leah's twelve or more coat-options are piled on top of mine, life is a little harder for me. I decide not to. 'So was my *event* Magaluf? Am I a different person now?' Let's hope so. My coat-hook concerns are bothering me, telling me I might indeed be a tad uptight, perhaps even self-righteous.

'You don't look or sound different. Do you feel it?'

'I've been feeling the urge to swear.'

'Do it!'

'Bloody.'

'Ooooh!'

'Arse.'

'Try in context: think Xano.'

His name makes me panic about Mum. 'She won't do anything to jeopardise her job, will she?'

'I don't think so, she's too clever. She was careful with those videos. Jeez, you are hopeless. Say it: *Fuck Xano!* Say it!'

'To hell with Xano.'

'I love you Su-Jin, my genius, kind, generous, beautiful – like I'm talking breath-taking-beautiful, so stunning I often want to stab you in the chiselled cheekbone – sister, but you just had the perfect opportunity to insert an expletive into a sentence and enhance it as a result, and you failed.'

'It'd be like me making you read the *Financial Times*.'

'I'd give that a shot. I don't know for sure that I won't find emerging markets and the FTSE enthralling. Isn't life dull when you know exactly who you are?'

The taxi drives past the main strip in Magaluf. The Coconut Lounge is in there somewhere, and I'm thinking: *But isn't life terrifying when you don't?*

Chapter Twenty-two

Always a quick thinker, Ruth decided that if the tiles didn't render her unconscious when she hit them, she would pretend. Xano . . . John . . . she didn't know what to call him now that she hated him so much, so MUCH. He had no name, and he paused after the blow, perhaps shocked by what he'd done, then kicked her shoulder quite gently with a foot. He leant down and slapped her face. He pressed a finger against her neck to check for a pulse. She heard him walk to the kitchen, run the tap, bang a cupboard door. She heard him take his washing out and put it in the dryer. She heard a metal click in the living room – he was removing his camera from the tripod, in all probability. He checked on her again, took her pulse, pressed a towel between her bleeding jaw and the tiles. She heard the television – news, in Spanish. The stories had started to repeat themselves by the time he took his clothes out of the dryer and got dressed (she guessed by the zip zipping). She heard the scratch of pen on paper. He returned one last time, checked her pulse, and placed a piece of paper on the floor.

She heard him shut the front door. The pool of blood around her face was thick and widening, but she should wait a minute more, just in case. Sixty seconds later, Ruth lifted her face, mouth agape and dripping. She completed a series of movements in order to establish the extent of her injuries (head a centimetre to the left, right, up, and so on, then arm, other arm, foot, and so on). Her jaw was probably broken. She'd lost a fair amount of blood, but the bleeding had practically stopped and she wasn't dizzy or confused, didn't have chest pain or a rapid heart rate. Apart from the jaw, she was okay. Ruth moved onto her knees and picked up the note he'd left on the floor:

'I think you've been naughtier than I have, My Lady, but I won't tell if you don't. PS You can't just stream to some random site without a strategy ffs. 15 views, daft cunt.'

Ruth was about to stand when she heard a knock at the door. Shit. She fell back into her play-dead position and tried to smear the blood she'd stretched in lines because they documented her attempted escape. Another knock. What was the key situation here? Did you need a key to lock the door behind you when you left? (She hadn't heard a key.) Or was there a snib? Would the door automatically have locked after the man closed it and left?

No, no no, the door wasn't locked. She heard it open and close. He'd be able to see her from there, she thought (do not move). He'd be looking at her now. She heard footsteps: he'd be coming at her now.

'Mum!' A woman, not him, a woman.

Another woman: 'Mum, oh my God, are you okay? Mum?'

Chapter Twenty-three

Mum and I had been on the same track all along. She wanted to get Xano even more than I did. Mum always said my instincts were good and that I should trust them.

('What about mine?' Leah once whined. 'You should listen to your instincts and then do the opposite,' Mum had joked.)

If I'd sought out John Martin rather than Kim Su-Mi, Mum wouldn't be lying in a pool of blood, jaw broken, neck and face covered in a violent rash, with a note that says she's a daft c-word.

The peace I'd found talking to Leah in the taxi has vanished. I want to grab the hammer on the floor and run after him now but I have to take care of Mum first.

It hurts for her to talk, but she conveys overwhelming relief that we've come to rescue her, and that I've finally returned.

I tell her I'm sorry and she holds me to her shoulder and sobs.

I stick with the lie I told Leah and say I don't want or need to meet some stranger in Korea, and she gives me a questioning look. 'Really truly,' I say.

We can't call the police, because it's pretty clear from John Martin's note that Mum's broken the law, and after consulting Doctor Internet I feel confident that we don't need an ambulance either. The bleeding has stopped, her jaw is not crooked or shifted, there are no missing teeth, and no pieces of bone piercing the skin. I clean and bandage the wound, give her some painkillers from the elaborate medical bag she brought with her, and help Leah get her into bed. She falls asleep almost immediately. Leah and I bleach the house and the car (yuk), removing all traces of John Martin. We check the flights leaving tomorrow. We'll book when she wakes, as long as she's well enough to travel.

Business dealt with, we check on Mum, who's sleeping soundly. She'll be out for a while, I think. Leah lies on the other side and holds her hand. I sit on a chair by the bed and hold the other. I should trust my instincts, Mum had said, adding: 'but that doesn't mean you should react to them hastily.' I try to calm myself. I must think this through, make a plan.

Earphones in, I check out Mum's attempt at restorative justice. No one's taken the film down yet, probably because it's quite dull. (Twenty-five views, no shares on Twitter or Facebook because Mum didn't give it a good title or set up tags and links and I don't know what else, which makes her naïve but not daft.) John Martin looks fabulously vulnerable with his pink bob and warty knob. The film doesn't come over like a restorative justice circle at all. Mum never posted the videos of him soiling himself in the car. In the only one she did post, she doesn't say a word. She's never in frame! No one'd know she was there. Wow, she meant that! Good thinking! It's like he's completely alone, filming himself. He says: *I ruined jobs and hopes and futures and caused a heart attack. I feel terrible. I will never forgive myself. I'm going to make sure I never harm anyone again.*

I whisper to Leah: 'Have you looked at this? It's like a suicide note!'

Leah takes the phone from me and then immediately switches it off. 'Have you looked at *this*?' She gestures to herself, then to Mum. 'It's like your family. Enough, Su-Jin. It's over.'

I sigh as if in agreement, and leave Mum and Leah in bed. I do sit-ups in the living room in an attempt to quell the rage, but it only builds. I make a mental list of the pros and cons of killing the man who made my mother a widowed felon with a broken jaw and a slutty daughter but the pros are many and hefty and they stifle the cons. I imagine what Mum will say when she wakes: *Did you get him? Did you finish what I started? Tell me you fought for me, Su, like I've always fought for you.*

It makes no sense to take instructions from Leah all of a sudden. She can't have morphed into a genius overnight. Okay so she's right about my family being in that bed. (I'm taking a peek – they're both sound asleep.) But this is far from over.

I drive Mum's hire car into town. There's a store on the strip that sells a bizarre range of stuff, and I'm relieved to find it still open. Hat and sunglasses on, I go inside. At this time, people are buying chocolate and alcohol, mostly. I remember getting bandages and mosquito-bite cream around 3 a.m. during the holiday. I buy some normal things (bananas, crisps, water, a large bar of Dairy Milk) to dilute the unusual things (Paracetamol, a kitchen knife, gloves, a roll of green paddle wire, a cloth).

There's a Looky Looky man, I see when I exit the shop. I find myself drawn to him, and then to the Coconut Lounge.

It's not coincidence or luck that John Martin is sitting at the bar. When Leah filled me in about her investigations, she told me he spends most of his spare time here. I sit at a table and watch the goings on. A PR guy – not the one who was here last – is instructing a man to suck alcohol into a lengthy straw. Once filled, the man takes aim as required and attempts to strike the first of eight nipples with his liquid. The man is good, and he strikes the first target. He wins free drinks till three. Everyone is so pleased for him that they cheer.

The couple I'm sharing this table with are tongue-kissing. I have a bird's eye view of the man's hand, which is jiggling frantically inside the woman's pants. She seems too wasted to be turned on, but I doubt she'd be turned on by his technique even if she was sober. I feel sore just watching, so I stop.

John Martin, meanwhile, has handed a wad of cash to the bar owner and is stuffing something into his money belt. He looks around the bar, peruses the talent, hones in on a girl who's dancing alone, sidles up behind her, puts his arms around her stomach, and attempts to sync with her grind-twerk-whatever.

A man covered in tattoos is pushing John Martin on the dance floor. 'Hey, that's my bird, you prick!'

John – my John, who'd have liked to shag me – apologises, hands in surrender, and skulks from the bar.

This room is so hot. My jaw is stiff. Two small circles of sweat have appeared under my arms.

I follow him outside and watch from the pavement opposite as he smokes a cigarette at the door. He's looking out of it.

I text Leah: 'Gone to get some food. Back soon. Has she woken yet?' She still hasn't replied a few minutes later, when

John Martin starts walking back towards the entrance. The guy who just pushed him comes out and it starts up again. 'She's all yours, mate,' I hear John Martin say as the man violates his personal space, fists and teeth clenched to escalate the altercation. John Martin takes a step back, grinds his cigarette out with his foot, and punches the man in the head. The tattooed man swings back with fury, landing one on John Martin's eye, and one on his chin. John Martin is experienced, it seems, and has the strength and skill to return a blow which sends his opponent to the ground. Victorious, he strolls away.

I follow him along the strip, down a lane, and around the corner. I check my phone, but Leah's not replied yet. They must both still be asleep.

John Martin walks outwards from the beach, away from the centre of town, until he reaches a hotel on the outskirts. I cower behind a wall as he makes his way through the car park at the back of the hotel. There's someone in the basement kitchen of the hotel. I can hear music.

Beyond the car park is a dirt road. He stops at a beat-up Fiat, his, I assume, because he gets in.

Bugger, bugger. My car is a long way away. If he drives off, I'll never catch him. But he doesn't drive off. He unzips his money belt and takes something out. Phew.

There are several sturdy trees on the dark road. If only I could drug him and hang him from one of them with the green wire. My shoulders slump, because hanging is not awful enough, and I'd never manage it anyway.

I sneak across the car park, and hide behind the tree beside his back seat. He prepares three lines of cocaine on a magazine.

I'm a bit flustered. I wish I could ask Mum how she was going to do it. It's not easy to fake a suicide, not in this situation. At least Mum had a controlled environment.

But I am in luck, because John Martin has fallen asleep or unconscious pre-snort. His head has fallen back and his eyes are closed.

I run towards the car. I look in his window to check I'm right. Yes, out for the count. I double, treble, quadruple check – opening the door, saying his name, slapping his face, removing his money belt.

My speed and ingenuity surprise me. His suicide must be outrageous in order to knock my film off the top spot, and I recall the details of the video I managed to outshine: the loving couple, the tree, the ladder, the chainsaw.

I choose the hefty tree I'd been hiding behind. I do calculations in my head as I wind wire around the trunk, leaving the correct amount of excess wire between it and the car. I open the rear window, feed the wire in, loop it under his crisp white collar, back out the window again, and back round the tree. I wind two more times round the trunk, then use the knot Greg Jamieson showed me on the Duke of Edinburgh trek to secure it. I check the excess wire on the ground is even and that it will unravel with ease when the car is in motion. I'm not 100 per cent sure this will work. Low eighties, I'd say.

I adjust the back window so it's open twenty centimetres.

I choose a restaurant sign fifty metres ahead and complete a second series of calculations. If he accelerates at X speed, he will reach the sign-minus-three-metres in Z seconds (this being the length of the wire now coiled between the car and the tree).

If I run at X speed, I will reach the sign in Y seconds.

And Leah says maths is useless in everyday life!

I set up his phone as required, click it into the holder on the dashboard, point it at his head, and press record.

His money belt is filled with treasure: plastic bag stuffed with white powder, some dodgy-looking tablets, 300 euros, a photo of a woman dressed like Dolly Parton, and Oxln genital wart cream (*It's over, thanks to Oxln*).

And . . . Action. John Martin is live on air. For now.

Money belt in hand, I take my position at the front of the car, legs stiff and apart, with one hand on a hip, like a cool cowgirl. I lean over and knock on the windscreen gently, but he doesn't wake.

I decide against knocking again. I'll wait.

The cool cowgirl pose is very uncomfortable ten minutes later, but not as uncomfortable as his face, which is becoming too familiar to me now. He has a dimple on his left cheek. I bet it made adults ruffle his hair in supermarket queues when he was little. Will he ever wake up?

A tune floats over to me. It's incongruous for this resort, and for my mission. I turn my head but not my body – I will not be deterred! – and spot a chef's hat bobbing in the basement kitchen of the nearby hotel. The chef lifts his arms and conducts the music which I do not wish to identify.

I am a ruined mixed-race adoptee, just as they predicted. I require revenge. My mother requires it even more. I will not be deterred by classical music, however pleasant.

I return my attention to John Martin. When he wakes, he'll rub his eyes then see me, legs stretched out like a cowgirl, one hand on hip. His skin will turn yellowy green with anger as I wave his precious money belt at him, his bag of goodies.

It's violin. So what?

When he sees me, I'll run towards the sign. And he'll use the accelerator as a war-cry, setting off after me, arm jiggling with gear changes.

John Martin will be angry as he drives, all the way to the end, when the car bucks or swerves suddenly three metres before the restaurant sign, green paddle wire stiff from tree to neck, then loose again because the force has ripped his head off. It'll be so clean, so neat. Now you see it, now you don't.

I'll ready myself to jump out of the way.

His head will hurl backwards, bang on the rear windscreen, and bounce once or twice before finally resting on the back seat, eyes wide open for ever. And my film will be forgotten, this the next number one, because nothing beats a good beheading.

He is never going to wake up. He's dreaming, I think, a bad or sad one. He's got cracked lips.

My rage is subsiding. I'm wondering if he had an *event* too, if something happened that turned him into the pathetic mess I'm looking at now.

Why won't he wake up?

My phone vibrates and I divert my eyes from John Martin to read Leah's text: *Where are you?*

I return my eyes to my target's gaunt and troubled face. Where am I? *Who am I?* I find myself imagining that I am him and that he is me.

And we're in the Coconut Lounge.

I'm John Martin, a thin, talentless, uneducated mess, with

genital warts, a drug problem, and a phone. I'm chatting up an Asian chick who no one else wants. She's gagging for it – everyone says so. She's rat-arsed but tense, so I top her up at my own expense. She reels me in and I feel good. Then suddenly she pushes me so hard that I fall back and hit a table and everyone in the bar stops and looks at me. This girl is treating me like scum and everyone is looking at me like I'm scum. I try to explain myself but it comes out wrong. Soon everyone's looking at the girl 'cos she's going nuts. She's centre stage on her knees, about to do something she'll regret big time, and I have my phone in my hand.

What do I do?

Leah's text interrupts my skin crawl of a fantasy. It's in capitals this time. *WHERE ARE YOU?! ANSWER!!!*

If I replied honestly, this is what I'd type: *I'm standing at the front of John Martin's car waiting for him to wake so I can behead him using a tree trunk, green paddle wire, an accelerator, and basic maths.* I'm not fond of how that answer comes over, so I reply with this instead: *Is Mum ok? Awake?*

She woke a few minutes ago. Come back. You're worrying me. What r u doing?

John Martin's crying in his sleep but there are no tears. His head has fallen forward and the paddle wire's quite tight against his neck now. Shit, he's gonna wake, any second.

But no, even with wire digging into his flesh he doesn't come round. I've grown tired of the cowgirl pose. I'm just standing like a normal(ish) girl now. I ignore Leah's last question and text: *What did she say when she woke?*

Leah's quick with her thumbs: *She talked about Dad, about what we could do to celebrate him properly. Then she realised you'd gone and freaked – btw Mum wasn't . . . Hang on, Mum's gonna text u.*

I feel panicky as I wait for Mum's text to come through. Before I drove into town, I felt sure she would want this. What was Leah about to type? – *Mum wasn't* what? *Mum wasn't going to murder him? Mum wasn't finished – she asked if you could please murder him for her?*

I don't know what I'm doing here! I'm not sure of anything! I blame his dimple and his cracked lips and Mozart's Serenade in G major coming from the kitchen over there – turn it off! This is Magaluf!

Mum's taking ages to text me. Or is it my signal? No, not the signal. Mum's taking ages.

What will I do if John Martin wakes before she's confirmed I should go ahead? Maybe I should just do it if he wakes now. I was confident she wanted this an hour ago. What's changed?

Maybe I should knock loudly on the windscreen, wake him, get it over with. Yeah, I should, I think. Yeah. I'll just give Mum ten more seconds.

My phone vibrates a minute later and he's still asleep. This is all Mum's written, don't know why it took her so long: *Don't let it be the thing that defines you.*

I'm walking along the strip towards my car. I don't know what time it is, quite late probably, because the Looky Looky guys have gone home and the PR guys are all in dark basement rooms convincing girls it's a good thing to be spat at by boys; convincing boys it's sexy to spit at girls and also lucrative if done with accuracy. There's a girl asleep or dead on the pavement ahead and so far no one's checked on her. I slow down as I pass and take a glance. She's vomiting, alive. 'Happy holidays,' I say, but she can't hear. Like everyone else in this place, she left her senses at home with her raincoat.

The car's still where I left it, but an artistically inclined young man has drawn a pair of breasts on the bonnet using shaving foam or squirty cream. While I'm intrigued as to which, I decide not to taste test. I get in the car, and close the door. My breathing sounds so loud. I'm not sure I've breathed properly since this whole thing began and it feels celebratory, like having a ciggie feels according to Leah (I had a drag once, never will again, ugh!). I inhale way too much air, hold till it hurts, and exhale slowly. I breathe like this for a while, filling, holding, emptying, refilling. I don't think it's just because of the breathing, but I feel larger and stronger when I dial the number I must dial.

Kim Su-Mi answers her secret phone immediately, must be quite attached to it. An exhalation of smoke would definitely add a little something to my lines: 'Hello, Mother! I've thought of something you can do.'

Chapter Twenty-four

This room is comfortable. Leah and Mum and I have been asleep in the king-size bed together and have just woken to our phones pinging. Our Ri7s are just three of the two hundred million that tinkled in unison a moment ago. Because two hundred million people have just received a video they didn't request in their Ri-Play folder. That's straight to number one, folks, thanks to the diligent Kim Su-Mi.

Which means Euan Grier and Beardy could watch it any moment. James could be watching it already. I've never known Millie and Natasha to ignore an alert – they'll be well into it by now for sure. Ashleigh from netball and Jen from debating will watch it at some point but not necessarily today because they both waste a lot of time interacting with actual people you could catch colds and stuff from. Aunty Louise and Aunty Marie and Bud and Cherry and Gran will definitely all watch it, share it too. Leah's checking it out and showing Mum. They're confused then transfixed then sitting up and trembling. Millions of people are watching this video. Even if no one shares it, it's the new number one. But they *are* sharing it, and it's not horrendous or outrageous or embarrassing. It doesn't make you grimace, scream, or hide your face behind your hands.

It makes you laugh. It's impossible not to laugh as Dad plays Caledonia to his babies, the bigger one bursting into an infectious and unstoppable chuckle at his deliberate bum-notes, the smaller one joining in, not quite sure why. Baby legs and baby arms flail with delight at their lovable and kind and funny Dad. Then the camera shakes because Mum's losing it too.

John Martin, if he's awake, might be smiling now rather than crying.

Mum and Leah and I are laughing and weeping at the same time and it's a painfully wondrous sensation.

That Dimwit social worker could be chortling this very second, then thinking: *Hang on, pause. No! Is that? Can't be! Is that Su-Jin?*

It is, you know.

And I am cute as fuck.